PRAISE FOR

# *LOVE, COFFEE, AND REVOLUTION*

"I frequently found myself laughing out loud. The book was ultimately moving and profound. I can't wait to see what Stefanie Leder does next."

**—ROBIN SCHIFF**

award-winning screenwriter of *Romy and Michele's High School Reunion* and producer of *Emily in Paris*

"Romance meets roasters in this frothy bungee jump of a novel that combines undeniable attraction, caffeine, and social justice in equally delightful measures."

**—MARK HASKELL SMITH**

author of *Rude Talk in Athens*

"In her spot-on depiction of a young woman facing a future she hasn't mapped out, and the exciting, if potentially troublesome, options she encounters, Stefanie Leder serves up dazzling storytelling that resonates."

**—JOSH SABARRA**

bestselling author of *Enemies Closer*

"Stefanie Leder is a true original and *Love, Coffee, and Revolution* is an audacious debut filled with equal amounts of adventure, romance, and laugh-out-loud humor. I loved it."

**—IVY POCHODA**

award-winning author of *Sing Her Down*

"[Leder's] unique voice and the integrity of her humor come through on every page. I marvel at how many layers she has folded into her young protagonist's caffeinated journey of tropical self-discovery."

**—DAVID KENDALL**

director of *Boy Meets World*

"A resonant, whip-smart, laugh-out-loud tale of love, politics, and personal growth...Bold, brilliant, inspiring, and impossible to put down. Tell a friend."

**—YVETTE LEE BOWSER**

creator of *Living Single*

"*Love, Coffee, and Revolution* manages the impossible: it not only tackles the big topics—love, identity, the question of ethical consumption in the age of capitalism—it's also fun, funny, and romantic. Stefanie Leder has written a delightful and smart romp of a novel, and I am so here for it."

**—EDAN LEPUCKI**

author of *California*

"As romantic and striking as its Costa Rican setting, Leder's engrossing and hilarious debut may just inspire you to veer off-road in a quest for adventure, romance, and a bracing café chorreado."

**—ERIN EHRLICH**

cocreator of Netflix's *Boo, Bitch*

"*Love, Coffee, and Revolution* is a tour de force. Smart and witty, with an unforgettable heroine who you can't help but fall in love with. I didn't want it to end!"

**—KATE RUBY**

bestselling author of *Tell Me Your Lies*

# LOVE, COFFEE, AND REVOLUTION

# LOVE, COFFEE, AND REVOLUTION

STEFANIE LEDER

Copyright © 2025 by Stefanie Leder
Published in 2025 by Blackstone Publishing
Cover and book design by Candice Edwards

All rights reserved. This book or any portion thereof may not be reproduced or used in any manner whatsoever without the express written permission of the publisher except for the use of brief quotations in a book review.

The characters and events in this book are fictitious. Any similarity to real persons, living or dead, is coincidental and not intended by the author.

Printed in the United States of America
Originally published in hardcover by Blackstone Publishing in 2025

First paperback edition: 2025
ISBN 979-8-8748-1183-9
Fiction / Romance / Contemporary

Version 1

Blackstone Publishing
31 Mistletoe Rd.
Ashland, OR 97520

www.BlackstonePublishing.com

# PART ONE:
# PLANTING THE SEEDS

# PROLOGUE

DECEMBER

ALAJUELA, COSTA RICA

I was hurtling forty meters above the Río Colorado, suspended from a bridge by a cord attached to my ankle *only by some flimsy Velcro,* and all I could think about was that goddamned Valrhona chocolate bar. I had gone all the way downtown to get it, because the only place I could find dark chocolate here was at the kosher deli next to the Virgin Mary kiosk by the bus terminal. But then I had remembered my mother telling me candy bars had enough processed sugar to kill a rat—*wait, that couldn't be true, could it?*—so I had eaten some papaya instead. But the experience of hanging headfirst over a mean-looking body of water made me realize that when the opportunity arises, you should eat the freaking chocolate.

And that's not all I realized, but it wasn't during the journey down. It was in the post-fall jiggling. All that downward rushing took one second, two, tops, and then I was jerked back to safety. The cord snapped upward, then downward, then upward, then downward, and after all that ecstatic flying, I was at the bottom, upside down. River, rocks, trees, and sky all blurred together fantastically. A sense of oneness enveloped me. The cord stilled.

The bungee guide with the eyes of honey called down to me. "Do you want to come back up?"

"*¡Sí!*" I said. "*¡No!*" And then I broke into a peal of laughter.

"Are you okay?" he asked.

And it was at that moment, choking on my own saliva because I was laughing and I was upside down, that I knew, finally, I was alive.

# CHAPTER ONE

ONE MONTH EARLIER

BERKELEY, CALIFORNIA, USA

The first step to becoming alive was realizing I was dead.

"Did you remember the wings?" Cody asked.

"I thought you were bringing the wings."

Irritation crossed his face as he rooted through the trunk. "What about the talons?"

"Nope."

"Dammit, Dee. How are we going to be Vultures of Capitalism without wings and talons?"

It was a good question. A better question is why we were going to be Vultures of Capitalism in the first place. Cody and I were in Berkeley to protest capitalism, which I was down for. It was the predator cosplay I was questioning. But Cody was giving me a very stern look.

"Well, why don't we go back and get them?" I asked.

"Because then we'll miss the protest." *And it will be all your fault.* He didn't actually say the last part. But he was thinking it.

I was accustomed to guilt, deserved or not. I was also

accustomed to discomfort. I had been uncomfortable my whole life; with my parents, my hair, my teeth. Things were different at age twenty-one. Now I was uncomfortable with my mind.

"The protest is already starting," he said, radiating displeasure. I tried not to own his feelings, like they advise in #selfhelptok, but it didn't work. I closed the trunk with a thud, and we started toward the small group on the corner.

"Is that Starbucks?" he asked, noticing the disposable coffee cup in my hand. His face turned an even whiter shade of white.

"No! Of course not. I just reused the cup."

"Why do you have a Starbucks cup in the first place?" he asked, as if it were a handgun.

"They had them at the Teamsters picket last week in Contra Costa. I thought if I was going to take a disposable cup, I should at least reuse it."

Horror washed over his face. "We can't be seen with that."

"But I haven't finished my coffee."

"We. Cannot. Be. Seen. With *that.*"

"Fine."

I couldn't deny that Starbucks was a megacorporation, but most of their coffee was actually ethically sourced. Still, it wasn't worth the fight. I went back to the car, took one last sip, and put it in the cupholder. Then we joined our friends, many of whom were decked out in talons and wings. They had signs like Boycott Oil, Housing Justice for All, and Team Orca. If you're thinking the protest could've used some specificity, you'd be right. All the causes were important, and on a deeper level related to each other, but it was hard to see what protesting them together in wing-and-talon gear was going to accomplish.

Marlowe, a young woman in ragged jeans and impressive fairy wings, addressed the group with a bullhorn. The bullhorn was a bit much—there were only thirty of us. "Okay," she said, awkwardly gripping it with her talons. "Those of you willing to get arrested, block the street." She fumbled the bullhorn. It crashed to the ground, giving off a horrid screech. She carefully plucked it back up. "We're going to march up the on-ramp to the 580."

"Isn't that a little dangerous?" asked Rory, the girl next to me. "I mean, I don't want to get hit on the freeway." I nodded at her; fair point.

"Those of you unwilling to get arrested, protest on the corner," said Marlowe. "You will serve as witnesses when the cops arrest the rest of us. Don't forget to record it. *For history.*"

Cody, chest puffed out, stepped into the street, ready to charge the freeway.

"Wait," I said, grabbing his elbow. "We can't get arrested today."

"Come on, Dee. Put your body where your words are." He looked at my picket sign: Eat the Rich.

"We have to drive down to my parents after the protest. I can't miss Thanksgiving."

"Why? So we can celebrate the genocide of native people?"

I didn't know how to reply. Yes, Thanksgiving had a problematic origin. But it was also a tradition that brought your family together. Maybe in his dysfunctional Wasp family you could miss holidays, but in my dysfunctional Jewish family, not showing up was on par with familial abandonment.

Cody stared at me. "I thought you were committed to the fight."

*But which fight?*

"Of course I'm committed," I said. "But what will getting arrested today actually accomplish? This is a really small protest. There isn't a unified message. There isn't even any press here."

"That's not the point. Little actions build into movements."

Maybe that was true. But maybe it was also true that Cody just wanted to get arrested so he could post it on TikTok.

"I can't do it today," I said. "I'm sorry. If you want to get arrested, that's fine, but I'm still going to LA this afternoon. I need to be with my family."

"Fine," he said, peeved, stepping back onto the corner.

So we grimly chanted, "Capitalism, no thanks! We'll burn your evil banks," while our comrades marched toward the freeway. They didn't even get to the on-ramp before the cops showed up. And much to Cody's chagrin, the cops didn't arrest anybody. They just closed the on-ramp with orange traffic cones.

♥ ◊ *

But Cody wasn't going to let me off the hook that easily. A lifetime of heteronormative cis male white privilege, family money, and an Aries placement had made him very obstinate. Or maybe it's because we were prelaw seniors at UC Berkeley, and if you're prelaw, you're probably at least a little bit of a jerk. I didn't think he was a jerk when I met him at a bicycle street-takeover in the summer. I thought he was brilliant and decisive and committed to justice. Those things were still true. They just didn't add up to being a great boyfriend.

"God, I hate this freeway," he said as he hit the steering wheel of his silver BMW coupe. We were bumper-to-bumper on the 580 East—just a few miles past the on-ramp we had failed to occupy—heading to LA. "Driving on a holiday weekend was a huge mistake."

Perhaps it was. I was already regretting it. But I had a lot of regrets. Like the mounting debt I was accruing to get a BA, so I could go to law school and accrue . . . more debt!

"Next time we're flying," he said.

*Sure, why not, add it to the pile. I'll never pay it off anyway.*

"You know, it's not too late to turn back. We could tell your parents there was just too much traffic. That way we won't miss the Black Friday protests."

"Look," I said. "I'm dreading it as much as you, but I have to go home."

"If you dread seeing them so much, why do you visit them so often?"

How to explain the dynamics of my close-knit family? That we loved each other so much that boundaries ceased to exist? That there was, in fact, such a thing as *too much* love?

"I don't dread seeing them," I said. "I dread seeing them all at once. When I go there, it's like I'm the new panda at the zoo."

"How?"

"They hyperfocus on me—Have I been eating enough? Sleeping? Did I know that highly successful people get at least seven hours of sleep a night, but not more than nine?"

"Tell them the questions make you uncomfortable."

I laughed. How naive of him. "They care about me. They want to know how I'm doing. It's just . . . a lot of pressure. They expect a lot out of me."

"You need to separate their expectations from your own." That was ironic coming from Cody, who was constantly pushing his expectations onto me. "Like, if you don't want to apply to law school, don't apply to law school. I'm not. I told my parents last week that they couldn't buy my complicity."

"They did buy you this car." He grimaced. The car embarrassed Cody because money embarrassed Cody. Just not enough to give it up.

"Can you change the playlist?" he said irritably. "You know I can't stand sad-lady guitar songs." That was another thing. He liked EDM. I liked music. It all added to a gnawing feeling that things weren't going to work out between us. While I respected his passion and commitment, sometimes I wished he could be a little less black-and-white about things. But maybe I was projecting; I had that problem, too.

We got into Van Nuys sometime after two a.m. and conked out. The next morning we had two waking minutes alone before my mother knocked on my door. Had she been listening in the hallway to hear when we woke up?

"Could you come out here for a second, Dee?" Her voice whistled through the space under the door. I put on a robe and joined her in the hallway. She looked incredible, as always. Fitted dress, glossy nails, hair freshly blown out.

"We've got a lot to do this morning," she said. She looked me up and down. "Your hair isn't done."

"I just got up." I smoothed my unruly brown hair down. My mom's hair was always perfect. Everything about her appearance was refined. My appearance was what I would call *natural.*

"Did you forget your tweezers?" She was staring at my eyebrows. "You can borrow mine. I know the big eyebrow look is all the rage with your generation, but they don't do your face justice. You could be so beautiful."

*Could be.* I didn't mind that she was perfect. I just didn't understand why she couldn't let me be . . . not.

"You know, *your* eyebrows look fantastic," I said.

Her expression brightened and her tone softened. "Thanks, honey. I just had them done." She unconsciously patted them. "The rest of the family will be here in an hour. Please get dressed. And wear something nicer than your 'good jeans.'" She hustled off to fluff the living room couch pillows, surely for the fourth time this morning.

After showering and finding an actual dress in my closet, I went to the kitchen, where Cody was meticulously measuring freshly ground coffee and adding it to his Chemex—which he traveled with, along with his scale and burr grinder. Coffee wasn't just coffee to Cody—it was science. And a chance to prove he had superior taste to everyone. I took a mug from the cabinet and served myself from my parents' old-school drip coffeemaker.

Cody choked a little. When he recovered, he asked, "Why?"

"Because it's ready. And I want coffee."

"But this will be ready in three minutes." He gestured to his Chemex. "This is a single-origin light roast."

"Mmph," I said as I drank my parents' second-wave blend. "Don't you have to wait for the bloom or something?"

"It bloomed." Cody finished brewing his magical coffee and poured me a cup. "Here."

"Wouldn't that be wasteful? Since I already have this cup?"

"Just try it."

I took a sip. "It's okay."

"*Okay*?! It's Ethiopian Yirgacheffe longberry. One of the highest-quality beans you can get."

"Yeah, it's okay."

Cody's head was about to explode. "Try it again. What do you taste?"

I sipped it. "Coffee."

"No." He shook his head. "What flavors? What undertones?"

". . . Dirt?"

He shook his head again, then tasted it himself. "Wildberry and lemongrass."

"What even is a wildberry?"

"It's a wildberry, Dee." He didn't know. Of course he didn't know.

"Did you just read that on the bag?"

"No!"

I took the bag and read the tasting notes. "'Wildberry and lemongrass.' Wow, you were remarkably accurate for someone who hasn't read this." He set his jaw. I perused the rest of the bag. "Huh. No type of fair trade certification. No Rainforest Alliance either. Even my parents' coffee is USDA organic."

"There are so many different fair trade organizations now, how do you know which ones are legit? This is *directly* traded. The roaster guarantees a living wage. And it's shade-grown."

"That all sounds great. But direct trade is a marketing term. There's no enforcement. So who verifies that it's true?"

He busied himself with cleaning the Chemex to avoid answering.

"The company itself?" I asked. "Seems weird to just take their word for it."

He took my mug of Yirgacheffe back and handed me my drip. "Enjoy your second-wave mediocrity."

I took my mediocre coffee and grabbed a second cup for my dad. It's not that I didn't like coffee—I loved it. It's that I didn't like pretense. If I was making it myself? French Press. Dark roast. Organic. And fair trade.

My dad was in his study. He was simultaneously watching a basketball game, scrolling on his desktop, and listening to music. And they say *my* generation has no attention span. I handed him the coffee.

"Thanks, Dee. You turn in your international relations paper before you came here?"

"Still working on it."

"You can't afford a B. Without scholarships, you're not going to law school."

*Hmm. Maybe that was the way out of it. Just . . . stop studying. Don't get a scholarship.*

"How are your applications going?" he asked. "You know you've already missed early decision."

"You're right. I do know." I couldn't have this conversation again. I needed a diversion. "So, just curious. Why do you have the TV, your computer, and music on at the same time?"

My dad muted the TV. Rhythm and blues wafted from his smart speakers. "Because I enjoy burning fossil fuels."

"Seriously, Dad. Don't you think this is a little wasteful?"

"Saving the world is your battle, Dee. Paying the mortgage is mine."

I stood there for a moment. I hated how life had changed him. But mostly, I hated how life had changed us. We used to be on the same team. On his desk was a picture of six-year-old me taking a swing at a T-ball. My pigtail braids were falling out of my blue batting helmet and onto my striped jersey. My dad had been standing right behind me, coaching my swing. He taught me to play baseball in the backyard when I was still a toddler, with a big red plastic bat and white foam ball.

*"C'mon Slugger. We have half an hour before dark."*

*"Mom said dinner."*

*"Dinner can wait."*

"I have to finish some work before everyone arrives," he said. "Why don't you go talk to the dog about her carbon footprint? She's been eating a lot of beef lately." He unmuted the TV and turned to his computer. Conversation over.

I went to check on my mom in the kitchen. I could see by the stray hair in her face that she was in a state of chaos that needed to be handled with extreme care.

"The turkey isn't even close to done and the house is a mess!" she wailed. "I'm never going to finish in time."

I put my hands on her shoulders. "You're a wonderful hostess, Mom."

"You really think that?"

"I do. You've got this."

She gave me a tiny smile.

"Now hand me that absolutely fabulous cheese platter."

I headed to the living room with the cheese platter, which must've weighed ten pounds. Through the window, I could see my Aunt Sarah and Uncle Stephen getting out of their new Porsche with their teenage daughter, Nicole. They had parked in our driveway, blocking in my dad's used Corolla. I don't think they realized it was his main (and only) car; they thought of it more as a golf cart. We weren't exactly in the same economic bracket as the rest of our family.

I went to the front door to wait for them. Nicole was staring at the front of our house, confused. My mom had hung wreaths even though we were Jewish. ("Relax, Dee. Christmas is *pretty*." "But it's the birthday of *Christ*, Mom." "Who made you so literal? Your father?") There were also white 'ornamental' lights on the eaves of our house. They were Christmas lights, and everyone knew it, especially all our Christian neighbors who brought us nativity scenes to put in our front yard, just in case. ("Just in case *what*, Mom? In case we decide we don't want to go to hell?" "Can you just *relax*, Dee?")

"Dee, you look like you've gained weight!" said Sarah, coming through the front door in her leather fashion sneakers.

"I'm just a little bloated."

"Your skin is so red. Have you thought of giving up gluten? That will help with the bloat."

"I've actually been increasing my gluten consumption. Am I doing this wrong?"

"When you're in LA for a longer period," said Stephen, "you should see Cousin Ally. She does this whole stool analysis that identifies your food intolerances."

"Can't wait."

Stephen handed me a tofu ham. "Are you going to be in LA next fall for law school? Maybe at USC?"

That was purely rhetorical. He knew my parents could never afford USC. Nicole snorted as she pushed past me into the house. "I hear DeVry has openings," she said.

"What will you and Cody do if you get into different schools?" asked Sarah.

"Guess we'll figure it out then," I said, as brightly as possible.

I dropped the "ham" off in the kitchen and went straight to the empty living room; I needed a respite from all the questions. I settled on the couch and poured myself a glass of sherry from the decanter resting on the table and wondered where Cody was. Probably making an "UnThanksgiving" TikTok in my room.

Uncle Ben, an actuary with overzealous facial hair, entered the room. He pushed past the pillows and sat in the middle of the couch. "So, Dee, I hear you're getting a sociology degree." He pronounced *sociology* like *dog shit.* "What are you going to do for work? You know protesting isn't a real job, right?"

"It is, though."

"Be serious," he laughed. "What are you *really* going to do?"

I felt trapped. My family would never understand me. I would never be able to convince them that what I was passionate about mattered. Suddenly, a better path than arguing occurred to me: *double down.* If they were going to give me a hard time about my future, I could give them a more exciting reason. It didn't even have to be true!

"I'm going to join the Peace Corps in Kiribati."

"What?" He glowered. "Never heard of it. Is that a real country?"

"Sure is." I gulped the sherry. Family functions were more bearable when you were plastered.

"To do what?"

"To save . . . endangered sea turtles." Were sea turtles

endangered in Kiribati? Surely some of them must be, the world was basically on fire now.

Gossipy Aunt Jackie, wife of Doctor Ralph, sat down on the couch next to me. "Hi, sweetie! How's school?"

"Never better."

"What are you doing after graduation?"

"She's going to join the Peace Corps." Ben's voice boomed with disapproval. "In Kubati. Kosovo. Keurig?"

"*Kiribati.*"

"Really?" asked Jackie, excited by the promise of drama. "Where is that? It sounds far."

"Oh, it is," I said.

"If you're going to do the Peace Corps, why don't you go to Monaco or something?" she asked.

Ben sneered at Jackie. "Monaco is a rich country. They don't have the Peace Corps."

I hemmed. "Actually, they do."

"*Why*?" asked Ben.

"No one knows."

"Wow, I would go to Monaco, maybe you could meet a rich husband," said Jackie. She snuggled up to me, all confidential-like. "What about Uncle Aaron's firm? You're not going to work there? No law school?"

"Nope."

"Do your parents know?"

"Food's ready!" said my mom from the hallway, rescuing me from Jackie and Ben. Gratefully, I headed into the dining room. I had no intention of my Peace Corps fantasy going past the hors d'oeuvres. I may have been unhappy, but I wasn't stupid.

I sat next to Cody and unfolded my napkin. Dad was in the kitchen grabbing a beer, and my little improv act might have gone unnoticed if not for chatterbox Jackie.

"I think it's great you're supporting Dee's plan to go to Corgi," said Jackie to my mother, while they were getting seated around the dining room table.

"Corgi is a dog, Jackie. It's *Kiribati*," said Uncle Ben, like he didn't just learn the name two minutes ago.

"That's so brave of her," said Jackie. "I mean, I couldn't even find it on a map. And it takes guts for you, too, Debbie, when you think about it. It's hard to let your kids go, but you know what they say, if you love someone . . ."

"You want to do *what*?" My dad entered the room, stunned. "You want to go *where*?"

Mom couldn't even speak. Shit, she had very high blood pressure. So did Dad. Could this give one of them a stroke?

"Wait," said Cody, confused and irritated. "You're leaving the country?"

"I thought you were going to law school so you could work *for me*," said Uncle Aaron, basically apoplectic. "I didn't give you a loan so you could waste it in the Peace Corps."

It was time for this conversation to end. For everyone's health. But I couldn't get a word in.

"This is crazy," said my father. "I knew I shouldn't have let you go to Berkeley."

"Huge mistake," said Uncle Aaron to my father. "Which I told you. You send a kid to Berkeley, they're going to come back a communist."

"Not everyone has the money to send their kids to Dartmouth," said my dad, pissed.

"Better a communist than a heartless capitalist," said Cody.

"Doesn't he drive a BMW?" whispered Aunt Sarah to Aunt Jackie.

"Generational war!" snickered Nicole, pleased this diverted attention from her.

"But the diseases!" said my grandmother. "Just think of the diseases!"

"That's true," said Doctor Ralph. "They have leprosy there."

"Leprosy?!" said my mom, on the verge of fainting.

"I still think she should go to Monaco," said Aunt Jackie.

"Hold up," said Sadie, my cool, older, union-organizing cousin. "First, y'all are being wildly first world. Check your privilege, please. Second, I think we're losing perspective here. This is Dee's life."

Silence descended over the table, and I could see them wrestling with that idea. It was harder to digest than the kale salad.

My mom turned to me. She looked genuinely surprised. "Is it true, Dee?"

*That it's my life?*

"No," I said. Everyone was staring at me, even Cody. "It was just an idea."

And then the unbearable slowness ended as ten pairs of eyes stopped focusing on me. My rebellion was squashed and forgotten in under two minutes.

"They lost," my dad was saying. "Worst referee in the league."

"If they had a decent backup center the refereeing wouldn't be a factor."

Cody leaned over my plate and speared some of my potatoes. "What was that?"

"A joke that got out of hand."

"Even when you're joking, you don't stand up for yourself."

I put my utensils down and fled to my room.

Maybe Cody was right, but he didn't have to be so insufferable about it. I put on my meditation app—should I do "self-love" or "setting boundaries?" I wasn't good at either. But I couldn't shake Cody's comment. Was he right about other things, too? Was I truly committed to our causes? Sure, getting arrested yesterday would've been objectively stupid, but was I ever willing to get arrested? For something that really mattered?

I heard footsteps in the hallway, then a cursory knock on the door. Sadie entered. Sadie was the black sheep of the family and my absolute favorite relative. She had dark curly hair, olive skin, and a punk vibe. She was carrying two plates of pumpkin pie. My stomach turned. Pumpkin pie makes me aggressively ill.

"I think joining the Peace Corps is a fantastic idea," she said, handing me a plate and sitting on the corner of my bed. She kicked off her Birkenstocks and shoveled in a mouthful of slimy brown paste. "That sounds way more you than law school."

I took a very small bite of the nasty pie to be polite. "I'm not really joining the Peace Corps."

"No?" The ring through her bottom lip sagged.

"I have no idea what I'm doing after graduation. I thought I wanted to be an organizer, and maybe I still do, but . . ." I pushed some pie around on my plate. "I feel like all I'm doing is theater. Like I'm going through these motions, but I'm not changing anything."

"Some actions are effective, some aren't."

"That's not the only reason. It's also that I'm really bad at it. I get nervous when I have to speak to strangers. Which is basically the whole job. I'm not brave like you." I felt so pitiful I decided to have another bite of the pie. Bad idea. I tried to spit it into a tissue without her noticing.

"I'm not that brave," she said.

"You've been arrested like a dozen times. You chained yourself to a tree in front of a bulldozer. You even lost a toenail."

"But I didn't start there. You gotta build up to it. Try getting a parking ticket first." We laughed. "Look, Dee, you don't need to decide what you want to do *right now*. I didn't know what I wanted to do for years after I graduated. Nearly killed Jackie." She always referred to her parents by their first names, which drove them crazy. She said she was trying to break down the patriarchal bondage that parents inflict on children.

"You'll figure it out." She patted my hand. "Just remember, don't do anything you don't want to do, don't worry about what your parents think, and don't have sex for money. And don't dance for money, either. It may seem all right at first, but trust me, it's a slippery slope. Wow, this pie is delicious." She wiped some whipped cream off her lip. "You have to do what's best for you. That's what Grandpa would've told you."

"How do you know?" But I could imagine how she knew. He had been the pole around which our whole family spun.

"I know," her eyes began to mist, "because that's exactly what he said to me when Jackie and Ralph were on my case."

I looked over at a framed photo of my grandfather. He stood in his bathing suit on Brighton Beach, twenty years old, chest puffed out, covered in suntan oil. He was so handsome then. He had died when I was nine. I was jealous of Sadie, who had known him. *Really* known him. I just had fragments of memories and an obituary. Medic. Vietnam Vet Against the War. Hero.

"What else did he say?" I asked, cheated.

"He said you should look at your life like a work of art. Make it beautiful. And important. That way, when it's over, you've created something."

I sat with that for a moment. "I wish I knew how to do that."

"You can begin by not living for other people. What do *you* want, Dee? What do *you* like? What do *you* think?"

"I *hate* pumpkin pie," I said, with a vehemence that surprised us both.

"That's a great start." Sadie laughed and took my plate. "I wanted seconds anyway."

# CHAPTER TWO

Knowing what *I* wanted was going to be hard; I'd spent my whole life trying to ignore it. But advocating for myself was going to be even harder. People had gotten used to pushing me in whatever direction suited them. Especially Cody.

The ride back to Berkeley was like a root canal without Novocain. He was still angry I had even *thought* about making a life decision without him. Plus, our friends had had a great time ruining Black Friday for everyone else and he was suffering from major FOMO. It was shocking how much our relationship had changed. When it started, we were perfect companions; on picket lines, in marches, in the bedroom. But had it really been that perfect? Or had I just made my needs secondary to his? It's easy to keep the peace when one person stays silent.

When we arrived in Berkeley, I requested a timeout. But Cody didn't really get the concept of a "break." Evidence A, these texts from him:

Hey! I know we're on a break, but
good news. We got the jobs!

What jobs?

Didn't I tell you? I applied for us to work for SEIU when we graduate. In Chicago. What do you think about these apartments?

*https://hotpads.com/chicago-il/apartments-for-rent*

Unbelievable. As soon as I broke free from my parents, my boyfriend took the reins. He literally got me a job without my knowledge. I wouldn't be surprised if he had adopted us a rescue dog. This had gone *way* too far.

So I started googling summer jobs, anywhere but Chicago, which got me thinking . . . why not *really* get a job? Like, *now*? What was college doing for me, anyway? Preparing me for the law school I didn't want to go to? Why not work for an NGO, preferably in another country? I'd like to see Cody and my family try to rule me from halfway across the world.

I made a list of job postings that were sufficiently far away. Then I drank the half empty bottle of Jägermeister in my fridge, uploaded my resume to a few sites, and clicked Submit. I knew it was crazy. As a not-yet-graduate, I didn't think I was qualified for any of them. Not unless one of these organizations desperately needed someone whose longest-held job was "dog walker" and whose greatest skill was "can handle large breeds." But I needed to do *something*, anything, that made me feel like I was the one in charge of my life. Even if it was only symbolic.

♥ ● *

Much to my surprise, it wasn't just symbolic. I actually got an interview! It was with a nonprofit called Justice Alliance. Maybe they were impressed by my chutzpah? I was terrified—and ecstatic. Justice Alliance was one of the coolest and most influential nonprofits on the West Coast. They had a slew of environmental and social justice campaigns, led by executive director Suzanne Lyon, who was legendary in Bay Area activist circles for her extraordinary ability to bring in funding, her unusual beauty, and her predilection for making CEOs cry. There was a project-based position open in the ecotourism division, which supported their organic and fair trade coffee campaign. This was a worthy cause that had a real-world impact. And importantly, the position was in Costa Rica, which was thirty-five thousand miles away.

My interview was at eight-thirty a.m. They seemed very keen to meet, which was inexplicable to me given my paltry work experience. I waited inside the surprisingly chic lobby sipping a complimentary cup of coffee. I tried to identify the tasting notes. Were those undertones of ash, paint thinner, and ennui? As I swished it around my palate, an intern with an undershave called my name. I followed her to a corner office, staring at the geometric pattern on the back of her head, realizing how basic I was. Unremarkable brown hair, unremarkable brown eyes, olive skin, and only two piercings in my ears—one per lobe. I was definitely not cool enough to work here.

The door to the office swung open and I was face-to-face with Suzanne Lyon. I was taken aback. I knew she was the executive director. I just didn't know I was going to be interviewed by *the executive director*. She had persimmon-red hair, leaf-green eyes, and limbs fit for a giantess. She was striking. She was scary.

"Let's get straight to business." She was hovering in front of her desk in a white shirt and light linen pants, simultaneously answering texts on two different cell phones. It was hard to imagine her not getting down to business. "We need a project-based organizer for one of our Truth Trips. How much do you know about them? Or how our organization works?"

I bit my lip. "I'd love to hear how you describe it."

She launched into a practiced spiel. "Justice Alliance has two main wings. One is Organizing, which runs our environmental and social justice campaigns. The other is Ecotourism, which funds Organizing. The eco-tours are crucial for us: people pay big bucks to feel like they're doing something important."

*Huh—maybe that explained Tesla's success. Surely no one thought they were* good *cars.*

"The Truth Trips are learning vacations for socially conscious travelers," she continued. "Currently we're putting together a trip to Costa Rica. The travelers will learn about organic, fair trade coffee, and hopefully have a good time doing so." I tried to imagine my parents on one of these trips. I failed.

"But first they learn why commodity coffee is problematic," she said. "Commodity prices are determined by supply and demand, with no thought to labor or the environment."

I took the opportunity to use progressive buzzwords. "It's extractive capitalism."

"Exactly. Then we teach them about direct trade, which is basically a marketing label." *That's what I told Cody!*

"That's why regulation is crucial," she said. "It ensures that the land isn't destroyed, that laborers are paid a living wage and are not exposed to dangerous chemicals."

I glanced down at my nail polish. What were *those* chemicals doing to the environment? I hid them in my lap.

"Which fair trade organizations do you work with?" I asked. "All of them?"

"Mostly. Our preferred partner is Ethical Coffee International.

They focus on both environmental and social regulations, not just a single issue."

*Ooh! I knew that one!* "I love their coffee-beans-on-the-scale-of-justice symbol. So impactful."

She raised an eyebrow, not impressed. "A pretty picture isn't why they are our preferred partner."

"Of course not," I backtracked. "This all sounds very comprehensive."

"It is," she said. "We want the travelers to come away with the understanding that what you buy has real consequences for real people. Fair trade and organic networks have pulled a lot of farmers out of poverty. And we want people to not just know that theoretically, but to *feel* it. Because people learn with their hearts, Dee, not their minds."

Wow, if she was inspiring in a job interview, what was she like on a picket line?

"So here's what we're looking for in a candidate. Someone who is independent, self-motivated, and speaks excellent Spanish."

That's me. Independent. Or . . . *independiente.*

"You'd be responsible for setting up every aspect of the first Costa Rican Truth Trip. Arranging homestays, finding social excursions, and most importantly, visiting coffee farms to determine which ones should be on the trip." This seemed like a bigger position than I had thought. I couldn't possibly be qualified for this.

Suzanne scanned my resume on her iPad. "I see you worked for the Living Wage League. Did you work on the Fine Hotels campaign?"

I flushed. I most certainly had *not* worked for them. But Cody had. "Can I see that for a second?" I asked. "Just want to make sure I sent you the most recent document."

She gave me an odd look and handed me the iPad. I scanned my resume. Except it wasn't exactly *my* resume. Cody must've embellished it to get us the jobs in Chicago! I pinched my fingers together. Which was worse? Admitting I had gotten drunk on Jägermeister and hadn't reviewed my resume before posting it? Or telling her the truth: that my experience was thin?

"The Fine Hotels campaign was groundbreaking," I said, handing back the iPad. "The energy on the picket lines was palpable."

She didn't seem to notice I hadn't answered her directly. Or if she did, she wasn't letting on. "And you managed a law office? For Aaron Feinstein?"

*Cody!!!* At least I *had* worked there. And *manage*, *assist*—were they really so different? "I have tremendous organizational skills."

She put down the iPad. "You've done a lot for someone so young. When did you graduate from college? How old are you?"

I happen to know it's illegal to ask someone their age in an interview, because when I "managed" Uncle Aaron's law firm in the summers, I interviewed his assistant candidates. He went through a new one every six months. But how to tell the person you want to hire you that the question she's just asked is illegal? Or that you're planning on dropping out of college?

"I take good care of my skin." I pushed some hair behind my ears. "I have a great antiaging cream, something with AHA. I can email you the name of it later if you like."

"That's all right." She looked at me with barely concealed surprise, causing her forehead to crinkle with lines. I guess my mom was right—it's never too early to start taking care of your skin. "If you'll excuse me, I need to call your references."

"Right now?!"

"We're in a time crunch. Unfortunately, a new hire dropped

out last minute." So *that's* why they were so keen to meet me. Someone quit before they even started. Hello, red flag. Was it because of the shitty pay? Because Suzanne was a difficult boss? Or something worse?

Suzanne headed to the door, then paused, looking at the iPad. "So your direct supervisor at the Living Wage League was Sadie Weiss? I thought she organized for SEIU?"

Something twisted very slowly under my rib cage. My cousin emphatically did not work for the Living Wage League.

"Sadie is a multitasker." I gave Suzanne my best smile, which really wasn't any good. Plus, I was short of breath from stabbing pains in the general vicinity of my heart. "She consults for many progressive organizations."

"Huh." Suzanne gave me a queer look and left the room. I quickly texted Sadie to ask her to cover for me. Then I placed my hand just under my left breast. The pain was so acute I couldn't breathe. After five minutes I really started to sweat. Who was Suzanne talking to? Was I going to get caught? Was it illegal to lie on a resume? Could I *go to jail*?

The searing pain flashed through my rib cage and I bent over. I had seen a doctor about this once in high school and had come away with this explanation: *It's your organs growing.*

*Your organs growing?* my mom had asked when I told her in the car.

*That's what he said.*

*Unbelievable, Dee. Next time I'm going in with you. If you don't want to feel like a baby, don't act like one.*

After that my mother had accompanied me into the room for each doctor's visit, causing almost unbearable embarrassment. The worst was my first gynecological exam, done by my male pediatrician.

*You're fifteen now,* he said. *So we're going to have a peek in there.*

*Can you tell if she's had sex?*

*Mom!*

*Sometimes,* he replied. *The hymen can give you* a lot *of information.*

"Well, that was interesting," said Suzanne, gliding back into the room.

*Interesting how? Like "you are a fraud" interesting, or . . . ?*

"Sadie really sang your praises." She sat across from me. "Just one last question. How good is your Spanish?"

*"Hablo muy bien."* Which was true, more or less. I definitely read and wrote academic Spanish. Would that hold up in the real world? *No sabía.*

"Great. If you take the position, you'll be working with my colleague Matías Khalil. He works in the organizing wing, but he'd be lending you support. Too bad you couldn't meet him today, but he's in Ecuador."

"Matías Khalil? *The* Matías Khalil? No-More-Capitalism-in-the-Age-of-AI Matías Khalil?"

"Yes." Did she look slightly annoyed?

"God, he's so brilliant. I loved his TED Talk."

"Everyone does." She was definitely annoyed. She uncrossed her slim legs and looked at her calendar. "The position begins immediately. You'll be leaving for Costa Rica next week. Do you have any pressing commitments?"

*Just breaking up with my boyfriend and dropping out of college.* "Nope."

She reached out her hand to shake. "Welcome aboard, comrade."

# CHAPTER THREE

Cody didn't want to accept the breakup at first. He told me I'd regret my decision. He said I'd never find a relationship like the one I had with him. The thing was, I didn't want another relationship like that. One where my needs weren't even an afterthought.

My dad took the news about me leaving worse than Cody; it was like I was breaking up with him. He would only speak to me in clipped sentences, then pass the phone to Mom. His disapproval of me was so total I couldn't bear to examine it. I clung to the belief that this was rock bottom for us. Surely, things would get better. One day, he'd be proud of me again.

The rest of the family was only slightly less upset. Grandma threatened to cut me out of her will, Aaron said he'd be needing that loan repaid soon, and Jackie kept emailing me State Department Travel Warnings for any country in a thousand-mile radius. Mom was the big surprise, however. She sent me three bottles of sunblock and some very trendy flip-flops. But all this familial disruption was the price I had to pay for freedom. I wondered, when literal birds flew the nest, what did the mom and dad birds do? Did they give their bird offspring the cold shoulder? Or did they tell their baby birds that yes, they were ready to fly?

I spent the next few days reading everything I could about Costa Rica and the coffee trade. I also rewatched Matías Khalil's TED Talk on capitalism in the age of AI. Matías was a mesmerizing speaker. He used his voice like a classical pianist. One moment he was practically whispering, the next he was thundering.

*"Capitalists justify their riches by saying they've earned it,"* said Matías, his voice low and measured. *"By taking risks with their capital, by working harder, or by being more innovative. But in the future, when AI does all the work, when humans effectively cease to contribute to the economy—what would be the rationale for one person to have more than any other?"* He mopped wavy hair off his brow, his voice now loud and assured. *"With no human 'work,' we'll need a new framework for distributing resources. Will we finally realize that our value as humans comes not from our labor, but from our souls?"*

Damn. He was so inspiring. And uncomfortably cute. Late twenties. Floppy hair, long eyelashes, and actual dimples. I couldn't believe I was going to be working with him. Some light Google-stalking revealed he was a committed vegan, avid recycler, and dog foster dad. There were quite a lot of female friends in the pics, but he appeared to be single. I stopped myself—what was I doing?! I just got out of a relationship. I did not need to be checking someone's relationship status, much less that of a coworker. I had a lot to prove with this job. It was somewhat curious I'd been hired despite my thin work experience. I tried not to think about that too hard. Or why the last hire dropped out. I was so used to asking myself, *What could go wrong?* What if instead, for once, I wondered, *What could go right?*

♥ ◐ *

Who was I fooling? Optimism was not in my birth chart. When my "direct supervisor" Sadie took me to the airport Friday morning, I was already nervous. It was five a.m. and the entire bay was blanketed in fog. That meant the pilots would be relying exclusively on their computers. The only thing I trusted less than computers were the people who had to interpret them. I patted the Xanax in my pocket. I would be needing a lot of pharmaceutical assistance to make it through this flight.

"Here," said Sadie, at the edge of the security checkpoint. "This was Grandpa's." She placed a black velvet jewelry box in my palm. I lifted the lid. It was the necklace he had always worn. Two golden snakes with flashing tongues, wrapped around a staff. Caduceus—the symbol of medicine. The alchemy of turning illness into health, bad into good.

"How'd you get this?"

"He gave it to me right before I went to Amsterdam." Sadie lifted it out of the box and unhooked the clasp. She stood behind me and pulled it around my neck.

"I can't take it," I said. "It's yours."

Sadie hooked the clasp and it fell to my chest. "Don't you know the story?"

"No." I didn't know most of his stories.

"A wounded soldier gave it to Grandpa during the war. The soldier's mother had given it to him for protection. Anyway, it wasn't much of a good luck charm, because the soldier's wound turned out to be fatal. But Grandpa had risked his life to bring the soldier into the camp hospital, and the soldier wanted him to have it." I felt the cool gold against my skin. "Grandpa never felt worthy of it. He felt guilty that he couldn't save that soldier. But he said his memory inspired him to try harder, to be braver. I hope it does the same for you."

I touched the point of the staff. Could anything alchemize my fears into courage?

"Thanks, Sadie. And thanks for . . ." God, I hated getting

mushy. But I was feeling mushy. "Thanks for always being on my side."

"Of course I'm on your side! We're family."

"It doesn't always work like that."

"Not on the surface, maybe. But way down deep. It does." She gave me a huge hug and pushed me into the line. *That* was the way a mama bird was supposed to send off her young, I was sure of it. She waved at me until I was out of sight. Was that water in my eyes? Ugh, I hated getting mushy!

After I made it through the shockingly matter-of-course violation that is airport security, I walked to my terminal, caressing my gold chain. I had no idea how I would ever feel worthy of that necklace if even my own grandfather didn't. He was an actual hero; I was afraid of my own shadow. But my anxiety manifested atypically. I hated the idea of giving into my fear even more than I hated being scared. So I still did many of the things that frightened me. It was exhausting and excruciating, but I didn't know any other way to be. Would moving to a foreign country miraculously change that? As I mastered a second language, would I also master my anxieties? Myself?

My phone started buzzing as I boarded the plane. It was Suzanne. I still couldn't believe I was on a phone call basis with *Suzanne Lyon.*

"Dee," she said. "Glad I caught you. Ignore the list of *cafetales* I gave you in the training packet. Matías or I will email you a new one."

"Something wrong with it?"

"We've decided to narrow our search," she said, breezily. "We want to avoid the northern parts of the country, near the border."

That sounded not great. "Something happening at the border?"

"Well, part of the reason we're opening a Truth Trip in Costa Rica is that we've had to close the one operating in Nicaragua."

*Uh.* "Why?"

"A bit of unrest, you could say. There's increased drug trafficking throughout Central America. Costa Rica is more stable than Nicaragua, but we've still encountered some . . . irregularities. Better safe than sorry."

*Better safe than sorry?!* There had been no mention of *unrest* or *irregularities* in my interview. Oh my god, is that why they hired me?! Because I was the only one naive enough to take the job?

"Anyhow, didn't want to worry you. Just avoid confusion. Also, while I make the decisions about the Truth Trips, Matías, being on the ground, will have actionable information. You'll be in touch with him regularly. Okay, gotta jet, have a safe flight."

A safe flight? What was the point of a safe flight if, when I landed, I would have to avoid *drug traffickers*? This was *not* what I signed up for. I signed up for organizing tours of coffee farms. Nice, peaceful, drama-free coffee farms.

The person behind me coughed politely, wordlessly telling me to get a move on. I took my seat—a middle one, of course—next to a businessman with a red tie and a nasty bronchial infection. I considered my options. The plane hadn't left. I could still deboard. Berkeley probably hadn't processed my notice of withdrawal yet.

But before I could properly assess the situation, the flight attendants announced they were sealing the cabin. A Central American woman wearing a large cross around her neck walked down the aisle, coming straight for the empty window seat next to me.

"*Perdón*," said the woman, wriggling into the seat. "There's so little foot space," she continued in Spanish. I smiled at her, then gripped my armrest as the engines roared to life. "I used to be scared to fly," she said, looking at me with pity. "But not anymore, because I've accepted Jesus."

I kept quiet, because I didn't want to have the Jews-killed-Jesus conversation. I figured telling her my parents were nominal Jews who said "Jesus was a communist" and "Religion is the opiate of the masses" would upset her. Or at least cause her to crack open the worn blue leather book she was taking out of her purse.

"You know that Jesus died for our sins?" she said.

"Mm-hmm."

"And he bled on the cross and suffocated on his own blood, all to redeem us?"

I nodded.

She gave me a piercing gaze. "*Pobrecita.*" She patted my hands and put the book on my lap. "If you receive the Lord in your heart, you will never know fear again. Can you do that now?"

I shrugged noncommittally.

"*Oye*, when you're in danger, say, '*Señor*, cover me with your sanctified, precious blood.' He will protect you."

"That's it?"

"That's it. Keep this Bible. I want you to have it."

I looked at the Bible and wondered how what she was saying was possible. All I had to do was repeat a couple of magic words and Jesus would make sure nothing happened to me? What an appealing idea.

I thanked her, ordered a scotch on the rocks, and used it to chase down my Xanax. Religion was okay, but I preferred modern drugs. As my head began to swim, I vaguely wondered if combining had been a bad idea.

Soon I was having a psychedelic dream about Jesus, who

looked and sounded *a lot* like Mandy Patinkin. I had just accepted him as my savior when someone started shaking me.

"Wake up," said the old lady. "We're landing soon." As I shook off my brain fog, I wondered: Did my dream count? Had I converted to Christianity? Or to the religion of musical theater?

"*Por favor, señores pasajeros,* please put your seats in an upright position," said a voice over the speakers. "We are preparing for landing."

Suddenly the plane made a radical tilt; this was no normal descent. Bottles and purses rolled down the aisles. A hundred and fifty people started screaming; me the loudest. And then, just as suddenly, we were at a normal angle again. I sighed with relief.

But then the cabin tilted two hundred and thirty degrees and the screaming resumed. I put my head between my knees.

"*¡Dios!*" screamed the Costa Rican passengers, clasping their hands together and bending over their laps.

"Help!" screamed the Americans, clutching their iPads.

"COVER ME WITH YOUR SANCTIFIED BLOOD!" I shouted.

The plane righted itself. It worked!

We continued in a gentle descent and then rolled to a stately halt. The old lady beamed at me, truly happy I was no longer going to hell. A cheerful male voice came from the speakers. "It's been a pleasure serving you. Please fly Tropical Airlines again."

*Sure. Right after I get Alzheimer's.* I joined the rush to exit the plane. As we stepped onto the tarmac and into the muggy air of Alajuela, I felt like I'd been smacked in the face. The air here was not the nonentity I was accustomed to. This was a presence that fought back with diesel, decaying green, and surprising density. But I didn't have time to wrestle with something as mundane as air, because the old lady who had saved my soul tripped over her shoulder bag, sending fifteen brand-new Bibles flying onto the pavement.

"*Perdón,*" she said, her face turning the same shade of red as the airplane seats. When I bent down to help her pick up her books, she broke out into a beatific smile. "*Que Dios te bendiga.*"

"God bless you, too."

We entered a cavernous room with shiny beige tiles. She headed to the returning nationals' line, leaving me alone in the visitors' line. It was while standing in that massive queue, full of families and couples and tour groups, that I realized the extent of my solitude. I was in a foreign land with nothing to hold onto but the holy book of another faith, the sneezing man's business card, and the name of the host family that was supposed to greet me in the airport. I had wished for independence. Now would I find the courage to take it?

# CHAPTER FOUR

SAN JOSÉ, COSTA RICA.

After an unnecessarily thorough interrogation at Immigration—I didn't see what my relationship status had to do with anything—I waited in a Xanax daze for the green light to signal me through Customs. I was grateful I had ignored Uncle Ralph's advice to bring some Oxycontin "just in case." I was worried enough about making it through with Sudafed; the last thing I needed to carry was time-release heroin.

The light flashed green and I stepped into the lobby area, which was enclosed by glass walls, creating a greenhouse effect. Sweat trickled from my forehead into my eyes. I was surrounded by anxious tour operators, reunited lovers, and vending machines selling fifteen varieties of peanuts. It was total chaos, and I wondered if I would faint right here from heatstroke, because that would be a very anonymous way to die.

I also wondered if my host parents would show up. Suzanne had arranged a homestay for me when I had gone by the Justice Alliance office to pick up my training packet last week. I had asked for an apartment, because really, I had enough problems with my own parents. I certainly didn't need another set. But Suzanne had been adamant in her silky-smooth way. "This will make things much easier for you," she had said, standing and sitting and standing and sitting, because she seemed to have a problem not doing ten things at once. "They'll show you the ropes, teach you how to get around. Trust me, you'll be thankful."

And I was, at least right now, because my host parents, Eva and Luis Marín, were carrying an enormous sign that said, "Welcome Dee Blum." In all that strangeness, at least something was familiar. I lugged my bags toward the sign and put them down. My host mother, Marilyn Monroe fabulous with bouncy hair, magenta lipstick, and an hourglass figure, stretched her arms toward me. "*Bienvenida*," she said in breathy Spanish, her mouth near my ear. "I hope you will be like a real daughter to me." Her breath was minty. Her teeth were whitened.

"I'll take those," said Luis, picking up my bags. He was short and sturdy, with the build of a boxer. I guessed they were both in their forties. As we walked toward an exit, Eva pointed to a small food kiosk.

"Here's the concession area," she said. "They have great coffee, and the empanadas are adequate. I'd stay away from the *bizcochos* though, they're very oily. Would you like anything?"

"No, thanks." We stepped out of the airport and walked across the road to the garage. Independent vendors were selling fresh-cut fruit and chili-lime peanuts. "Oo—maybe we can get some mango."

"No!" said Eva, surprisingly severely. "*Never* eat street food." She considered. "Unless you want to lose a few kilos." She sounded like my real mom.

After paying the parking fee, Eva and Luis deposited me and my bags in the back of their sedan. I was squished between stacks of glossy pamphlets and pharmaceutical samples. Apparently one of them was a drug rep. What luck! Now I wouldn't need to worry about running out of Xanax.

"So you just graduated from college?" asked Eva, as Luis got onto the highway. I smiled noncommittally. Why get ticky-tacky about details? "What kind of work are you doing here?"

"I'm organizing tours of organic, sustainable, fair trade coffee farms."

"Oh." Eva paused with the nail of her pinky finger at the corner of her mouth, looking at me through the rearview mirror. Then she looked back at herself and scraped away some excess lipstick. I imagined how strange my job would sound to two people who had grown up surrounded by coffee farms. For them, that would be like vacationing in Iowa to learn about corn. "Who goes on those tours?" she asked, gamely taking a second stab.

"People with a social conscience who want to use their money and time to educate themselves." That did it. It was the last question Eva asked about my work in Costa Rica, and that was just as well with me.

"You're going to love Costa Rica," she said, changing tack. "It's the most beautiful country in the world. And we're the Switzerland of Central America."

I'd read this propaganda in my guidebook, but as we left the airport environs, I could see why Costa Rica inspired such exaggerated praise. The clouds were bigger, the colors were brighter, and everything was more immediate. And there was life everywhere. Palms, ferns, fruit trees. I grasped my grandfather's gold snakes, overcome with gratitude. I had asked to be delivered from my sterility, and here I was, smack in the middle of a flowering nation.

Eva turned to face me. Apparently, she was not a big fan of silence. "I love your carry-on bag. I got some great luggage in Miami." She went on to list the comparative advantages of shopping in different countries. I didn't tell her that all Americans don't go to Europe to buy their wardrobe, because I figured we had so little in common to begin with, why start digging a greater divide?

"Yes, it's true nothing compares with Italian leather," I said. I noticed her posture had become very rigid, and I wondered if I had said something wrong. But as we started going higher up a hill, passing through nicer and nicer neighborhoods, she seemed to relax. Corrugated tin and old tires gave way to turquoise houses and banana trees. The road was also smoother.

"We'll give you a list of approved neighborhoods," she said, rubbing hand sanitizer between her fingers.

"You really want to stay at the top of the hill," said Luis.

I looked at him, askance. Did he mean that literally or figuratively? Were they bougie elitists? But before I could prod further into their class politics, Luis took a turn at full speed and then slammed on the brakes. Dozens of pamphlets fluttered before my eyes, and little blue pills zipped by my forehead. When the pamphlets settled and the pills stopped flying, I opened my eyes. Our car stood not ten feet from a smoking taxi and a man crumpled on the ground. Holy shit. Was he alive?

Some pedestrians rushed over to the man. Suddenly, he sat up and started cursing the taxi driver in colorful slang. The crowd burst into applause. Dogs and roosters howled in concert.

"What luck," said Eva. Some men helped the injured guy to the side of the road, where he continued to impugn the chastity of the taxi driver's mother.

"Luck?" I asked.

"He's standing," she said. "Most people who have accidents at this intersection leave in a bag."

I gulped. That was a grim detail. Luis turned off his engine.

The taxi was in the middle of the street, along with two dozen gawkers. Trying to pass was futile.

Eva went on to give me a detailed history of the accidents at this corner while we waited for Emergency Services to arrive. I learned ES here was like the Tooth Fairy; you had to lose a body part to get proof it existed.

"You must stay alert when you walk here," she said. "The water tanks reduce visibility." I looked at the huge blue cylindrical steel water tanks and wondered why they had been built in the location most likely to cause problems.

Suddenly I heard a groan. Orange-suited emergency workers were attempting to put the man's knee back in place. This elicited a new round of exciting profanities; I would have to look them up later.

"You have to be careful everywhere," added Luis.

"Yes," said Eva. "Walking isn't safe. Especially not by yourself."

Wait. Hadn't she just said we were in the "Switzerland of Central America"?

"I thought this was a very safe country."

"It used to be," she said, nodding. "But the murder rate has gone through the roof. Organized crime and drug cartels act with impunity. But our neighborhood is still okay. As long as you don't walk."

Cool, cool, just drug cartels and organized crime. Sounded like home! Finally, the road cleared and Luis restarted the car.

When we arrived at their house, I began to suspect that my host mother and I shared a preoccupation with *safety first*. An iron gate stood a good ten feet tall, protecting their two-story white fortress from the outside world. All the doors and windows were covered with iron bars. But preventive measures didn't stop at barriers; coming straight at us was a snarling attack dog, carrying a chewed-up doll in his yellowed teeth. As soon as the dog saw me, he dropped the doll and lunged.

"*¡Rambo! ¡Basta!*" Eva waved her acrylic nails in his general direction.

"AAAAAHHHHHH!" I said, throwing elbows and knees. When the dog put his paws on my chest, I lost my balance and fell to the ground, knocking the one-eyed, one-legged baby doll with my foot. The doll must've had a machine in her torso, because she began to wail.

"Waaaah!" said the doll.

"Aaaaah!" said I.

"Down boy," said Luis, in my opinion, way too calmly.

"He's not going to hurt you," said Eva, motioning for me to get up, even though Rambo's paws were pinning me to the ground. Luis jerked the dog's collar. Drool from his snarling face trickled onto my neck.

"*¿Qué está pasando aquí?*" asked an elderly woman in Spanish, coming out from the house. "Here, doggy." The old lady held out a handful of shelled peanuts from her apron. The dog stopped snapping at me, took his paws off my chest, and went to the front door.

"Come on, Dee, get up. He was just saying hi. Come in the house." Eva held out her hand to me. "This is your grandmother, Abuelita Ivelise."

Abuelita Ivelise was standing in the doorway. Her brow was furrowed and imposing. Her hair was an engineering marvel.

"Pleased to meet you," I said, in hesitant Spanish.

"The pleasure is mine." She grabbed my arm with surprising strength. "Come sit, you look tired."

She pulled me through the threshold and down a hallway. I was even more startled by the decor. The entire interior of the house was white. White walls, white tile floors, white couches, white curtains. Eva and Luis dragged my luggage up the white staircase, while Abuelita led me into the white kitchen.

"What did you eat on the plane?" Abuelita Ivelise was pouring two cups of very black coffee. The light was blinding, because it was refracting off every surface. "Was it lunch or dinner?" Now I was in familiar territory. "How much sugar do you take?"

I noticed a thin skin on the milk in the saucer. How natural. "I don't take sugar." It was too late. She had already stirred in four heaping teaspoons. She pretended she couldn't hear me. Once again, familiar territory.

"Did they serve meat?"

"I think so."

"You Americans never eat enough meat. You're not a vegetarian, are you?"

She looked at me with such distrust I feared I had to lie. Would she even know the word "flexitarian"? And would it torpedo our relationship before it even began? "I try to eat a varied diet."

"Our last homestay guest was a vegetarian. And an *atheist.*" She swilled her coffee in one gulp. "You're Catholic, right?"

I sipped my coffee. Such an interesting mix of incredibly bitter and incredibly sweet. I kind of liked it. Abuelita continued to stare at me and I considered. I knew my religion would upset her, and it was purely nominal anyway. Besides, I had sort of converted on the plane. "God is very important to me."

"Good." She sighed. "I'd be very sorry if you went to hell." She seemed genuinely relieved. I decided I liked Abuelita. "Eva's a Protestant," she said, darkly. Like how you might say, *Eva is a pedophile.*

"Oh," I said, with what I hoped was the appropriate level of dismay.

"She was Catholic when Luis married her. But then . . . she converted."

"I'm . . . sorry." It was then I realized how very little I knew about Christianity, or for that matter, Costa Rican culture.

"But divorce would be a sin," she continued, glowering impressively.

"What's that?" asked Eva, coming into the kitchen in her fuchsia high heels. Something that wasn't white! Abuelita didn't bother answering her, and Eva didn't press it. Ooh . . . these two were *not* friends.

Eva dragged me off the white stool. "Let me show you your room." I looked wistfully over my shoulder at Abuelita, who was just taking steamy golden things out of the oven. But Eva pushed me forward.

"We recently redecorated," she said, leading me up the spotless spiral staircase. "At first we thought we would have a child." I couldn't see Eva's face, since I was following her, but I detected a hint of melancholy in her voice. "But that wasn't God's plan." We got to the landing, and Eva directed me toward a door on the right.

I gasped. Everything in my room was white. And scaled for an eight-year-old.

"The bed's fairly new." She pressed down on it to show me. I touched it. It was like a rock. A small, child-sized rock. "And we added the dust ruffle. What do you think?"

The dust ruffle was the only thing in the room that wasn't white. It was beige. "Chic."

"I'm glad you like it. Well, let me know if you need anything. This is your home now." She gave me a warm smile and closed the door.

I put my purse on top of the dresser, which was also clearly intended for a child. I thought about why they had signed up to host homestays. Some people did it for the money—but I doubted that was the case for Eva and Luis. It seemed they were doing it to fill a hole.

I sat on my bed, suddenly feeling a bit sad and overwhelmed. I had just left my family, friends, school, and the only part of the world I had ever known. Now I was in a completely new place with new people and new expectations. Plus a job I had exaggerated my way into. What made me think I was qualified to organize other people's lives when I couldn't even organize my own?

I was starting to go down a dangerous hole of what-ifs. I needed to concentrate on something concrete, fast. I checked my phone, but it was dead. I tore off my dirty clothing, then unpacked my laptop. Abuelita had said they were going to stop at the neighbors for five minutes for coffee, so I knew I had at least an hour, having read all about "Tico Time." In Costa Rica, the word for "now" was flexible. *Ahora* was the technical translation. But in reality, *ahora* meant, "at some point." *Ahorita* meant "at some even vaguer point." But how to convey *now*? As in, there is a fire, please hand me the extinguisher *right now*?

I sat at my little white desk and tried to connect to the Wi-Fi. I had to wait for my computer to find the weak signal, so I opened the window that took up the better part of the back wall. Mistake. Hordes of mosquitoes flew into my room, going straight for the little lamp on my desk. I shut the window, but it was too late, my room was now Dengue Heaven. Stupid, stupid, stupid. I turned off my lamp and cracked the window so they'd fly back out, but the brainless bugs just flew straight into the glass. Great, now my window looked like a killing field. I tried to see past the brown smudges into the garden. The yard was like an erotic still life, overflowing with opening pink flowers and virile banana trees. I could get used to this, I thought, until a marble-sized mosquito buzzed up and zapped me.

I went back to my desk and opened my email. I wanted to see if I had the new *cafetales* list from Suzanne. And maybe more specific guidance than "find the best coffee farms for the Truth Trip." She wasn't kidding about needing someone independent. There was nothing from her, but there was an email from Matías Khalil. I felt a ping of excitement.

TO: Dee Blum
FROM: Matías Khalil
SUBJECT: Buena Suerte in the Land of Pura Vida
cafetaleslistrev.doc (112 KB), contact_info.doc (24 KB)

Hello Dee,

Sorry our introduction has to be virtual. We're battling a proposed gold mine in Ecuador that would wipe out indigenous water sources and it's getting dicey. I had to pull one of our organizers for safety reasons. I hope you're enjoying the tranquility of Costa Rica—has anyone taught you the national phrase? *Pura Vida*, or Pure Life. Basically, "It's all good."

Here's the revised list of *cafetales* to check out. Things have been shifting quickly with the co-ops over the last few years, so some of these farms may be unsuitable. Many have gone to direct trade, and it's hard to verify if they are complying with regulations. Your job is to visit the *cafetales* and determine which ones would make the best candidates. Our goal is to pick one or two for the trips. I know it's Friday, so we don't expect a progress report right away. Take the weekend to get acquainted with the country, maybe check out some fun activities for the social side of the trips.

I've enclosed the contact info for some people you should get in touch with. One is Professor Eugenio Ramírez, a close friend of mine. Have you heard of him? He's pretty well known in Costa Rica, and he should be able to help you narrow down your list.

In Solidarity,
Matías

*Professor Eugenio Ramírez?* Had I heard of Professor Eugenio Ramírez? He was only the most famous revolutionary academic in the Western Hemisphere. He had worked with Liberation Theology priests in El Salvador during the civil war, served as a human rights observer in the Zapatista communities, and supported the indigenous people's struggle against oil drilling in Venezuela. Professor Ramírez's work didn't just consist of tidy interviews conducted in the quiet sanctuary of a university office. This was research that entered the world and changed it.

I leaned back in my uncomfortable white desk chair, awed. This is what I'd been searching for the whole time I was at Berkeley: the chance to be involved in something bigger than myself. Now I was breaking into a world bigger than I had dared to imagine. Suddenly, *overwhelmed* turned into a good thing. My life was a blank slate, and instead of seeing it as an empty wasteland, I saw it as an opportunity.

TO: Matías Khalil
FROM: Dee Blum
SUBJECT: Re: Buena Suerte in the Land of Pura Vida

Hello Matías! Nice to e-meet you. Although I almost feel like I know you since I've read all your essays in *The Nation* and watched your TED Talk on capitalism in the age of AI. It's a little unfair, isn't it? I know so much about you, and all you have is my resume. At the risk of sounding like a fangirl, I have to confess, it's a thrill to work with you.

It's also a thrill that I'm going to meet Professor Ramírez. He's literally my idol. I'll call him first thing Monday. Good luck in Ecuador.

*¡Hasta la victoria siempre!*

Surprisingly, Matías wrote back right away:

TO: Dee Blum
FROM: Matías Khalil
SUBJECT: Re: Buena Suerte in the Land of Pura Vida

Dee, you flatter me. Stop. (Don't.)

Let me know after you meet Eugenio—I can't wait to hear how you two get on.

M

I closed my laptop, lay on my tiny white bed, and smiled. I had been looking for my people for such a long time. It appeared I was finding them.

# CHAPTER FIVE

Later that evening my host parents took me on a driving tour of San José. They showed me the neoclassical *Teatro Nacional*, the flagship of the revered POPS ice cream chain, and oddly, the Coca-Cola bus terminal. They wanted to make sure I never went there: it was in the infamous *Zona Roja*, full of pickpockets and prostitutes. Surprisingly, there was also a Taco Bell. I made a note of that for later.

But I had been too jetlagged to appreciate what I was seeing, so early the next day, I decided to explore downtown. After all, part of my job was finding interesting social activities for the Truth Trip. Eva and Luis reluctantly offered to accompany me, but I declined. I didn't want their impressions to color my own. In less than one day, I had turned into a Christian. Who might I turn into today?

I waited for the Guadalupe bus against their advice. Luis had wanted me to take the less direct Sabanilla bus, which traversed our upper-middle-class suburb, instead of the Guadalupe bus, which went directly through working-class neighborhoods to downtown. Luis seemed to think poverty was contagious, like the flu. The green-and-blue Guadalupe bus lurched to a stop near the blue water tanks. The front window was lined with chili pepper string lights, and a small piñata hung over the driver's head. How festive!

I sat down next to a little boy in a faded Superman T-shirt, eating sticky *dulce de papaya*. He offered me some of his candy. I didn't want to tell him there was no way I was going to eat something that came out of a plastic bag that was wet with his drool, so I just cradled my stomach and said, "*Dolor.*" He gave me a sympathetic look, then calmly resumed chewing. I looked over his head out the window; trees, houses, and buildings flew by in a blur. It filled me with this incredible sense of dislocation and excitement. Sure, I was only going downtown, but I felt like I was at the beginning of an epic adventure.

Soon we were in the middle of the city, but I didn't know where to get off. I didn't want to miss my stop and end up at the Coca-Cola bus station, so when most of the bus disembarked, I followed suit. I stopped a middle-aged lady to ask for directions to the Plaza de la Cultura. She answered in rapid-fire, colloquial Spanish, which made me question *everything*. I thought I spoke Spanish! So why couldn't I understand her?!

"Go north and turn right at the old post office," she said in Spanish, pointing to the corner.

"I don't see a post office there."

"No, love, I said turn at the *old* post office. Currently it's a bank."

After turning right at the current bank/former post office, I stopped a man in painter's pants for clarification.

"*Mi reina*, go fifty meters to the west," he said, "and then turn at the scar of the obelisk."

"There's an *obelisk* downtown?" I asked, confused.

"No, there's a *scar* of an obelisk."

"What is a *scar* of an obelisk?"

He looked at me like it was the most obvious thing in the world. "The mark that remained after the obelisk was removed."

After three more similar conversations, I finally realized it wasn't my Spanish. I mean, it was that, too. But Costa Ricans had a fundamentally different way of giving directions. It was based on landmarks, but the landmarks didn't need to exist—at least not currently. This was an *existential* way of giving directions, where the past and present were one. *Deep.*

Forty minutes and many loops later, I finally made it to the Plaza de la Cultura. I stood in the center and looked around. It was a juxtaposition of colonial buildings with eighties modernism, full of tourists, birds, and entrepreneurs selling turtle-shaped flutes. I took out my camera, a Canon Rebel. I always had a real camera on me, ever since Sadie gave me one on my thirteenth birthday. At first it was a novelty; who had a camera in the age of cell phones? Then it was a self-defense mechanism. Photographing family parties was a welcome relief from participation. But somewhere along the way, I fell in love with it. I marveled at how when you changed the angle, you changed everything. If only I had that kind of control over myself.

After I posted some obligatory shots to Instagram, I struck out from the plaza to explore. The streets were much narrower than the ones at home. Some were paved with stones, and many of them were closed to automobile traffic. Vendors were selling things on every corner: lotto tickets, platano chips, fresh fruit, cheap necklaces. I decided to check out the Central Market. I'd read that you could buy anything there, including your dinner while it was still breathing.

I stepped into the street, and a pink bus with a sign reading, God Loves Everyone, Even You, Poor Sinner, almost ran me over. Huh. Apparently pedestrians did *not* have the right of way here. I would need to remember that. I walked east to the Central Market, where I learned that refrigerating eggs is optional and there is something called shelf-stable milk. I went through the whole cramped bazaar, passing dead chickens, live chickens, herbs, plants, leather, and every food item under the sun *except* dark chocolate.

I left the market and stumbled upon a kosher deli four blocks away, squished between a knockoff sunglasses store and a Virgin Mary paraphernalia kiosk. I could see the infamous Coca-Cola bus station looming in the distance. I stood outside the shop and took a good look. The windows were filled with musty bottles and foreign items; this was no Jerry's Deli.

As I stepped over the threshold, little bells jingled. The interior of the shop was dark and smelled like spices. A middle-aged Sephardic woman looked at me from over the top of her purple rhinestone–studded reading glasses. She said something in an unfamiliar language that I was guessing was Ladino.

"Can I help you?" the lady asked, switching from Ladino to Spanish.

"I'm looking for dark chocolate."

The lady went through her chocolate selection. While I was waiting to see if she had any 70 percent dark, I promised God I'd convert back to Judaism if he'd give me a Valrhona. The lady handed me a Valrhona, and I handed her a couple hundred colorful Costa Rican *colones*. Sweet. The reconversion was on.

When I stepped out of the store, a born-again Jew with a bona fide bar of dark chocolate, I received my first *piropos*—catcalled "compliments."

"*¡Ay, corazón, take me to heaven!*" A yellow taxi zipped by, leaving diesel in my nose.

"*¡Ay, you with those curves and me without brakes!*" said an old man sitting on a curb in front of a fruit stand.

"*¡Guapa!*" said a construction worker. "*Turn off the lights so I can see you better*!"

I wondered what, exactly, these men got out of these transactions. I knew from other women that I was supposed to be offended, but I found it neutral-to-positive. It's not like I received tons of compliments from people I knew.

As I wandered on, a sign in English caught my eye: Coffee Time. The logo was green and white, and looked suspiciously like a mermaid with a crown. This reeked of home. But across the street was an inviting Costa Rican café named Café Pura Vida.

I entered Café Pura Vida and surveyed the bar. It was clear these people took their coffee *very* seriously. The single barista was dressed formally, in a vest and slacks. There was a Chemex, a Hario V60, a French Press, a Marzocco espresso machine, and something I had never seen before. It looked like a combination of a ceramic pitcher and a vase. I approached and asked the barista what it was.

"A Vandola," he said. "This is the Costa Rican way to make *café chorreado*—pour over."

"Okay," I said. "I'll have that."

"Hmm." He raised his eyebrows. "I'm not sure you're ready for *café chorreado*."

"Not ready?!"

"No offense, but you seem more like a pumpkin spice latte person."

I bristled. "For your information, I hate pumpkin spice."

He laughed. "I'm just kidding. Everyone is entitled to their preferences. Even bad ones. Now, for your *café chorreado*—we have eight varietals. Please choose."

I looked at the chalkboard menu, overwhelmed. He was wrong about pumpkin spice, but he was right about me being basic. "What do you recommend?"

"Do you like single origins or blends?"

"Please don't judge me. I don't really know the difference."

"Well, blends are safe. Single origins, they are adventures. Like any adventure, they can go great—or they can go off the rails." *How could a coffee varietal be an adventure?* He read my mind. "Blends smooth out the differences. They give you a uniform, pleasant drinking experience. But single origins take you on a journey. They tell you the minerality of the soil, the humidity, the altitude. Even, perhaps, the dreams of the farmer." He leaned over the counter, closer to me. "In the single origin, you taste the terroir. You taste the soul."

I have to admit, he made it sound intriguing. He wasn't pretentious, like Cody. He was *invested.* "Okay. Give me your favorite single origin."

He reached for some whole beans in a canister with a smile. While he poured boiling water into the Vandola from a gooseneck kettle, I read the flyers on the wall. Many were in English. One in particular called out to me:

LOOKING FOR THE THRILL OF YOUR LIFE?

A TRANSFORMATIVE EXPERIENCE?

COME TO EL RÍO BUNGEE,

RIGHT OFF THE PAN-AMERICAN HIGHWAY, TODAY!

Below the words were pictures of cheery blond girls suspended in midair over a river.

"One *café chorreado* from Tarrazu, *listo,*" said the barista. "Tarrazu means from the land of the saints."

"Does it come with any miracles?"

"No. That costs extra."

I took the coffee and was about to add milk from the counter when he stopped me. "No, no, no. At least try it first." So I did. "How do you like it? What do you taste?"

"Um . . . cocoa?"

"Good."

"So I'm right?"

"There is no right. There is only what you experience." He saw me looking at the flyer. "You should go. You'll never be the same." I blew on my coffee, contemplating. I had sworn I would never, ever, *ever* bungee jump. What could be stupider than jumping off a bridge, essentially imitating suicide? But never being the same was so appealing. Plus, this would surely qualify as investigating a social activity for the Truth Trip. I could expense this!

"Take that bus right there," said the barista. He pointed toward the glass wall of the café. There was a yellow bus parked outside. "Tell the driver to let you off at Salón Los Alfaro. Then just walk to the bridge. Easy."

"Throwing myself off a bridge is easy?"

"You don't even have to jump," he said. "You just have to let go."

♥ ● *

So that's how I found myself approaching the bridge over the Río Colorado. Because the barista told me I would never be the same, and because being in a foreign country made me think nothing was real anyway. This was like a video game; I couldn't die. Actually, my whole life had been like a video game, except someone else had the controller. At least that's what I was thinking when the God of the Bridge stopped me. He was so overpoweringly handsome that I forgot to breathe.

"What's your name?" he asked, in Spanish, slapping Velcro onto my ankle.

"Dee."

"I'm Adrián."

Adrián had curly hair, a quick smile, and a level of sex appeal that seemed frankly unfair. He looked up and down my body, which made my heart race and palms dampen. Then I realized he was assessing me for harness size. As he straightened out cords, he asked me, "You came here by yourself?"

I nodded, unable to speak. Was it because he was so hot, or because I was potentially going to jump off a bridge?

"Bit of a daredevil, huh?"

"The opposite, actually," I said.

"You came to leap off a bridge, by yourself. You seem pretty brave to me."

"Then why am I frozen in place?"

"Isn't the definition of being brave being afraid of something but doing it anyway?" His eyes twinkled. How could I back out now? He held out the harness for me to step into. Then he bent down by my hips to fasten it. The closeness of his face to my waist made me blush.

"Is that tight enough?" he asked. I nodded. When he took my hand, heat filled my body. "You're going to jump on three."

I stepped onto the platform and looked down at the river. The sight of all that water rushing so far below me sent panic flooding through my body in one enormous wave. As I stood on the precipice, the reality that my life wasn't a video game hit me with the force of a forty-meter plunge. This was real.

I backed away from the ledge. Some tourists waiting to go next pointed at me and laughed.

"I'm sorry," I said to Adrián. "I can't. This is a mistake."

"It isn't," said Adrián. "Something brought you here."

"Wimp," said one of the tourists, a drunk frat boy.

"Hey," Adrián said to the jerk in English, "that is no way to speak to a woman!" Then he put a hand on my shoulder and spoke softly into my ear, his breath hot against my skin. The baby hairs on my neck bristled. "I know you can do this, Dee." He took my hand in his and gave me a gentle smile. "Do you trust me?"

I don't know why, *but I did*. "Yes."

"The trick is not to think about it. If you hesitate, you won't do it. When I say three, just go for it. One"—he squeezed my hand hard—"two"—he squeezed tighter—"three!"

I let go.

# CHAPTER SIX

The flyer wasn't wrong. Jumping off the bridge *was* transformative. At the bottom of that rope, I had an intense, direct experience of oneness. The river and sky were indistinguishable. My body had no beginning and no end. My skin was no longer a border. Doubts, fears, self—they all drifted gently away with the current. How long would this feeling last? Could I find a way to hang onto it? Or would I be destined to spend my life chasing it, one jump after another?

After Adrián reeled me back up to the bridge, I stood there shaking and laughing and staring at him like a lunatic. But my unhinged laughter was contagious, and he started laughing, too.

"Looks like we have a convert," he said. "Want to go again?"

"Hey, it's my turn!" said the jerk American.

"Sorry," Adrián said to him in English, "We're closed."

"What?! You just offered her another jump!"

"It's siesta time." Adrián turned to me. "Come on. Let's get a beer. *Bien fría*."

Ten minutes later we were at a little bar down the road.

We sat at a scratched wooden table that the employees had brought out of the back room just for me. Everyone else sat at the bar, watching *fútbol* on the tiny TV, pushing away the plastic yellow flags that the fan kept whipping into their faces. I was the only female.

"Why did you come to Costa Rica?" he asked in clear, simple Spanish, over a pair of Imperial beers. I knew he was slowing it down for me. It was nice. "Are you studying? Vacationing?"

The real answer bubbled up to my mouth, but I hesitated. How would it sound? Because I had known other people were living, and I wanted to be one of them? Because my life was so tightly controlled that I felt like I couldn't breathe? I needed a slightly less intense answer. "I was bored."

Adrián laughed. He was watching me pick the label off my sweaty beer bottle. I had shredded it, and little sticky pieces stayed glued to my fingers. "You came here because you were bored?" he asked. "When I get bored, I don't go to a foreign country."

"You don't really seem like the type to get bored."

"Busted." He smiled, and goosebumps somehow managed to raise themselves on my arms, even though it was five hundred degrees plus humidity. "But I don't believe that's why you came here either."

"I came for work."

"Don't you have jobs in America?"

"No, we're totally out!"

He laughed. "So you came with coworkers?"

"No."

"A boyfriend?"

"No."

"He at home?"

"He doesn't exist."

Adrián smiled wider. "So you really came to Costa Rica all by yourself?"

I nodded.

"And you were trying to convince me you're not brave? Sorry, don't take this the wrong way, but I think you're an unreliable narrator."

I laughed. "Isn't everyone unreliable about themselves?"

"Maybe to a degree. But some people have more self-awareness than others." He looked right into me. Like he could see my bones. My DNA. "We've established you're not very self-aware," he said with a smile, "but let's try anyhow. You came to a foreign country by yourself, then flung yourself off a bridge. So, Dee, are you running toward something, or away from it?"

I ran my hand underneath the table, feeling the exposed ridges of the rough wood, the hardened knobs that must have been old chewing gum, and the deep grooves of carved initials. When I looked up, his eyes met mine. They flashed with challenge and sugar.

"Can it be both?" I asked.

"You tell me."

Boldness surged over me—perhaps residual hormones from my jump—and I took my hand from beneath the table and placed it squarely next to his. "Maybe I came to find a new version of myself."

"Maybe I can help you find her." He took my hand. It was warm and firm. Somehow both comforting and exciting. "Let's start tonight."

♥ ● *

That night around nine, Adrián came roaring up to Eva and Luis's house in a silver Jeep. He was wearing a white button-down guayabera, with several buttons unfastened, revealing a breathtaking expanse of deeply tanned skin. He jumped out of the Jeep and gave me the Costa Rican double-air kiss—except with no air. His lips brushed my cheeks lightly, politely, but it was enough to make me unsteady. He held the passenger door open for me and I hopped in. To my surprise, I was into this. Was that strictly speaking a feminist reaction? Did I care?

I suddenly felt incredibly shy. I had vowed to myself not to get into a relationship while I was in Costa Rica. I was here to figure out who I was, and to learn to be independent. If I didn't know how to be autonomous without a boyfriend, how could I be autonomous with one?

Yet here I was staring at Adrián's hand casually gripping the steering wheel. Marveling at his long fingers. His smooth skin stretched over compact muscles. What was I doing?! I tried to keep my eyes on the road, but I couldn't stop myself from sneaking looks. I figured he was in his early twenties. Relaxed, confident, athletic, with curly hair that couldn't pick a direction. His smile was the standout feature though—wide, genuine, infectious. And just a little bit naughty.

"Is it common to drive in the middle of the road here?" I asked. Adrián was veering around a large speed bump, known colloquially here as *muertos*—dead people.

"Sure is." He was now playing chicken with a taxi driver. In any other circumstance, I would bet on a taxi driver, but Adrián seemed in control. Cody would never in a million years challenge a taxi driver. "*Hijueputa*," Adrián shouted through his open window as we whooshed by the taxi driver, who was meekly clinging to the right side of the road. Adrián returned to the proper lane and then reached into my lap to take my hand. "*Disculpe, corazón*," he said. *Heart.* I could get used to this.

We arrived at Tuanis, one of San José's largest nightclubs.

Women in short skirts and men in shiny shirts packed the large dance floor under flashing strobes and hanging TV screens. I caught a glance of myself in a mirror; I was seriously underdressed in my "nice jeans." God, I hated it when my mother was right. Tables ringed the dance floor, and upstairs there were little booths for couples to eat, drink, and dry hump. I was thrilled by all the color and noise. This was *living.* Adrián pushed through the crowd, got us two Cuba Libres from the bar, then led me through the dancing throng.

"Do you know how to dance?" he asked.

"I can do the FriYay TikTok dance."

He shook his head, pained, then taught me how to salsa, utilizing the male-endorsed "thigh method." He grasped me close to his body, put his right leg between both of mine, and told me to "feel the rhythm." At first, I thought this was a blatant attempt to get between my legs. After a couple of minutes, I realized I didn't mind.

"I have to go to a wedding tomorrow," he said.

"Yeah?" I was busy counting. Even while "feeling it," I had to pay close attention. Tropical rhythms were totally counterintuitive to me.

"Why don't you come with me?" he said.

He spun me in a circle. I considered going to a wedding with him. I imagined how he'd look *in a tuxedo.* I also imagined the alternative: going to Mass with Abuelita and Luis. "Why not?"

Several Cuba Libres later, Adrián was showing me how to merengue. Much easier than salsa, and much lewder, too. It afforded me a very clear idea of Adrián's anatomy. So now I knew he had a body. I wanted to know if he had a brain.

"What kind of requirements are there for being an extreme guide? Did you have to study physiology? Take a certification course?" I asked.

"Oh, no, there's no training at all." I gulped. Not putting bungee jumping on the Truth Trip. "But it's just a weekend job for me. I recently graduated from the university."

"What did you study?"

"Philosophy."

"Really?" I stepped on his toes. "That's pretty esoteric."

"Well, it was one of my majors. My dad owns some hotels, and he wanted me to study management so I could help him. But that's not my passion."

"Wow, two majors." I stepped on his toes again. "But why philosophy specifically?"

"Because it helps me find my place in the world."

*It helped him find his place in the world.* Could he help me find mine? I stopped dancing. "Can we sit for a bit?"

Adrián led me off the dance floor. We stopped at the bar to get fresh drinks, then went upstairs, which was considerably dimmer and quieter.

"So," I said, settling into one of the soft magenta couches. "Did you?"

"Did I what?" Adrián was trying to figure out how close to sit. First, he sat next to me, but not touching. Then he scooted closer, until his thigh was pressed next to mine.

"You know, find your place in the world?"

Adrián's face lit up with some interior sun, and he leaned closer. One arm was around my shoulder and the other was hovering near my knees. "It's not exactly something you find. It's just somewhere you go." He placed his hand on my knee. I shivered.

"What does that mean?"

"You think you know where you want to go, so you go." Adrián's hand lifted off my knee and fluttered in the air as he spoke. "But when you get there, you have new questions. So it's a process of constant reevaluation. You never get 'there,' because 'there' keeps moving. So you just keep going, keep questioning."

"But you said philosophy helps you find your place in the world."

"It does."

"But you just said you don't get there."

"You don't."

"So how does it help?"

"It helps with the looking."

"Oh." I grabbed my drink.

"You don't like that answer."

"Not at all." I looked up at Adrián and recognized the expression on his face. Not from experience, but from the movies. Like I was a new land he had just discovered. I put my drink on the table and stood up. "Let's dance again."

Adrián hesitated, then put his drink down. "Whatever you want." He took my hand and guided me to the dance floor. Dancing was nice because I didn't have to look at him directly. I didn't want to think about never getting "there." And I certainly didn't want to think about what it meant that my body wouldn't stop shaking. So I asked him questions about his family and the wedding.

"Will they think it's weird you're bringing some random North American as your date?"

"No. Just pretend you're my girlfriend."

"What?! Wouldn't that be weirder?"

"Nah. It will be easier that way." He sent me on a double spin. I felt a little uncomfortable out there. Adrián spun me back into his arms.

"But *why* will it be easier?" I reluctantly removed my legs from Adrián's and took a step back, forcing him to look at me. "Can't they think we're friends?"

"That's not really a thing here." He wrapped his arms around my waist. "But you don't have to pretend if you don't want to. Whatever makes you comfortable." He put his cheek next to mine and spun us in endless circles, his arms circling my waist and shoulders. The room flashed around me in muted reds and blacks. The only solid thing was Adrián, and the only thing I knew was that while he was holding me, I was safe. "Forget about it," he whispered, and I did.

"Spin me around again."

"As much as you like," he said. We were spinning. I was laughing. "Always."

# CHAPTER SEVEN

I woke up the next morning excited and jittery, and it wasn't from Abuelita's double-strength coffee. I was supposed to be researching coffee farms, but instead I was fretting over what outfit was appropriate for a Costa Rican wedding. Just because I wasn't Adrián's real girlfriend didn't mean I didn't want to look good.

So I needed a dress. Eva was thrilled—*thrilled*—to play dress-up with me in her bedroom. She pulled out every dress she owned and spread them out on the bed. Her generosity was trumped only by her love of sparkles. I didn't understand how she could be in an uber-conservative church yet have the wardrobe of a drag queen.

"What does he do for a living?" she asked, as I modeled a particularly short red number. She was sitting on her bed with her knees pulled up. In that position and without her makeup, she looked like a teenager.

"He works for his dad. His dad owns some hotels."

"Oh, that's *perfect.*" I could see her calculating his net worth in her mind. I shimmied out of the red dress and tried on another. "*That's* the dress." It was a short green frock with a deep

V-neck. It was the most conservative dress she owned. "He's going to be very happy."

That was a really weird statement. Was I getting dressed *for him*?

But it turns out Eva was right—the dress did make him happy. Or possibly the person inside it. His eyes widened when he picked me up a few hours later.

"Thanks for coming with me, *novia*," he said, eyeing the plunging collar of my dress. Maybe I should have been offended that he was staring at my chest, but honestly, I was flattered. I didn't even mind that he called me girlfriend. After all, it was only for one day. And he was completely breathtaking in a tux.

So I perved on Adrián as he drove us to Escazú, admiring his broad shoulders and trim waist. Was it wrong to objectify him? Or was it a needed rebalancing of gender norms? I wrested my eyes off him long enough to check out the scenery. Escazú was incredibly posh. "This is like Costa Rican Beverly Hills," I said.

"Isn't it beautiful? I'm going to buy a house here someday."

We parked and entered the vestibule of the church. If the neighborhood was Costa Rican Beverly Hills, then the church was the Beverly Hills Hotel. Other than the pictures of Jesus on the cross, you'd have thought it was a hotel lobby. It was all marble, drapery, and flowers. I stopped to examine a flower arrangement. It had massive birds of paradise, hibiscus, and orchids in deep shades of purple and fuchsia; so different from the pale pink roses I was used to. Adrián pushed me deeper into the room. "You've got to meet my mom."

Even if I wasn't his real girlfriend, this was still intimidating. I had no idea what the social rules were here. Was I supposed to call her by her first name? Hug her? Bow? No, that would be overkill. Adrián led me to a strikingly attractive and regal woman, Doña Teresa. She was wearing an ice-blue dress and black pearl earrings.

"Pleased to meet you," I said in Spanish, grazing her cheek in the Costa Rican hello-goodbye kiss. I didn't have the hang of it yet—were you supposed to make contact, or just get in the vicinity?

"*El placer es mío.*" She eyed me up and down without any attempt to hide it. "You look so pale," she said, in Spanish. "You'd look better in lighter colors."

"*¡Mamá!*" said Adrián.

"It's true, she's such a beautiful girl!" She said something rapidly to Adrián that I couldn't understand. *She hated me. She hated me. She hated me.* "And so polite, too." *Oh god, did she hate me!* "So what do you, Dee? Are you a student?"

I looked at her perfectly smooth pearl earrings, which probably cost as much as a small car. How could I tell her that *I was a professional radical*? This was not the right audience for that. And I *was* a student until just two weeks ago. If Costa Ricans gave directions based on former landmarks, maybe this flexible attitude toward time could extend to other contexts?

"Yes. I'm a student." Adrián looked at me, surprised, but didn't say anything.

"Where are you studying?" she asked.

Crap. I had hoped to keep this to a temporal-based almost-not-lie. Well, if I was going to be a fake girlfriend, I might as well be the best fake girlfriend I could be.

"I'm in an exchange program at UCR, doing my last semester before law school."

Suddenly, Teresa's expression turned from mild distaste to interest. "Wonderful." People were drifting from the vestibule to the nave of the church. "Come, dear, sit with us."

So it was flanked by pheromone-spewing Adrián and his prim mother that I watched the wedding ceremony. The priest started hemming and hawing, and I sat up straight and tried very hard to understand what he was saying. Would I have to *eat the body of Christ*? Do they do that at Catholic weddings?

It turns out, they do. Everyone was going up to the altar. I was pretty sure this was just meant for Catholics. Would it be a sacrilege if I, as a Jew, took the communion wafer? And if I didn't take it, would everyone assume it was because I had unconfessed sins? Like having strictly forbidden premarital sex with Adrián? This was a lose-lose situation. I hesitated as everyone in our pew rose. Adrián held out his hand and looked at me quizzically. Teresa was also looking. I reluctantly followed him to the altar.

As the priest put the wafer in my mouth, I closed my eyes and prayed. First, to my God. *Sorry, My God, this doesn't mean anything.* Second, to Jesus. *Sorry, Jesus, I hope you understand. Also, I hope you will still protect me when I say cover me with your precious sanctified blood.*

I went back to the pew with Adrián and was relieved not to be struck with lightning. I *almost* made it through the rest of the ceremony without issues. But when the priest offered the final blessing, I started tearing up. Why did this always happen?! Would Adrián's family mistake my tears as a desire to don the white gown?

Perhaps. Teresa nodded approvingly when she noticed my sniffles. After the final benediction, we exited the nave and entered a beautifully maintained courtyard.

"Go stand with all the other girls over there, 'college student' Dee," said Adrián, pointing toward a fountain, where young women in multicolored finery were swarming.

"Why?"

"My cousin's going to throw the flowers."

"I don't want to." The girls looked like they were going to topple over the flower arrangements. Someone was going to get crushed, I just knew it.

"Ok, but it'll look weird if you don't," he said.

Just then, a young woman grabbed my arm and tugged me with her into the middle of a flock of blushing and giggling girls.

"Use both hands to catch it," shouted Adrián. I glared at him from the middle of the pack, now trapped. If I tried to escape, Adrián's mother would notice and make him "break up" with me. And at this point, it was about pride. I was good enough for him, dammit.

"Blah blah blah blah," said the groom.

"Blah blah blah blah," said the bride, and suddenly there I was, right at the end of the bouquet's trajectory. I tried to bobble it, and the flowers bounced back into the air. Other girls dove for it and pushed and scratched, and those flowers kept flying back to me like I was a freaking magnet! I'll be damned if those other girls didn't absolutely place it in my hands by pushing each other out of the way. So there I was, the reluctant winner of the bridal floral arrangement. The other girls pretended to congratulate me.

The bride came up to me. "This means you're going to get married next!" She kissed my cheek, actually making contact. "Congratulations!"

"You caught it," Adrián said. "With only one hand!"

"What luck," said Teresa. "Do you intend to get married before law school? If you wait to have children until after, won't you be too old?"

My shock must have been apparent, because Adrián distracted her by waving at someone. "Look, Mom, it's Tía Marisol." Teresa followed Adrián's gaze to Marisol, who was wearing a pink silk dress and an entire chest full of jewelry. Marisol approached and kissed Teresa and Adrián. She looked at me with frank curiosity.

"Marisol," said Teresa, "This is Dee, Adrián's new girlfriend."

Marisol smiled and pulled me in for an embrace, horribly crushing the ill-fated bridal flowers. I felt the spike of a bird of paradise prick my chest.

"Pleased to meet you," I said in Spanish, again awkwardly attempting the hello-goodbye air kiss.

"Dee's an exchange student," said Teresa. "She's going to be a lawyer."

"I'm so proud of her," Adrián said, giving me a devilish look.

"*¡Qué maravilloso!*" said Tía Marisol, clasping her hands together over her ample bosom. "We could always use a lawyer in the family." Whoa, slow down, lady. How did we go from new girlfriend to family?

"What is your area of focus?" asked Teresa.

Adrián looked at me. "Yes, I'd like to know as well. Since we never discussed it."

Was he mad I lied? I was just trying to be a good fake girlfriend! I looked at Teresa and Tía Marisol, then stammered, "Corporate." They kept looking at me. "Maybe in-house for a coffee brand?"

Marisol smiled. "My sister and her husband own a coffee farm. Café Bavaria."

I perked up. "Is it organic? Sustainably produced?"

Marisol laughed. "It sustains their lifestyle."

Teresa gave a wry grin. "Only Americans use fad terms like that. All our farms are 'sustainable.' We've been growing coffee in Costa Rica for over two hundred years."

Adrián turned to me. "It's a conventional farm." *Translation: full of chemicals and awful labor practices.* "You know, the kind you want to work at? After law school?" He was trolling me now. He was enjoying this!

"I could arrange a private tour for you," said Marisol. "So you can be certain it's the field you want to go into."

"That would be great."

"But if you go to law school, when will you have kids?" Marisol asked.

"That's what I said!" said Teresa.

My face must've betrayed my alarm because Adrián jumped in again. "Oh, listen, my favorite song . . . 'La Vaca.' Come on, Dee, let's dance." He took me to the dance floor.

"What was all that about?" he asked, as he began the basic merengue steps. I tried to follow.

"Yeah, seriously, I'm not a breeding mare."

"No," he laughed. "You telling my mom you're an exchange student. I thought you were here to organize some sort of justice tours?"

"Truth Trips. To learn about organic and fair trade coffee. I thought that would bring up more questions than necessary."

"Are you embarrassed by your job?"

"What? No! I'm proud. This just doesn't seem like the right crowd."

Adrián looked at me, confused, as he sent me out on a spin. I returned.

"I'm an activist," I said. "I work to take down the capitalist system." I looked around me at the majestically jeweled women, hoping he would get it. He did.

"So we're The Man, huh?" A hint of a smile tugged at the corners of his mouth.

"Basically."

"*You're* the North American."

"I know. It's ironic."

"Don't you think you're being a little judgmental?" he asked. "How do you know people here wouldn't understand your point of view? Or at least respect it?"

"Fair point. So what do you think of my point of view?"

"I think it's really naive and first world and privileged."

"See?!"

"But I respect your right to be naive."

My face flushed. He held me tighter and put his cheek close to mine. And suddenly I couldn't tell if I was hot with anger or hot with desire. He spun me around, using his leg as an anchor between my thighs. Okay. That was desire. But I was still annoyed.

"Why do you think I'm naive? What do you have against ethically produced coffee?"

"When you choose to buy a product from someone, you are choosing *not* to buy a product from someone else. What happens to all the workers picking coffee at conventional farms if you stop buying that coffee? 'Fair' trade coffee isn't a no-cost solution. Someone gets hurt. In this case, the most vulnerable."

"It hurts the rich owners, not the laborers."

Adrián noticed my furrowed brow. "Hey. We're at a wedding. We're supposed to be drinking and dancing. Maybe even kissing." He looked at me with a twinkle. I tried to frown. "Besides, you're my girlfriend, if even just for one night, and I want to enjoy it. Truce?" I nodded. He pulled me in closer. "You can try to convert me to your radical cause tomorrow."

After the wedding, Adrián dropped me off at the gate surrounding my host parents' fortress. I fished my keys out of my purse and began the elaborate process of entering the citadel. Top lock. Middle lock. Bottom lock. That was just the gate.

By the time I was putting my third key in the front door, Rambo was barking furiously. I didn't want my host family to wake up, so I tossed a handful of cake crumbs I'd saved from the wedding and sprinted to the stairs. I could hear Rambo licking the tiles as I crept toward my bedroom door. All the lights were off upstairs, so I knew I was safe. Perhaps they were tired from their big day. Abuelita and Luis went to Mass, which I gathered was a long affair with a lot of kneeling, which couldn't have been great for Abuelita's knees. Eva went by herself to a Pentecostal service. I wasn't sure what that entailed, but I had heard Abuelita dismissively refer to the congregants as *panderetas*—tambourine-shakers. Abuelita knew how to throw some shade.

I slipped out of my dress and took it to the hamper in my closet. Before I tossed it in, I caught a scent of Adrián. Cedar and sweat. Shit, I was in trouble. I pulled on my pajamas and went to my laptop to write to Matías. I wanted to see what he thought about me visiting a corporate farm. He was slightly less intimidating than Suzanne.

TO: Matías Khalil
FROM: Dee Blum
SUBJECT: Espionage?

Hi Matías! I've been offered a private tour of a conventional farm. I thought it might be useful if I got photos and interviews with the laborers. We could use them in the promotional materials for the Truth Trip. Showing the enemy to sell the hero—what do you think?

Again, Matías responded immediately:

TO: Dee Blum
FROM: Matías Khalil
SUBJECT: Re: Espionage?

> Look at you, already hustling up opportunities. Going to a conventional farm would be great. I have to warn you; it will be difficult to witness the true working conditions. Management will only show you what they want you to see. But if anyone can do it, it's you. I know all about your sleuthing skills. We're honored to be working with such a top-notch gumshoe. Turns out the fangirl(boy) thing goes both ways.
>
> *¡Buena suerte!*

*Fanboy?* My intellectual idol was fanboying *for me*? Impossible. And gumshoe? Sleuthing skills? The only mystery I'd ever solved is where the Tooth Fairy had put my teeth—in a mason jar under my mom's bathroom sink. That was a fun surprise for an eight-year-old.

It didn't make sense; but then again, little made sense right now. I'd only been here a few days and already my entire previous world felt like a dream. I had come here to change my life, to become a different person. Well, my life here was definitely different. I looked at the bridal bouquet on the desk, an explosion of color and hope. I wasn't sure if experience equaled identity, but either way, I was getting closer to a breakthrough. I could feel it.

# CHAPTER EIGHT

When the sun woke me at five in the morning, I knew I was in a completely new realm of existence. In my old life, if I had been woken up at five, I would have thrown sharp objects at the rioting birds. But now I rejoiced with them. This was a new land, and I was a new person, willing to forgive my winged friends for their noisy transgressions.

Minutes later, my phone buzzed. It was Adrián. "We have a meeting at Café Bavaria this morning," he said. "Be ready in an hour."

I was both excited and nervous. Excited, because I was going to document abuses in Corporate Hell, a.k.a. Café Bavaria. Nervous, because I'd be spending the entire day with Sexy Junior Oligarch Adrián. He was a whole lot of temptation wrapped up in a whole lot of potential aggravation. We were obviously politically incompatible. And there was that pesky "vow to focus on myself" thing. So, despite his astounding hotness, I would resist a romantic entanglement. We were going to be friends. Friends with incredible, yet resistible, chemistry. But I still needed to know more about him. Just, you know, in case.

"How often do you work for your dad?" I pretended to occupy myself with Google Maps, but I was making a mental list. Did he smoke? Did he have a Madonna-whore complex? What were his thoughts on cobalt mining?

"Pretty close to full-time."

"So why were you working at El Río Bungee?"

"It was my part-time job in college. I don't do it very much anymore. But a friend was sick and asked me to cover his shift." He turned off the road leading out of Carmen and into a roundabout. "So I guess our meeting was fate." He winked at me and then whipped out of the roundabout and onto a main artery. Right on the side of the road was a twisted motorcycle, surrounded by police and an ambulance. Jesus Christ, I couldn't go more than ten kilometers without seeing a traffic accident. Was I going to get used to this? I looked at Adrián, who was silently crossing himself. "*Pobrecito*," he said. Then he looked back over to me. "I had a motorcycle. But I totaled it."

I wasn't ready to speak again until we got to the Pan-American Highway. A tollbooth station was blocking the road. Adrián pulled coins out of the glove box and tossed them into a plastic bucket. They clinked loudly on their way down the pipe.

"So you're all set to be a semi-reluctant hotel mogul, huh?" I asked.

"Pretty much." He looked at me and smiled. "What do you want to do? Be a professional radical?"

"Is that an actual position? If so, yes."

"But why on coffee farms?"

"Because I'm interested in economic justice *and* sustainable environmental practices."

"Then why are you drinking out of a plastic bottle?" He gestured at my Alpina water bottle. "Is that sustainable?"

I gulped.

"I don't understand why you Americans are so obsessed with the origin of your coffee. I don't see you making sure your breakfast cereal is sustainably sourced. What is the terroir of your oat milk?"

"Fair point. Maybe we should be examining all of our products this way."

"But you don't. So your fascination with 'ethically sourced' coffee is virtue signaling."

Damn. He was good at this. I decided to go back on the offensive. "I don't understand your problem with sustainable production and fair trade. You say you're concerned about the pickers at the conventional farms losing their jobs. But if the market share shifts, they'll go work at the ethical, sustainable farms. They're migrant labor. This way, they migrate to better working conditions."

"That's a lot of assumptions. Most of the fair trade organizations create price floors, which artificially manipulate prices. How is that fair to the sellers who invested their money and deserve to make a profit?"

"But the commodity prices aren't fair," I said. "They don't include social and environmental costs."

"Sure they do. The market takes negative externalities into account through supply and demand."

"That's not true! Even the IMF admits all costs aren't factored into pricing. Ignoring social costs causes social problems. And ignoring environmental issues causes *the literal death of our planet.*"

"Dee." He casually passed another car on the right shoulder. "Price floors have knock-on effects. They can create surpluses. Which means the farms are stuck with coffee they can't sell. Which means they hire less labor. Which means more hungry families." Ugh, I hated that this made sense. "Intervening with the market creates more problems than it solves."

I turned toward the window, little sparks of anger flying off my fingers. The whole this-is-the-way-the-world-is-and-we-can't-do-anything-about-it thinking really drove me up the wall. Because you hit a complicated situation, you're just supposed to do *nothing*?

"Hey," he said, reaching out for my hand. "Let's not talk about this. I hate politics."

The softness of his voice took the edge off my anger. Besides, it was so freaking humid today, it was easy to get irritable. "What do you like, then?"

He paused to consider. We were now out of the city and into a more rural part of Costa Rica. Nothing but green lined the highway. "Smart women." He stopped looking at the road and looked right at me. "Smart, passionate, naive, idealistic women."

"I'm not naive."

"I was talking about women in general."

"Right."

Adrián started slowing down the Jeep. "*Preciosa*, I think Google Maps is trying to drive us straight into a waterfall. Can you check the directions?" *Preciosa*. It was impossible to stay mad at this guy. I looked at the map. I had never navigated anything well, even metaphorically, so how was I supposed to interpret directions in a country that didn't use addresses or labeled street names? Plus, I was completely overwhelmed by the scenery. This was my first time out of San José and I couldn't believe the roads. They were barely wide enough for one car, twisting in and out of mountain passes, skirting streams, and bordering ravines. I felt like I was on a green-and-blue rollercoaster that took dips through the hills and did loops through the clouds. I was disoriented, dizzy, and awestruck. What did east or west mean to me now?

But Adrián didn't say anything about my navigational

incompetence. He just squinted at his phone as he drove. After a few wrong turns, we saw a small sign almost overtaken by the massive leaves of *sombrillas de pobre*—a plant aptly named poor man's umbrellas. Adrián turned right and we both caught our breath.

Calling the road a road was an act of charity. It was a narrow swath of earth carved out of the mountain on the left and buffeted by tumbling hills on the right. It was paved, in a sense. In the sense that someone thought it would be fun to fill it with different-sized rocks. I swallowed hard, and Adrián pretended to look blasé. It would take just one awkward roll over a large rock . . . or a sharp stone puncturing a tire . . . or a little bit of earth giving way . . . and then we'd be over the side, rolling like children down a grassy knoll, except on fire and with glass shards in our eyes.

Adrián put the Jeep into four-wheel drive and we puttered on, getting out occasionally to remove sloth-sized rocks or push the Jeep out of a rut. I relaxed a little when I realized that even if we did skid off the road, there were lots of cushy bushes to break the fall. People survived stuff like that all the time . . . probably. But then the road veered to the left, narrowed, and dropped precipitously. That's where I lost any pretense of being okay. The road was now lined by a sheer rock wall stretching down into the abyss.

Adrián stopped the Jeep and we got out to assess our chances. Where the road turned stood a lone tree trunk, stretching up to the sky in barren stillness. Its singed branches were an ominous sign; beyond there was nothing solid, just fog rolling over the valley a thousand feet below. I clung to the trunk and watched light rain fall in almost horizontal sheets. Adrián turned to me. "What are you thinking?"

*That we are going to die a painful and slow death, impaled on the gearshift, hanging upside down in the Jeep, flames just beginning to flicker at our feet.*

"Mmmph," I said.

Adrián kicked a little rock and watched it free-fall down the side. We couldn't hear or see it touch the bottom. "You know, we don't have to go," he said.

"Are you scared?"

"No!" He laughed a hollow laugh. "Concerned, maybe." Then I started shaking. If Adrián was scared, and Adrián was the driver, and an extreme guide on top of it, there was no way I was going down that road. Adrián walked away from the tree and puffed out his chest. "What the hell," he said. "We all have to die someday." He took my hand and led me back to the Jeep.

"What are you talking about?" I stood in front of the door. "I'm not going if you think we're going to die."

"We're not going to die."

"But it's a possibility."

He shrugged. "It's always a possibility." And without another word, he guided me back into the Jeep, turned on the engine, and started down the Road to Hell. I could see its blood-covered maws opening up for us, smiling. Sweat trickled down from the small of my back to my thighs. All I could see out the windows was gray, because the fog was thick and the rain was kicking up dust. My body was at an extreme angle pointing down, and I was hanging on tight to the door so I wouldn't go flying out the windshield. Blood shrieked in my ears, rain lashed at the windshield, and the wheels whined against the rocks. We started rounding a boulder and hysteria took a hold of my body. *I'm going to die, I haven't accomplished anything with my life, and my parents are going to go bankrupt repatriating my body! Why didn't I buy the good travel insurance?!* I closed my eyes and braced for impact.

And then, curiously, we weren't tumbling down a cliff, and we didn't seem to be descending. I opened my eyes. The cliff was gone! The road was level! We weren't dead! Adrián hit the brakes and we both opened our mouths and shouted:

"Yes!"

"We're alive! YES!"

And then, out of nowhere, I leaned over and kissed his lips.

"Oh!" he said, surprised, but evidently in a good way.

"Oh!" I said, embarrassed, and surprised, but not in such a good way.

"See," he said, putting his foot back on the gas. "That wasn't so bad. It just looked bad."

"Right," I said, thinking that if I was ever going to take up smoking, this was the time. "It was nothing."

We sat silently in our separate parts of the Jeep. I was too embarrassed to look at him and much too embarrassed to speak. I couldn't believe I had kissed him. I was supposed to be *resisting* romantic entanglements!

"I think that's it," said Adrián, pointing toward a sign that said Café Bavaria.

"Looks like it." I rolled down my window and put my hot face out. Cool air rushed at me, turning my cheeks even pinker. I snuck a look at Adrián. He sure did look good, his muscles tensing as he expertly shifted gears, his hair flying in the breeze. Would a brief fling count as a romantic entanglement?

Adrián turned right onto a little access road lined with banana trees. At the end of the road, there was an iron gate. Adrián parked next to it. I jumped out, relieved to have my feet on terra firma. Adrián came up to me. "Thank you," he said.

"For what?"

"For this." And then he leaned over and kissed me. Heat exploded all over my body with little popping sounds. Blood rushed out of my head and swelled all the cells in the more sensitive parts of my anatomy. My lungs began to fail. Adrián pulled back and looked into my eyes to see if this was okay.

*He's still young,* I thought, my resolve wavering. *Maybe he will reject his bourgeois ways.* He looked like he was coming in for the kill, so I started hiccuping, flushed beet red, and then said something incomprehensible. Adrián looked utterly bewildered.

I pushed open the iron gate, and we walked down a long drive with trees on both sides forming a canopy. I'm sure Adrián was thinking I was nuts, because after all, I had initiated the first kiss, and if he asked me about it, I would have said, *Yes, I am nuts.* It's not that I didn't find Adrián attractive. In fact, I was *turning bright red with the thought of his lips exploring other areas,* but lust was not a sufficient determining factor. One had to use reason. One had to use one's better judgment. One had to stop concentrating on Adrián's *lean muscles rippling under his clothes.*

I had to get a hold of myself. I was here to work. I was here to find purpose in my life. I was here to stop being controlled by stronger personalities. I was not here to become the girlfriend of a risk-courting junior hotel mogul . . . *or was I?*

"Nice day, huh?" said Adrián, searching for a way out of this terrible discomfort. The normalcy of his voice brought everything back into perspective, and the blood returned to my brain, where it belonged.

"Sure is." And in truth, it was glorious. Sure, the humidity must've been 90 percent, but the landscape was stunning. Costa Rica was like a box of crayons with all the ugly colors thrown out. We walked down the drive until we saw a Costa Rican–style plantation house, blinding white in the sun. It was surrounded by palms and jacaranda trees and had a massive wraparound veranda. Light reflected off the many windows and flitted across the manicured lawn.

"Wow," said Adrián. "That is big."

That was an understatement. It was massive. How could only two people live there? Were they planning on having forty children to form two opposing soccer teams? I took out my Canon and snapped several shots of the plantation house, doing my best to evoke images of corruption, greed, and exploitation. I posted one quickly to Instagram (#cafetales #corporategreed #eattherich). Then Adrián and I headed toward the house. I looked around for the coffee fields, but they weren't visible. The plantation and its trees blocked the entire horizon.

When we reached the veranda, we were met by Mr. Dieter Hess, third-generation inheritor of Café Bavaria, and new husband of Tía Marisol's sister Ana. He was of indeterminate middle age, German ethnicity, and dressed in an immaculate white linen suit that fit exactly on his spare frame. He had a comb-over; tiny, circular, steel-rimmed glasses; and a manicured mustache. His handshake was limp and his palms were clammy. He gave me the creeps.

"It's so nice to finally meet you," he said to Adrián, in German-accented British English, as he led us from one indistinguishable hallway to the next. It was difficult for me to participate in the conversation because I was trying to keep track of where I was going. I was also trying to figure out what was behind all the shut doors. What do you do with so many rooms? Keep them empty and lock the doors, or buy useless stuff to fill them?

"Ana was anxious for me to get acquainted with the family," he said. "But we've been on a whirlwind of a trip. Berlin, Hong Kong, Dubai. You know how it is."

Adrián was nodding agreeably, unaware that we were both outclassed and out-moneyed. Adrián's parents were wealthy, but this was on a whole other level. This was has-a-chauffeur/

personal chef/gets-invited-to-Davos money. I covertly cleaned the dirt from beneath my fingernails. Should I start getting professional manicures? At what age is it necessary? And why do we have to pay for that shit when men don't?

Dieter stopped walking and opened a door. We entered a sitting room that looked out onto a courtyard with palms and orchids. The moment I sat down, a maid appeared out of nowhere with coffee. I took a steaming cup and checked out the collection of photos above Dieter's head. They were old black-and-whites of men in uniforms, circa 1940.

"I've spent two months every winter here since I was a child," Dieter said. "But imagine—I barely speak three words of Spanish!" Adrián smiled as required, but I don't think he thought it was funny. "This could've caused dire marital problems, but fortunately Ana speaks both perfect English and a smattering of German. We met at the Oxford and Cambridge club." Adrián still looked calm, unaware that we were out-educated, too. "I suppose it would be marginally helpful if I learned the language, but we spend most of the year in Berlin and London. But you didn't come here to learn about my life! You want to know about coffee."

I nodded, then noticed an ornately framed photo above his head. Were those German soldiers? *Oh my god—was one of them Adolf Hitler?!*

"People often assume that coffee grows best in hot climates, but this assumption is false. Coffee grows best above nine-hundred meters, where temperatures range between fifteen and twenty-eight degrees Celsius, quite a bit cooler than one would suppose."

*No. Who would put up a framed photo of Hitler? It had to be a different German soldier . . . with a short, thick mustache.*

"People also assume that coffee is indigenous to Central

America, when indeed, it is not. Coffee was brought to the New World by Spanish, French, and Portuguese colonists. The original coffee came from Ethiopia and Arabia."

*Wait. Wouldn't* any *German soldier from the '40s be a Nazi?*

"When the first coffee plants were brought here to Costa Rica, they were considered purely ornamental. Colonists used the plants to decorate their patios and courtyards. They had no idea of the future significance of the plant."

*HOLY SHIT—the soldiers had* eagles *on their pockets—these* were *Nazis!*

"I don't know how familiar you are with coffee bushes, but they are lovely. What with their green glossy leaves, seasonal snow-white flowers, and blood-red berries, they can be quite breathtaking."

"How did coffee go from being an ornamentation to the mainstay of the economy?" asked Adrián, in Spanish, oblivious to the *photos of war criminals.*

Dieter answered, belying his claim to zero Spanish comprehension. "Demand was soaring in Europe. And the climate and soil conditions here were perfect—it was as if God had destined Costa Rica for coffee cultivation. By 1840, coffee had become their largest crop. It was carried through the mountains by oxcart, all the way to Puntarenas, where it was then shipped to Chile, and from Chile, shipped to Europe."

I still could not believe the whole wall was covered with SS. *Was Dieter descended from Nazis?*

"And the rest, my dear, is history."

*Did he know I was Jewish?* Maybe it was time to talk about how much I loved Christmas. "You know, coffee bushes look almost like poinsettias," I said.

"Not at all, my dear, they only share the same colors. I do love poinsettias."

"Me, too!" I said, "And Christmas! *And* Easter."

Dieter pushed his glasses lower on his nose and stared at me. "You haven't even touched your coffee."

"It's hot."

"It's supposed to be," he said. "It's coffee."

I took a very tiny sip. "Delicious."

He rose from his chair. "Let's start the tour, shall we?"

Dieter led us into the courtyard, his Italian loafers clicking loudly against the tiles. The sound ricocheted off the stone walls like bullets. "Café Bavaria has two hundred and fifty hectares of fields. Currently, only seventy percent are being used. We rotate the fields to preserve the integrity of the soil."

Dieter opened a low wooden door on the far end of the courtyard and held it open as I passed through. "The first half hectare of land is for private consumption." Dieter closed the door and pointed at the garden in front of us. "We have potatoes, mangos, and chilis." He snapped off a green chili and handed it to me. "They're rather mild. Costa Ricans aren't big on spices." He snapped off another for Adrián. "Taste it."

What were the negative side effects of eating a chili of unknown origin? Weren't some of them weapons-grade? I watched Adrián with apprehension.

"I knew a fellow at Oxford who burned eighty percent of his tongue eating a chili," said Dieter. Adrián had just placed the tip of the chili in his mouth. "Tragic, really. He lost almost all of his taste buds." Adrián stopped chewing. "You do get some of them back. Follow me." Dieter stepped onto a stone path that skirted the vegetable garden. I looked at Adrián, who was discreetly spitting out his chili. He held out his hand for me and we followed Dieter.

"Watch your step," said Dieter, who was waiting for us on a flat patch of dirt a couple of feet up. "Don't want you getting bitten by anything. We have quite a few venomous snakes."

I stepped closer to Adrián. "What kind of snakes?"

"Too many to list. We have twenty-two venomous species." He thought for a moment. "And Africanized bees."

Was there any horror that didn't exist on this plantation?!

"Here we are," he said, gesturing. In front of us was a small field covered with short coffee bushes. They were planted in uneven rows, interspersed with trees. Small green cherries hung from the branches in thick clusters. This wasn't what I expected a conventional farm to look like. Dieter stepped off the stone path and walked through an unevenly planted row of young coffee bushes.

"This is your first coffee farm?" he asked. I nodded. "You'll find that this is exemplary of Costa Rican *cafetales*. One of the finest in the Central Valley."

"It's lovely," I said, snapping pics with my camera. "But how do you cultivate so many hectares in this small family-farm style? This doesn't look like a big commercial farm"

"I'm glad you asked. Café Bavaria is at the cutting edge in agriculture. We're one of the pioneers in returning to natural farming methods. The slash-and-burn method has been discredited. It turns out that what's best for the environment is also best for the coffee. Which is best for our bottom line." He gestured toward some trees. "As you can see, banana trees have been planted along with *poró*, the short wide-blooming trees that were traditionally used to provide shade for the coffee plants."

"But genetically engineered coffee doesn't need shade, right?" I asked.

He turned and looked at me intently. "Someone did her homework." His voice was tight. He glanced down at my hands. "How quaint. A real camera."

Was he onto me? "They're kinda making a comeback," I said. "There's a whole Reddit thread about it."

He looked at me in noncomprehension. "Right."

We continued through the fields as Dieter chattered on about the minerality of the soil. But something wasn't sitting right with me. These coffee bushes seemed awfully short, and possibly immature. Matías's warning was echoing in my head—*they'll only show you what they want you to see.*

"This is wonderful, Dieter, but where are the pickers?" I asked. "Aren't we here during the harvest?"

If Dieter was uncomfortable, he hid it expertly. "Yes, they go field by field. Let me request that one of them join us." Dieter pulled out his phone and texted. A few minutes later, a tall, bony laborer in overalls and a blue bandana joined us.

"Don Rodolfo, thank you for coming." Dieter beckoned the scarecrow man to come closer. Rodolfo was *very* jittery. "This young lady is exploring the idea of working in the coffee industry. Could you tell her a little about your experience here at Café Bavaria?"

Rodolfo shifted his eyes from right to left. Then he cleared his throat and began to speak in spurts punctuated by deep rasping breaths. "Café Bavaria is an excellent place to work," *gasp*, "because the company is dedicated to producing fine coffee through safe," *gasp*, "and environmentally sound practices." *Gasp*. "We have the best wages of any coffee pickers," *gasp*, "in the entire country." *Gasp*. "We have full medical benefits . . ." Rodolfo stopped speaking for a moment to swallow several lungs full of air.

"And sick leave," added Dieter.

Rodolfo nodded, his irises darting from side to side. Then he gave the remainder of his speech in one rapid burst. "Housing is provided free was completely remodeled three years ago was modernized equipped with air conditioning hot water we have a recreation center includes a soccer field any questions?"

His voice contained a jagged edge of hysteria, so I decided not to press it. Perhaps his medical benefits did not provide coverage for his agoraphobia meds.

Dieter lifted his hand. "Thank you, Don Rodolfo. Why don't you go to the rec center and take a break?" Rodolfo nodded and hurried away.

Dieter turned to me. "I hope that answered your questions, Dee," said Dieter. "You certainly are a curious young lady." That was not a compliment. "You look a bit flushed. Shall we call it a day?"

"Let's," I said, much too quickly. "On account of the humidity. I'm not used to it like you."

Dieter pulled a handkerchief from his coat pocket. "I'm not sure that one ever does get accustomed to the humidity." He handed me his handkerchief and started down the stone pathway. "Or the political situation. You can't imagine how difficult it is to do business here."

"Hmm," I hedged.

"It's quite backward." I stifled a gasp and glanced at Adrián. He looked like he was chewing glass. "If you want a permit," Dieter continued, "you have to buy it from a politician. Business and power are hopelessly intertwined."

"But where aren't they?"

"Too true," he said.

Adrián was pissed but had evidently decided it was better not to say anything. So I tried to shift the conversation. "I've heard the situation has become more fluid recently," I said. "That there's been upheaval with long-standing contracts?"

"Correct. The Rust has put a lot of farms out of business. Many contracts to supply roasters are up for grabs."

Adrián turned to me. "The Rust is a fungus that is decimating the coffee bushes in Central America. It's gotten worse with global warming."

Dieter nodded. "We're relatively fortunate because we have large corporate buyers. They can extend credit to help through rough patches."

"I assume you fight the Rust with fungicides?" I asked.

"We use whatever is indicated," he replied, in a clipped voice indicating further questions were not welcome. We walked in silence until we were back at the plantation house. "Will you be joining us for lunch?" he asked, on the first step of his veranda.

"No," said Adrián, "we have to get going."

"A pity," Dieter said insincerely. He thumped Adrián on the back. "We have to get to know each other better, son. I could use someone like you in my sales department."

"Yes," said Adrián, "I could help you understand our backward culture."

Dieter nodded, oblivious to the sarcasm. "Come back any time," he said. "After all," he gestured at Adrián, "we're family now." *Family.* Adrián was related to Nazis. Sure, it was only by marriage, but still. "*Auf Wiedersehen.*" Dieter gave us a little wave.

Adrián and I walked down the long drive. When we lost sight of the plantation house, I sighed in relief. I looked over at Adrián. His poker face was slowly melting into a steamy twisted mess.

"Backward?" he spit out.

"I know. Particularly ironic given that *his* culture popularized genocide."

"The whole tour was a joke," he said as we got into the Jeep and pulled away. "I mean, I know the show was for you, but was I supposed to just play along? He could've at least warned me."

"Yeah. That picker was giving us rehearsed lines."

"And that field? Conventional plantations don't have shade trees or charmingly uneven rows." The Jeep went flying over a pothole, then returned to Earth with a thud. Without missing a beat, Adrián tapped the steering wheel and we returned to our proper lane. "Those plants weren't even mature. That field was just to show tourists."

I couldn't believe how far capitalists would go to cover their tracks! But this meant that there were real fields somewhere else; fields that we could potentially find and photograph. I turned to Adrián. "Do you think we could find the actual fields?"

Adrián fiddled with the radio. Nothing came in but static. "Probably." It was as if a curtain had fallen in front of his face.

"Do you not want to look for them?"

"Do you mean, do I want to trespass on my cousin-in-law's farm? The one descended from Nazis?"

"Didn't you tell me bravery was being afraid of something but doing it anyway?"

He smiled; I had checkmated him. He pulled a terribly dangerous U-turn. "Hope you know some good lawyers."

"You know what? I do."

# CHAPTER NINE

Half an hour later, we were still looking for the right turnout. There were farms all over here, and we didn't want to trespass on an unknown coffee baron's estate. At least if we got caught on Dieter's land, we'd be "family." Still, I was a little concerned when Adrián started circling the same stretch of highway, peering into the dense foliage on either side. What exactly was he looking for?

"Are you worried about Dieter finding us?" I asked.

"I mean, it would not be fun explaining it to my family. But I'm more worried about the guards."

"Wait . . . guards?"

"Yeah, the big farms have security guards. They do sweeps of the fields to make sure the pickers are productive. And to keep out union organizers."

*Oh.* I started fiddling with my seatbelt. "What about drug traffickers?"

"Yeah. Maybe."

"Like, we need to watch out for them, or the guards are looking for them?"

"Both, probably."

Suddenly I wondered if this was such a good idea. Adrián pulled over and drove through a pristine patch of greenery, then cut the engine. I looked at the path we had cut. It sprung back to life before my very eyes.

"Wow," I said. "Durable."

He smiled at me. "Tropical."

The Jeep was completely hidden from sight. We got out and headed toward an access road shaded by mango trees. As we went on, the greenery gradually disappeared, replaced by wheat-colored brush and a pervasive dryness. We passed a sign announcing that we were entering *Tres Aguas*. Three Waters. Someone had a nasty sense of irony.

"Why is it called *Tres Aguas* when there's no river?" I asked.

"Oh, there's gotta be a river here somewhere. Most farms use the wet-processing method to process the beans, which creates a lot of leftover pulp. So farms dump the waste in the rivers."

"That's got to be bad for the rivers, right? Isn't the pulp really acidic?"

"Yeah. Environmentalists are pretty upset about it."

"But not you?"

He shrugged. "The waste has to go somewhere."

We stepped onto a steeply ascending dirt path, bordered by oaks. I tried to read his expression. "So . . . your attitude is, it's horrible for the environment and too bad?"

"I'm just telling you facts. Everything has a cost." The forest was thick here and we couldn't see more than twenty feet ahead of us. "Your coffee grinds each morning? They release carbon dioxide into the environment." *They did?!* Uch, another thing to feel bad about.

"Is that good?" he continued. "No. But it doesn't help the environment to be naive about how things are produced. Or about what you consume."

I wrestled with this. Once you weren't naive—what did you do with the information? Stop consuming? Consume less? In a world where perfection was unattainable, when was less harm enough?

"Now you know more about the environmental impact, are you going to stop drinking coffee?" he asked with a puckish smile.

I shook my head; obviously not. "Are you?"

"I'm going to drink *more.* Sometimes I leave my faucet running just for fun. And I love burning trash."

"Trying to hasten the end of the world?"

"Exactly!" he said. "Usher in the reign of peace. Aren't your people bringing back Jesus for us?"

"Oh, yes, the *Mashiach.* You're welcome."

"We're very grateful." He pulled me in for a kiss and my body melted. *Impossible. He was just impossible.* I reluctantly pulled myself away from him, and we continued on the path. It turned north and we were no longer in a forest.

Mature coffee bushes stretched out under the sun in endless rows, with no shade in sight. No banana trees, no poró trees. There weren't even weeds. Just red dirt and neatly planted coffee bushes stretching out to the horizon.

"Well," said Adrián. "I guess we found the real fields."

"Yeah," I said, staring at the adults, adolescents, and children hunched over in the blazing sun, picking the bright-red coffee cherries. "I guess we did."

Unease settled over me. I noticed the angles the workers' backs were crooked at, and I saw the sweat dripping off their foreheads. They struggled under the weight of the baskets tied to their waists to hold the coffee cherries. You never saw images of this on your one-pound bag of specialty coffee. The backbreaking labor replaced—no, *hidden*—by the innocuous picture of a songbird.

The pickers noticed us as I took out my camera. Some were heading farther into the fields, but one old lady with raisin skin stood there looking at me. We walked up to her and I offered my hand. Hers was hard and dry. I introduced myself in Spanish. I told her who I worked for and asked if I might interview her. Adrián stood next to me, scanning the horizon.

"Are you an American?" she asked in Spanish. "Your Spanish is very good."

"That's very nice of you to say."

"You're a Tico?" she asked Adrián. He nodded.

"I want you two to interview me," she said. "And I want you to go back and tell your friends how it is for us *nicaragüenses* in Costa Rica."

I took out my phone and started recording.

"My name is Belén Chamorro," she said. "I want you to use my real name."

"What brought you to Café Bavaria, Doña Belén?"

"The Rust," she said. Her eyes took on a faraway look. "We lost our farm in Nicaragua two years ago when the Rust killed our plants."

A man nearby chimed in. "The Rust loves the heat. And every summer is hotter than the last."

"Did you plant new bushes?" I asked.

Doña Belén shook her head no. "The price of coffee dropped. Now it costs more to produce than it does to sell. So why would we buy new plants? If we could even get a loan." She pushed back her straw hat. I could see the folds of her skin hanging heavy under her eyes.

"How long did you have your farm?"

"Four generations. It was my life. Now it's just dirt." She kicked the soil at her feet. "Or who knows. Maybe it's a hotel for gringos now. With a swim-up bar."

I felt a knot form in my stomach. "What happened after you lost it?"

"All of my daughters came to work in San José as housekeepers, and my sons came to work in the fields here. My husband never recovered from the loss of our farm. He had a heart attack." She was unblinking. Unflinching. "After he died, I didn't want to stay in Nicaragua by myself."

"I'm so sorry," I said. The words felt so inadequate.

"I could've stayed with my sister. My kids sent home money. But I thought, why should young people work so hard to support an old lady like me? What's my life worth now that it's almost over? If I come here and work, that will help them save money, and then maybe they can return home and buy back our farm when the Rust is gone." She paused. "If it's still there."

My heart ached for her. It was all so unfair. Our lives were a lottery of where we were born and to whom. I noticed Adrián had started pacing in a wide circle around us. He seemed agitated.

"Have you been able to save money?" I asked.

She laughed, but it was mirthless. "No. They pay us dirt. They don't care what our labor is worth. They care more about their horses than us. When the horses get sick, they get medicine. When we get sick, we get replaced."

She didn't speak with emotion. Her matter-of-factness left me feeling empty.

"To them, we're disposable," she said. "But I wonder. The people drinking the coffee. Do you ever think about us?" She looked me directly in my eyes. "Do you ever imagine who sowed your beans? Who picked them?"

Her gaze was so intense I got goosebumps. I thought of how casually I would drink a six-dollar-latte in Cody's air-conditioned car. Sure, I paid a premium for ethically produced coffee. But did I ever *really* think about the people who made it possible? Or the costs they incurred?

Before I could answer her, an enormous roar startled us. We turned to see a dust cloud billowing hundreds of yards away. My heart began racing and I looked for Adrián. He was running toward me.

"*Oye*," said Doña Belén. The cloud of dust was coming closer and pickers were running. My mouth tasted like iron. "Tell our story."

"*¡La guardia!*" the man behind her shouted. "*¡Váyanse! ¡La guardia!*"

Belén didn't budge. She maintained eye contact as dust swirled around us.

I nodded.

Suddenly Adrián grabbed my elbow and dragged me toward the edge of the field. By now the dust had dissipated enough to reveal an old army Jeep rushing down the perimeter of the fields. Adrián and I were at a dead run heading toward the path when I suddenly fell to the ground, pushed down by Adrián's palm in the small of my back.

"Be still!" Adrián said in a fierce whisper, collapsing on top of me. I was face down in the dirt with black crud in my eyes and silt in my mouth. I couldn't see anything. The sounds of the engines stopped and heavy boots thudded onto the ground. I could feel the vibrations of their steps through the earth. The steps came closer. Blood pounded in my ears and the saliva dried in my mouth. My mind couldn't make sense of this. The transition from safe to unsafe was so quick. The footsteps came to a halt.

"Who were you speaking with?" asked a man in the distance, in Spanish. The sound of his voice froze me. This was a voice of metal, of gunpowder, of unchecked violence.

"I was singing," said Doña Belén. "While I worked." I writhed underneath Adrián. I had to see her. I lifted my head slightly and saw that we were lying in an irrigation ditch. We were behind some very thick bushes and wouldn't be visible to the guards. I could barely see them through the branches.

"We saw you from the highway," said a guard. "There was a group of you. You know you're not supposed to congregate while you work. Who the hell were you talking to?"

Belén shifted in and out of view. "No one. I told you. I was singing. Like a Disney princess."

I heard a smacking sound and saw her basket fly to the ground, berries cascading in every direction.

"You better tell me who you were talking to," said the guard. "Or you're going to lose a lot more than one basket."

"She was talking to me." It was another man's voice. "And my brother. We're sorry. We know it's not allowed."

Another basket went flying. Red berries arced through the air, landing softly on the ground.

"We have a duty to protect the farm. And from the highway, we really can't tell who's who. Who's a picker, who's a union organizer, who's a drug runner. You understand?"

Belén shifted and I could see her. Her chin in the air, her stance defiant.

"You understand?" he said again.

"I understand." Her lips curled into a smile. "I understand you're a son of a bitch."

I wasn't sure exactly what happened next, because I couldn't see whose hands were connected to whose bodies. I saw a raised hand, another hand grabbing it, and Belén flinching ever so slightly.

"You keep talking like that, old lady," said a guard, "and I'll cut your mouth right out of your face."

I shook in the ditch. Adrián held me tighter to stop the movement. I wanted to run at that guard and whip his gun across his face. I wanted to run straight back to Adrián's Jeep and drive to the airport and get on a plane back home. I wanted to run in one thousand directions at once. But I did nothing.

"*¡Vámanos!*" said a guard. There was the loud roar of the Jeep starting, a crunching sound as it mowed over greenery, then the hushed chatter of the pickers. Even that died down as they wandered to other corners of the fields. Finally, it was silent.

"They're gone," Adrián whispered in my ear, pushing back loose strands of my hair. He removed his hand from my mouth. "It's okay."

I breathed in and the air was harsh against my throat. Adrián rolled off me and crawled to his knees. Brown smudges covered his arms and face. He pulled a handkerchief out of his pocket and ran it lightly across my face. I saw streaks of red on the white cloth. "It's just a scratch, *Preciosa*," he said. He gently dabbed at my cut. "Let's get out of here."

Adrián took both of my arms and pulled me to my feet, then started back down the path. I hung back for a moment, peering out into the fields. The pickers had moved on to other rows. I couldn't see Belén. What had happened to her? Adrián grabbed my hand. "She's fine, Dee. I saw her go to a different part of the fields." I let out a sigh I didn't know I was holding.

Numb, I followed Adrián back down the path toward the road. I could feel my necklace clicking against my collarbone. I took the gold snakes between my fingers and rubbed them so hard the pads of my fingers ached.

*They say discretion is the better part of valor*, my grandfather had said to me in his sunny breakfast nook. He was teaching me gin rummy and life lessons at age eight. *But only sometimes. Sometimes, it's just valor.*

I wondered what my grandfather would have done if he had been here. Would he have jumped out of the bushes and identified himself? Or kept silent in the ditch?

Adrián stepped off the main trail and walked on a narrow, unkempt path. He pushed back the fronds of some overgrown ferns and we saw the Jeep twenty feet away. Within thirty seconds we were in the Jeep, racing toward the main highway. As soon as we were on the highway, the tension melted off Adrián's face.

"That was close," he said. He wiped sweat off his forehead. "I would've had a hell of time explaining that to my dad."

"Adrián." I searched for the right words. "Did we do the right thing?"

"What are you talking about?"

"Maybe we should've declared ourselves, admitted to trespassing, and said that the pickers had no knowledge of our visit."

"Are you crazy?" The Jeep hiccuped as it went over a big round rock. "Then they would've gotten into trouble for sure. At the least they would've been fired."

"It was our fault they got in trouble."

"They didn't get in trouble. They got a warning. Besides, that woman *wanted* to talk to us. She wanted us to tell her story."

"I hope you're right." I leaned back in my seat, suddenly feeling all the soreness in my body. Suddenly feeling the reality.

# PART TWO:

# HARVESTING THE CHERRIES

# CHAPTER TEN

Café Bavaria shook me. I realized I had just been playing at being a radical with Cody. Street takeovers, die-ins, pussy-power marches; they were theater. There was no real jeopardy. Even an arrest was something to brag about, not something to fear. Here, it was different. Here, there were consequences. I couldn't erase the vision of Doña Belén facing off with the guard.

When I came to Costa Rica, I had been running away. But now I had to choose—what was I running to? And if this new life required me to make sacrifices, to put myself in danger, would I have the courage?

After a restless night, I woke up a little calmer. But then I remembered *the kiss*. And the next kiss. And the lingering, amazing, frustrating kiss Adrián had given me when he dropped me off last night. My vow was going the way of the dodo bird.

I noticed my face felt hot, so I checked it in my phone camera. Oh. Wow. This was not excitement. This was a very interesting sunburn. Perhaps from driving with the window down while we went east? But no matter; no one besides my host family was going to see me in person for a few days. I'd mainly be researching farms and homestays, and constantly checking news sites to make sure no old ladies from Nicaragua had been harmed. I made a note in my phone to figure out the best way to get out Doña Belén's story.

As I was dressing, my phone beeped—miraculous! The signal in my bedroom was crap. I opened my email.

TO: Dee Blum
FROM: Matías Khalil
SUBJECT: Professor Ramírez

Hi Dee. Hope your conventional farm visit went well and you got to peek behind the curtain. With your super sleuthing skills, I'm sure you did. I wanted to let you know that I've taken the liberty of setting up a meeting for you with Professor Ramírez on Tuesday at ten at the university. I was Zooming with him this evening and he was very keen to meet you when he heard about your Living Wage League work. He loved your direct action where you glitter-bombed the Fine Hotels board to symbolize how the hotel rains cash while the laborers struggle to make ends meet. I have to agree; it was very creative.

Hope you are rested and ready to fight the good fight!

Wait, how did he know about the glitter bomb? It was true, I had helped Cody procure the glitter. But going to the craft store and taking photos were the extent of my contributions.

And what was with the "sleuthing skills" thing again? It's like he had some sort of alternate resume for me.

But more importantly . . . Tuesday at ten?! That was in three hours! When had he written this? I checked the time stamp. *Last night.* Now my geometric sunburn was of slightly more concern. Meeting my idol was nerve-racking enough, but looking like a cubist painting to boot?

TO: Matías Khalil
FROM: Dee Blum
SUBJECT: Re: Professor Ramírez

Hello Matías—

I did make it to the conventional farm, or as I call it, Corporate Hell. I managed to find the real fields and interview one laborer. But I didn't get very far, or take many photos, before getting chased out by the guards. I don't know how you found out about my sleuthing creds but I think your source is unreliable. I am a spying disaster.

Thank you for setting up a meeting with Professor Ramírez. He is my hero. So much so that I might be hyperventilating. And thanks for your support. As you can see, I'm going to need it.

I raced downstairs, where Eva, Luis, and Abuelita were having breakfast. When Eva saw my face, she dropped her coffee cup on the counter. "*Dios mío*," she said. "You look like . . ." She hesitated. What did I look like?

"*Una turista gringa*," said Abuelita. "Who forgot to put on sunblock."

"*Ay*," said Luis, briefly looking up from his newspaper. "She looks like a tomato."

"You can't let Adrián see you like that," said Eva.

"Who's Adrián?" asked Luis, looking back up from his newspaper. Oh no. My host dad did *not* get to weigh in on my potential dating choices.

"Is he Catholic?" asked Abuelita.

Eva gave Abuelita a dark look, then opened the sliding glass door of the kitchen and gestured for me to follow her to the patio. She cut off a leaf from an aloe plant and handed it to me. "Here."

"Here what?"

"Squeeze the plant. Put the gel on your face."

Wow. How DIY. After thanking Eva and slathering the aloe on my face, I said goodbye to Abuelita, prayed to my guardian angel like she taught me, and unbolted the three deadbolts on the front door. I walked outside and was immediately pleased. People think: Costa Rica, Central America, hot. But that just shows you how little most people know. San José was in fine temperate form this morning, with fleecy clouds lazing in the horizon and the sun giving one great big wake-up yawn. I exited the gates of my citadel, exalted in the balmy air, and set foot on the wet spongy ground outside the house.

My only companions on the road out of Carmen toward the Fatal Water Tanks were chickens and feral dogs. I carefully negotiated the potholes, mud patches, and marshes that lined the road in lieu of a sidewalk, praying constantly that an errant taxi would not whack me from behind and send me airborne and mangled into Guadalupe. When I got to the water tanks intact, I said goodbye to the rising sun and turned right, starting my descent into Sabanilla.

The thing I couldn't get over in Costa Rica was the sky. It was closer, it really was, closer and bigger and heavier, and right here on the road down to Sabanilla was where it was closest. When it rained, the giant gray clouds seemed only twenty feet up from the tops of the tin roofs. When it was clear, the blueness had a thickness to it that suggested it was an object like any other, something you could hold in your hand, pinch, feel. So as I walked down the steep hill to Sabanilla, I felt like if I slipped and fell down the slope, I would be caught by the giant blue arms of the sky.

Forty minutes, six *piropos*, and three perilous road crossings later, I was on campus. The University of Costa Rica looked like a typical Southern Californian suburban community college. Squat nondescript buildings, open spaces, large trees, and lots of benches. The main difference was that every tree had a family of parakeets and a resident sloth. There was also a brook snaking through the middle of campus, with a sign claiming it was a Geological Study Site. The sign reminded us to protect our natural resources, but it wasn't fooling anybody, that sucker was polluted as hell.

I crossed the brook, entered the Social Sciences building, and went to the third floor. There was a plant-filled anteroom where a voluptuous middle-aged assistant with bright-blue eyeshadow and turquoise pumps was filing her nails.

"Dee?" she asked. I nodded. "Go in, *corazón*. He's waiting for you."

I stepped into his office; all the windows were open. It was like entering a wind tunnel—literally and figuratively. It blew me away in the same way that Capitol Hill blows away twelve-year-old poli-sci nerds who want to be president. This is the intimidation that comes with the desire to emulate.

Hanging behind an enormous oak desk and surrounded

by a blood-red frame was a life-sized poster of Che. Che was looking straight at me with that mocking, seductive, mysterious smile. The smile that made you wonder—was he a revolutionary hero or a cold-blooded murderer? Was it possible to be both? Surrounding Che were thousands of newspaper clippings vying for attention and failing miserably.

But the most impressive piece of furniture was the professor himself. At six foot four, Professor Ramírez dwarfed everything in the room. His colossal frame was made even more intimidating by his inky eyes, set in stark contrast to his flowing white beard and cascading hair. He looked like an out-of-water Neptune.

"*Bienvenida, joven,*" boomed the living statue in Spanish, sending vibrations over me. He crossed the room and I could almost see plaster flaking off him as his muscles rippled under his clothes. He had to be somewhere in his seventies, but he was in incredible shape. I held out my hand and he shook it, American style. I felt like I had just got my hand jammed in a car door.

"Sit down," he said in Spanish. I acquiesced. "I'm not sure what Matías has explained to you, but my goal is to get all coffee produced in Central America fairly traded and sustainably produced by 2030."

"That's ambitious."

"That's just the beginning. Next is chocolate, then textile production. You're aware of the slow fashion movement?"

I self-consciously tugged at my Old Navy shirt. "I am."

"Obviously, coffee has to be first, it accounts for eleven percent of our exports. So I'm documenting all of the *cafetales* in Central America that produce their coffee under fair trade and organic standards. But coffee is also important symbolically. Did you know that wherever coffee has been introduced, it has been a harbinger of revolution?"

"No."

"There's something mind-expanding about coffee. When people begin to think, they become dangerous. And when they think in groups—in coffeehouses—they become powerful. It was from Café Foy in 1789 that the French Revolution began. It was in Boston coffeehouses in 1773 that the Boston Tea Party was plotted. A drop in coffee prices sparked the Brazilian revolution of 1930. Coffee, my dear, is the world's most radical drink."

*Wow.* I thought it helped me study for exams—I didn't realize it could take down governments.

The Professor sat down suddenly, then leaned across the table and looked me straight in the eyes. "Matías said you were passionate about cooperatives. Why?"

This was a test; there was no denying it. I took a sip from my (reusable) water bottle to buy time. I hadn't anticipated the necessity of defining my interest in economic justice. I wiped some sweat off my upper lip. "Cooperatives allow the farmers to organize for better working conditions and pay."

"Sure. But beyond that?"

"I think cooperatives challenge the current economic order."

He raised his eyebrows. "How?"

My adrenal glands were working overtime. "By providing an alternative. It's great to say you don't like capitalism, but what are you supposed to do? Secede from the world? That's not practical. But your average person can buy products from co-ops. And producers can join them. It's something ordinary people can do to better their community, and by bettering their community, better their world."

"Yes," he said, smiling.

I realized I had been holding my body rigid. But I had passed the test. Well, at least the first one. There were going to be more, I was sure of it.

"Matías was correct in sending you to me. He said that you were a dedicated and intelligent comrade. A sister in the fight." Matías said that about *me*? How did he know?

The Professor leaned back in his chair. "Since we're both visiting farms, it makes sense to join forces." I sighed with relief. If he went with me, I wouldn't have to worry about my terrible sense of direction or general incompetence.

"If it's all right with you," he continued, "we'll divide the labor, much as I detest the division of labor." Uh-oh. This did not sound as promising. "You're going to visit Café Alegre tomorrow. It's an Ethical Coffee International–certified cooperative that has risen to prominence over the last few years. It should be a good candidate for your Truth Trip."

"Wonderful. Is it in the Central Valley?"

"Central Highlands, Guanacaste region. Why?"

"Suzanne mentioned I should stay away from the north. Something about drug-related violence? Organized crime?"

"There has been an uptick in crime in the north, yes, but in reality, it's all over the country."

"Does it affect coffee farms?" I asked, my voice going up just a notch.

"It can affect any home or business. Drug runners need safe houses." My pulse quickened. *Could the farms be pitstops for drug dealers?!* "But I wouldn't worry about that," he said. "The kind of danger you're more likely to encounter is run-of-the-mill labor unrest. I'm sure you've heard about the activists who were murdered in Mexico in the last few years."

Gulp. I had not.

"Again. Very unlikely. Take normal precautions."

*Like not provoking guards?* "By the way," I said. "I went to a corporate farm yesterday. Café Bavaria."

The Professor looked surprised. "That's a particularly bad

one. Dieter Hess is well known for his dirty business practices."

"Yeah, I snuck into his fields and talked to the laborers."

Now the Professor looked impressed. I was flooded with pride. "Looks like I don't need to worry about you," he said.

*Um, no, you should still worry about me.*

"Anyhow," he said. "Since you're helping me with my research project, I need you to document their business model and ask the pickers some questions. In the meantime, I'll visit a few other cooperatives in the Central Valley. Then you and I will reconvene." He tapped his coffee mug. "I've already interviewed farmers from all the major networks in Nicaragua, El Salvador, Panamá, and Guatemala. I was saving Costa Rica for last."

What an incredible man. He was single-handedly attempting to change the face of economics in Central America. I couldn't believe he was entrusting me with his research. "Thank you, Professor Ramírez."

"Eugenio."

Then the Professor reached across the table and took my hands firmly in his. He smiled, baring all of his humongous white teeth, and I came this close to fainting. I had witnessed the dental work of God.

♥ ● *

Ten minutes later I was underneath a trumpet tree on campus, hoping the resident sloth wouldn't poop on me, and sipping a guanabana milkshake from the campus *soda*—a mom-and-pop traditional food stand. I was also wildly waving my phone around for a signal. I wanted to email Matías and find out why he had said such nice things about me to the Professor. But before I could write to him, I received this.

TO: Dee Blum
FROM: Matías Khalil
SUBJECT: Charismatic Leaders

I sent my best organizers down to El Salvador last year to check out some maquiladoras and they didn't even get past the front gates. So I don't know what you're talking about with this "spying disaster"—you sound like a pro.

You're probably meeting with Eugenio right now. Suzanne sent me your website, and as soon as I read your honors thesis, "The Role of a Charismatic Leader in the Development of Class Consciousness in a Moment of Struggle," I knew you two were a match. It got me thinking about my own political evolution. Eugenio was the charismatic leader who took *me* to the next level of class consciousness during the Colombian national strikes. It was a great idea to put your thesis on your website. And your protest photos—they're art-gallery worthy. You remind me of the great protest photographer Hoppy Hopkins.

One quibble. While there are hundreds of your photos on the internet between your website and social media, I couldn't find any with *you* actually in them. How is that even possible? I'm getting a little suspicious. Are you in Witness Protection?

Do you secretly work for a three-letter agency?
Are you catfishing Justice Alliance?

Curiously,
Matías

P. S. Do you think a person can still level up, class consciousness-wise, without a charismatic leader to help interpret things for them?

*My website?!* I didn't have a website! I googled myself, hit the link, and yep, there it was, "my" website. Could Cody have made it?

"*Hi, I'm Dee,*" said my bio that I had in no way written any part of. "*I'm in Costa Rica taking photos for several news organizations. I plan on going to law school next year. Please check out my photos, as well as my scholarly essays.*"

*Scholarly essays?!* Then it dawned on me. *My father.* He was trying to make my case stronger for law school. As if they would ever see this! I scrolled through the site. Dad had created links to all the papers I had ever written in school. And a gallery with all my protest photos he'd swiped from Instagram. Matías was right—there were no photos *of* me, but that was very much intentional. A big perk of being the one with the camera is you're not in any of the pictures.

But where had the "sleuthing" thing come from? I clicked through the links and found my dad had mistakenly taken some fanfic I had written for Veronica Mars and posted it as a personal essay. *Oh my god.* My dad must've either remotely hacked my computer or broken into the encrypted hard drive I'd left at home. Jesus Effing Christ! I moved to another country and my dad was still trying to run my life!

TO: Jacob Blum
FROM: Dee Blum
SUBJECT: not cool

Dad. How could you create a website *for me*? Don't you realize you're totally violating my privacy? How would you like it if I went and messed with *your* website? "Jacob Blum: Part-Time Real Estate Agent, Full-Time Sad Clown for Hire."

I wanted to really let him have it, but I knew if I kept going, I'd say something horrible that I'd have to apologize for and feel even more horrible about later. So I decided to leave it at that and write back to Matías. I couldn't believe he had taken the time to read my thesis and engage with it in a meaningful way. I mean, even I realized it was about a very niche topic.

TO: Matías Khalil
FROM: Dee Blum
SUBJECT: Re: Charismatic Leaders

This is awkward, but I didn't put those essays on my website. Or even create the website. It was the work of a cyber stalker who happens to have my same genetic code. How weird do you think I am? But I'm flattered that you read my thesis. Yes, I do think some people can level up without the influence of a leader, but I think those autodidacts are rare. Most people learn better when they have someone to help put things in context. Speaking of charismatic leaders, thank you for vouching for me to Professor Ramírez. That was pretty risky of you—now I can vouch for your bravery. Hope I don't disappoint.

Also hope my new photos won't disappoint. The pressure is really on with a comparison to the famed Hoppy Hopkins! I'll be visiting some co-ops soon, so keep your eyes peeled.

Regarding my identity: obviously since I'm a criminal mastermind I'm not going to reveal my methods or likeness. You'll have to look harder.

"Dee"

I hit send and headed to the bus stop. I couldn't believe that Matías Khalil, *the* Matías Khalil of No-More-Capitalism-in-the-Age-of-AI fame, had read my thesis. And liked it! It was a new, heady experience having people believe in me. But the flip side was the fear I would disappoint. I had earned the Professor and Matías's respect. Would I be able to keep it?

# CHAPTER ELEVEN

Tomorrow became today, and I was vibrating with excitement. Today I was going to my first cooperative—or as I preferred to call it, Cooperative Heaven. Some kids went to bed dreaming of sugar plums or magic lands, but I dreamed about *this*: a utopia of economic cooperation where everyone enjoyed the fruits of their labor—equitably. And I was about to experience it in the flesh.

With Adrián. I was surprised that he wanted to participate in my naive, imperialist activities, but he said he wanted to avoid work that day; his dad planned on firing two housekeepers. I couldn't deny that I was happy he was coming with me. But I preferred not to think too deeply about my weakening resolve to resist.

After a drive exceptional only in that we didn't pass any dead bodies, we saw the sign to Café Alegre rising twenty feet high out of the jungle. Cooperative Heaven! Adrián parked outside a gate with three horizontal bars. Then we walked down a dirt road shaded on both sides by large guanacaste trees. After a few hundred meters, pink and periwinkle plaster houses appeared.

Since this was a cooperative network, the worker-owners lived on or near their plots. Vibrant red heliconias decorated the path, and prickly green guanabanas littered the ground. I left the road to try to peer into the closest house, but Adrián pulled me back by the belt loop of my jeans.

"What are you doing?" he asked, a bit severely.

"I just want to look inside."

"If you want to see the place, just knock and ask for a tour." I looked at him with surprise. He wasn't exactly a follow-the-rules type. "I don't want to see anything happen to you."

"Nothing's going to happen. We're at a co-op. *Cooperative.*"

Adrián didn't speak. He just pushed an errant hair away from my forehead. His real motives for coming hit me. "Are you still hung up about the scratch? Did you come here to *protect* me?"

"You never know what kind of security they have on these farms. Coffee is big business here, Dee. It's not all roses and kittens just because it's a co-op." He grabbed both of my hands and wrapped them around his waist. "And I wanted to spend time with you." Then he began to kiss me in a way that made me worry about keeping our appointment. My sexual experience was limited to my high school boyfriend and Cody, and the heat dial never went past seven. But the way Adrián kissed me made me think that maybe there was a whole world I was missing out on. Actually, it made me not think at all.

"Um. Okay. Well," I stammered as I reluctantly pulled away.

"Is there a problem? Do you not like it?"

"No! I like it! I really like it! I super like it!" *Oh my god, could I just stop talking?* "I just don't want to be late for our appointment."

"Okay."

As I watched Adrián struggle to catch his breath, I realized

I'd have to make up my mind about what I wanted this to be soon. The word "slow" didn't appear to be in his vocabulary. And "fast" wasn't really in mine, at least not physically. Adrián straightened his shirt and took my hand.

We walked on, smelling the overripe guanabanas and listening to the birds. At the end of the road, there was a clearing with a soccer field, surrounded by laurel negro trees. Behind the soccer field stood a community center with a veranda. It was flanked by a large building to the west, and a drying platform for coffee berries to the east. A layer of bright and puffy clouds hung over everything. It looked like a cloud factory had just exploded.

Now that we were here, I became a little nervous. Was Adrián right to be concerned about our safety? When the Professor said, "take normal precautions," why hadn't I asked what those were? Why had I even come to Costa Rica in the first place? What had been so terrible about home? How did a pushy, overly invested family compare with the terrors of interviewing people you had never met in a foreign language you had barely mastered? I stopped on the path and turned to Adrián. "This was a bad idea."

"Bringing me?"

"Thinking I could do this in the first place. I'm a college dropout with limited qualifications. My resume had a lot of . . . embellishments."

"*Tranquila*." Adrián put his arms firmly around my waist. "Everyone exaggerates on their resumes. And nobody ever feels as qualified as they are. Maybe you don't have a lot of experience, but you're smart and you're passionate."

Huh. *Adrián actually made me feel better.*

"Remember when I told you you're an unreliable narrator?" he asked. "Maybe it's time to change your narrative about yourself."

I smiled at him. Maybe it was. We crossed the soccer field and went up the steps of the veranda. Adrián opened the thick wooden doors and we went inside the community center. The main room was a large, thoughtfully merchandised tasting room with an elegant coffee bar. Pounds of coffee were for sale: medium and light roasts, single origins and blends. There were also Café Alegre mugs and tees.

A genial, moon-faced man in his fifties came toward us with outstretched arms. "*Buenas tardes, amigos*," he said. "We've been expecting you." He gave me the Costa Rican air kiss. "You must be Dee," he said in Spanish. "I'm Manuel and this is Paula." Doña Paula, a serious woman in her late forties, nodded at us from the coffee bar. She was the only other person in the room. Manuel turned to Adrián. "And you're . . . ?"

Adrián looked at me with a mischievous smile. "Her driver."

"Ah. Great. Come with me!" Manuel led us to the coffee bar. "What will you have? Single origin or a blend?"

"I'm supposed to like single origin better, right?" I asked.

"You're supposed to like whatever you like," said Adrián. "No one gets to choose your preferences for you, Dee."

"Agreed, *profe*," said Manuel, using the local slang for driver—professor. He ground some beans from a canister, then poured boiling water from an electric kettle into a Vandola. After a few moments, he handed us two cups.

I sipped the coffee. It was balanced and smooth. Was I getting a hint of plum? Was I fooling myself?

"It's our house roast," he said. "From just three micro-lots. A light to medium roast."

"It's phenomenal."

"Glad you agree. We're closed to the public today, so you're going to get your very own private tour. But first I'm going to give you the history of the place. Would you like that?"

"Yes, please."

"Café Alegre was a dream of mine ever since I was a boy." He leaned against the coffee counter. "I grew up on a coffee plantation. At the age of six, I was already working in the fields, picking berries. My mother, my father, my seven brothers and sisters, and I lived in a two-room shack. We didn't have electricity or running water. We bathed in the river."

Adrián looked disgusted. I elbowed him subtly.

"My youngest sister was a child prodigy, but we had no money to send her to school. She continued picking coffee just like the rest of us. My younger brother lost his senses from meningitis because we couldn't afford the medicines. And the imperialists next door lived large while we suffered and starved. It was an outrage."

Paula nodded. Manuel wiped his face with a red bandana.

"So I took that resentment and I turned it into a dream. And that dream became Café Alegre."

Paula murmured, "*¡Gracias a Dios!*"

"And now my sister is getting her PhD in engineering at the University of Western Australia." I was too struck to say anything. What a success story.

"How does Café Alegre work?" asked Adrián, unmoved. Was he made of stone?

"I'll tell you, *profe*," said Manuel. "Better yet, let me show you. Let's go to the mill."

Manuel and Paula led us out of the tasting room, down the steps of the veranda, and into the building next door. The cavernous main room was humming with mechanized activity where coffee cherries were pulped, fermented, and washed. A few workers supervised the process.

"Do you mind if I take photos?" I asked. "I've never been in a coffee mill."

"Be my guest." Manuel pointed to some tanks. "This is called the wet-processing method. It provides a consistent, clean taste."

"What do you do with the coffee pulp waste?" I asked.

"We use it as natural compost."

Adrián raised an eyebrow.

"Where are the cherries roasted?" I asked.

"Most of that happens offsite, by the buyers."

"Why?"

"Because that's its own specialty," said Manuel. "Roasting is part science, part magic. You're not just heating up a food product. When you alchemize starches into sugars, you unlock *the essence* of the bean."

"That sounds very mystical," I said.

Adrián nodded. "My grandmother used to say, roasting reveals the true nature of the coffee. Transforming it into what it was always meant to be."

Could that be true? Could things have an innate essence, waiting to be revealed, through trial of fire? Were people like that?

But we were done with philosophy for now. Adrián had turned to Manuel. "How does the co-op work from an economic perspective? Who pays for what? The plants, the machines, the processing labor?"

"Great question. We are all brothers and sisters here, by blood or affinity. Every owner-member has their own small farm that they work with their family. We all pay fees to belong to the cooperative, and those fees pay for the labor of processing, the materials, and the equipment."

"How are the profits split?" I asked.

"By yield, from each lot," said Paula.

Adrián raised his eyebrow again. He was going to get wrinkles there. "So not evenly," he said.

"No, we're a co-op, not a commune," said Manuel, perhaps slightly annoyed. "But if one family is doing poorly one year, we all cooperate to help them out. We don't really view ourselves as *owners* of the land, per se. We view ourselves as custodians."

"*¡Amén!*" said Paula, nodding.

"That's why we don't use pesticides," said Manuel. "We believe that we are here to protect the Earth, not destroy it. It is through God's grace that we have this land. Everything we have is a gift from God. We are *borrowing* from God."

"*Praise God*!" Paula said.

Paula and Manuel seemed unusually religious. Perhaps they belonged to a cult?

"Can you talk to me about the costs involved in being certified by Ethical Coffee International?" I asked.

"Yes. The costs are thirty percent higher."

Adrián was visibly surprised. "That's a lot."

"It is. Fortunately, the profits are also higher. Also, Ethical Coffee International minimums are just a floor. We can sell the coffee for as much as the buyer will pay. But that's not the main thing. The main thing is that it's the right thing to do for the Earth, and the right thing to do for our laborers."

"*Praise God*!" said Paula, again.

Suddenly I realized I had urgent business to take care of. That coffee God gifted me with sure made me have to pee. I asked Manuel for directions to the bathroom.

Fortunately, the layout was simple. The center of the building was a wet mill, with small offices surrounding the main floor on three sides. I walked around the fermenting tanks, entered a hallway, and found the tiny bathroom. Coffee gifted back to the Earth, I walked back more slowly, peering into the offices, some of which were open. One room was stacked with massive hundred-pound bags of coffee. I went to inspect them.

Strangely, they didn't have the Café Alegre label. They had the word *Fuerte* stamped on them.

I passed by some other rooms, also full of hundred-pound *Fuerte* bags. Seems like they made a lot of this stuff, but I didn't remember seeing any in the tasting room. As I continued, I saw an administrative office with the door ajar. I decided to investigate further. I mean, if you don't want someone to go into a room, don't leave the door open, right?

Inside there was a desk, an antique armoire, and a framed map. I studied the map, which showed the layout of the buildings and fields. Then I turned toward the armoire. I touched the wood and the doors opened slightly from the pressure. I glanced inside. There were dozens of little drawers. I knew I shouldn't open them—but opening small boxes was in my DNA. If past lives are real, I'm certain I was Pandora. Or Bluebeard's wife. Or Eve. Why were there so many myths about women getting in trouble for seeking knowledge? I became *more* determined to open the drawers. This was a feminist issue.

I looked over my shoulder to make sure there was no one in the hallway. Then I opened a drawer. *There was a drawer inside the drawer!* Besides myself with childlike joy, I started opening everything. I found letters, coins in foreign currency, and small metal things that I assumed were washers . . . whatever the hell washers were. Then my hand hit a piece of hollow wood. Because I had spent so much time with my mom in antique stores being bored out of my mind when I was a kid, I knew that many older armoires had secret drawers. And hollow wood was a telltale sign that you'd found a false back. I wiggled the cheap piece of plywood, then heard a jangling sound. The compartment was hiding keys!

Just then I heard footsteps in the hallway. *Shit.* How was I going to explain that I was snooping in the offices? I quickly ducked under the desk. What had I been thinking? I was not a sleuth! I was barely a real organizer!

The footsteps sounded like they were headed to the bathroom next door. I heard the person peeing in the toilet—wow, that was a lot of urine. I decided to get out of there before they finished. But as I got up, I noticed the closet door was open. Inside were some black boxes imprinted with *skulls and crossbones.* My stomach sank. I picked up a box and read the label, which was in Spanish.

WARNING: THIS PESTICIDE IS INTENDED FOR USE OUTSIDE OF THE HOME ONLY. IT IS EXTREMELY TOXIC TO BOTH HUMANS AND DOMESTIC ANIMALS. IN CASE OF ACCIDENTAL INGESTION, PLEASE CONTACT YOUR NATIONAL POISON CONTROL CENTER.

I put the box down in disbelief. The "custodians of the Earth" used pesticides?! Manuel specifically said they didn't. And that would be in *major* violation of Ethical Coffee International regulations. I had to be mistaken. Maybe this was a translation error. I perused the ingredients statement, but I didn't even know what those chemicals were in English.

I heard the guy flush next door. No time to get out of here now. I squeezed myself into the closet and shut the door gently. After an interminably long hand wash (which was a good thing, I guess, since he handled food), I heard footsteps again.

*What if he came in to get the pesticides?!*

I began sweating. If he discovered me, what would I tell him? *I mistook this dark closet for a toilet?* But after a few tense moments, the footsteps faded away. I sighed with relief. When I was sure he was gone, I opened the closet door, stepped out, and quickly snapped photos of the boxes. As I went to shut the closet door, I noticed something large leaning against the back corner. It was too dark to make out the object, so I shone my phone flashlight on it.

*A shotgun.* Even stationary in a closet it filled me with dread. What was this for? Hunting? Or something else?

Rattled, I went back to the mill. No one noticed that my face was ashen, except Adrián. "Are you okay?"

"No," I said into his ear. "We have to leave."

"Leave?" said Manuel. "But you haven't even seen the fields!"

"We'll have to come back." I clutched my stomach. The click-click-click of the conveyor belt resonated through my legs. "I'm sick."

"What is it?" asked Manuel. "Let me call you a doctor."

"No." I teetered toward the door. "I just need to get home. We'll call you to reschedule."

I hustled out of the mill, and a worried Adrián followed. When the community center was no longer visible, the knot in my stomach relaxed.

"*¡Preciosa!*" said Adrián, grabbing my waist. "What's wrong? What made you sick?"

"Insect poison."

"What?" He dropped his car keys. "When did you eat insect poison?!"

"I didn't eat it. I saw it."

Relief flooded his face, and he bent down to retrieve his keys. "Where?"

"In a closet."

"I knew it!" He clapped his hands. "Anyone who says 'Praise God' has to be doing something bad." A large branch whacked Adrián in the face as he straightened up. God's revenge. The keys fell back to the ground.

"I can't believe they're frauds," I said.

"Get used to it. Hypocrisy is the one thing that's universal."

I looked at Adrián as he searched for the keys in the bushes. That just wasn't true. Not everyone was deceitful. Adrián, for one, was totally honest about his beliefs, pro-free market as they might be. But that made me realize something. I needed to be *sure* Don Manuel was a fraud. What if they didn't use the pesticides on the coffee? What if they were for insects in the community center?

"Adrián. We have to go back. I have to see the fields."

"Oh no, not this again."

"I need to get soil samples."

"Why?"

"Because I need to be sure they're actually *using* the pesticides on the coffee. If they are, maybe Suzanne can report them to Ethical Coffee International. Then they can enforce the requirements."

"You're not a spy." Adrián found the keys and stood up. "Your job is to organize trips for do-gooders, not to enforce regulations on non-compliant farms. Tell your boss this farm isn't suitable, and we'll go to the next farm."

"This isn't like Café Bavaria." *I hoped.* "It's going to be fine." As I said the words, I began to believe them. I had overreacted because the near miss at Café Bavaria had made me paranoid. I needed to woman up.

"I really don't think we should do this," he said. "It's not worth it."

I stared at him for a moment. "You're wrong. It really is."

Adrián tossed the keys from one hand to another. Then he looked up to the heavens for answers, then finally back at me. "You know you're crazy, right?"

"I do."

He shook his head. "So what's the plan?"

# CHAPTER TWELVE

"You're going to sit on the veranda with Manuel and Paula," I said, as we started walking back toward the community center. "Distract them. Talk about something exciting."

"*Fútbol.*"

"*That's* the most exciting thing you can think of?"

"To a Tico, yes." He looked at me. "What are you going to be doing?"

"Just keep your stories spicy. If you need to throw in a doping scandal, do it."

He shook his head but kept walking forward. I took his hand and squeezed it. "Why are you helping me?"

"I don't know. Maybe because of your eyes."

"I thought you liked my brain."

"I thought so, too, but now I have some questions. Particularly about your judgment."

I laughed. I had questions about my judgment, too. We stepped into the clearing with the soccer field.

Manuel and Paula were sitting on the veranda outside the tasting room, sipping coffee. When Manuel saw us, he sprang up from his seat. "Dee! You're back." He came to meet us. "Are you okay?"

"No. I returned to use your bathroom."

He nodded. Adrenaline swelled through my body as I ran into the mill. I went straight to the bathroom and locked the door behind me. I figured I had fifteen minutes before they began to suspect Adrián was stalling. I heard Adrián's low voice rumbling and then an explosion of laughter from the veranda. This was my chance. I opened the window and crawled out, then sprinted toward the thicket in front of me.

I tried to suppress my anxiety as I crashed through the bushes. The only things I could hear were the babbling of a small stream and the screeches of wildlife. The only things I could see were monkey tail ferns, poor man's umbrellas, and stigmata plants. I wiped some sweat off my forehead and ordered myself to calm down.

*You came to get soil*, I reminded myself. *Quickly.* I pushed my way through waist-high plants until I found the footpath I'd seen on the map. Bright-orange butterflies were crisscrossing in front of me, and I followed them until the trees disappeared in an explosion of light. When my eyes adjusted, I saw an unshaded field filled with hunched-over forms. There were no trees interspersed with the coffee plants, which was odd for a supposedly "shade-grown" organic farm. I stepped behind the thick trunk of a laurel negro tree on the perimeter, before any of the pickers could see me.

*Don't freak out*, I told myself. *No one's looking for you.* I pressed my body closer to the laurel negro and peered around the side. I saw dozens of pickers on the north side of the fields, spread apart from each other at standardized distances. I hugged the tree tighter and looked south. There were four short forms. Instead of spacing themselves out like the pickers on the right, they were all clumped together. I stared at them, wondering why they were so short, when suddenly it hit me. *They were kids.*

There were two boys who looked fourteen or fifteen, sixteen at the oldest. There was a little girl who seemed about eleven with tight curly locks sprouting out of her head like a doll, and a younger boy, no more than eight. Whose kids were they? It was totally against Ethical Coffee International rules to have children help with the harvest. As I was staring at them, the taller of the two teenagers turned around and looked in my direction.

I wrapped myself back against the tree trunk and prayed he hadn't seen me. I was in shadow and he was in direct sunlight. Maybe I looked like . . . a bird? A very, very large upright bird? What was I going to do now? I needed a soil sample if I was going to report Café Alegre for violations. But I couldn't risk the kids seeing me and telling Manuel I had been there. I heard footsteps approaching; there was no way to leave without being seen. I closed my eyes and hoped for divine intervention. *Would the sanctified blood trick work here?*

"*¿Quién es?*" asked a young male voice.

I sighed. No use hiding now. I came around the tree to face a tan, scrawny teenager with a broad forehead, thick straight hair, and shrewd brown eyes. His smile was angelic, but he had the voice of a hustler. "What are you doing here?" he asked in Spanish.

"Uh." I looked around me, hoping a plausible excuse would paint itself in the sky or spell itself out in berries. "I got lost," I said in Spanish.

"Are you an inspector for Ethical Coffee International?"

I looked at the boy's expectant face and considered his question. Did he *want* me to be an inspector? If he were exploited labor, I could say yes, and maybe he would confide in me. But if he were one of Manuel's relatives, then he'd tell him an American had been snooping around. And then, well . . . I'm not sure what would happen, but I didn't want to find out.

"Manuel told us a visitor was coming today," he said. "But not to here. To the visitors' fields." He gave me a probing look.

"I'm just a lost tourist," I said. I held up my camera as proof. "Okay if I take some photos?"

"That's too bad. I wanted to speak to an inspector." He stuck out his hand, confident. He had a sophistication that didn't match his age. "The name's Tomás."

We shook hands. I shifted, very uneasy. "Why do you want to speak to an inspector?"

His eyes darkened. "Because this is a terrible place. Café Alegre does not comply with Ethical Coffee International standards. Like, at all. See the people there?" He pointed to the pickers on the north side of the field. "They're the *nicaragüenses*. They come for the harvest, with their kids, and they don't even get minimum wage." I looked more closely. There were several kids working with the adult laborers. "And them?" He pointed at the shorter teenage boy and the two little kids he had been picking with. "Those are my brothers and sisters. We don't get paid anything."

"Why not? Where are your parents?"

Tomás's eyes narrowed slightly, but his voice stayed even. "Our mom went to the city looking for our dad, so she left us with Manuel."

"Why would she leave you with Manuel?"

He looked down. "He's our stepfather."

Ohhh. I felt a pang of compassion. "Why doesn't Manuel have you in school?"

"Because we're not his real kids. We only go to school when he doesn't need us." Jesus, Tomás was a real-life Cinderella. "The Nicaraguan kids don't go to school at all. That's why I want to speak to an inspector. If they bust the farm, maybe I can get emancipated and move to the city." His voice dropped. "And find my mom." The sophistication had left his eyes, replaced by sadness, and for a minute, he looked his age. "Can you send someone out from Ethical Coffee International?"

"I'll try. Do you know if the farm uses pesticides on the plants?"

"We put something on to combat the Rust, and something for the insects, but I don't know what they are. They don't smell great, and we have to wear gloves."

I grabbed an empty Ziploc from my backpack. "Could you put some soil in there for me?"

"*Por supuesto.*" Tomás walked over to the nearest coffee bush. While he filled the bag with soil, I took photos of the pickers with my Canon. After a moment, he returned and handed me the bag.

"Thanks," I said. "I'll try to get this to an inspector. And good luck. I hope you find your mom."

"Do you need directions back?"

"What?"

He looked at me keenly. "You said you were a lost tourist."

*Right.* That was my genius cover. "That would be great."

I followed his directions to the footpath and started down it. I could feel his eyes on my back, burning little holes into my spine. I felt terrible. *How could I leave him here?* But what could I do about it?

When I got to the edge of the forest, I looked at the back of the community center. I could hear Adrián and Manuel and Paula laughing on the veranda out front. They wouldn't be laughing if they knew I'd been chatting with their child labor and collecting proof of their pesticide use. An awful thought occurred to me—what if they *did* know? What if Manuel had seen through my pretense and was just waiting for me to come back? Would he have me arrested for trespassing? Or worse?

I sprinted toward the back of the mill. The bathroom window was still open so I hoisted myself through it. I looked at my face in the mirror. Sweat was running down my reddened cheeks and distress was pulsing in my eyes. I needed to pull myself together before I went back to the veranda. I sat down on the closed toilet and did breathing exercises. Breathe in. Breathe out. Breathe in. Breathe out.

But that made me hyperventilate—which made me *more* anxious.

*MANUEL KNOWS YOU KNOW AND HE'S GOING TO KILL YOU!* screamed my uncooperative subconscious. *JUMP OUT THE WINDOW AND RUN!*

Someone knocked on the door but I couldn't answer. Air would just not go all the way into my lungs. The knocking continued, my breathing slowed, and then all I could see was black dotted with little particles of light. *Was this a panic attack?* I wondered. *I'm pretty sure this is a panic attack. Unless it's a heart attack?!*

"Are you okay?" asked Paula, from behind the door. "Are you still sick?"

"Yes," I gasped, head between my knees in an attempt to make the floor closer should I faint. Why did Adrián let Paula come for me? Because he was *dead*!

"Yes, you're okay? Or, yes, you're sick?"

"I'm okay . . ." I wheezed, now lying on the cold tile, face up.

The voice was silent, and I heard retreating footsteps. A few minutes passed while I tried to regulate my breathing. Then there were different, heavier footsteps.

"*¡Preciosa!* Are you okay?"

*He wasn't dead!*

"Open the door, please. It's locked."

I looked up at the handle. I willed it to open itself.

"Open the door!"

I lifted my right arm into the air. It stayed elevated. *How strange,* commented my subconscious, *still working.*

"*DEE*!"

I heard a great thud, then a splintering, and then Adrián was in the bathroom standing over me.

"What happened?" he asked, falling to his knees.

"Nothing," I said, my lungs having resumed their regular functions. "Well, probably a panic attack. Do you have any Xanax?"

He shook his head. "Why are you on the floor? And why are you covered in dirt?" He put an arm behind my back and helped me up.

"Why are you here?" I tested out my legs. "I told you to distract them."

"I did. I already 'checked on you' twice. Then Doña Paula insisted on checking on you. I thought I heard you come back a few minutes ago so I figured it was okay. But then I got worried something happened."

I looked over his shoulder past the broken bathroom door to make sure no one was listening, and then I shut it as best I could. I turned to Adrián. "They use child labor. I talked with one of them and they confirmed it."

"I hate to tell you this, but lots of farms use child labor."

"That doesn't make it right. And they would lose their Ethical Coffee International certification if it got out. Manuel's not going to let me waltz out of here with information that could sink his business."

"He's not going to know," he said. "Let me do the talking." Adrián helped dust me off, which even in my panicky state was not unpleasant, then led me to the veranda. Paula and Manuel stared at me.

"Where's the closest hospital?" asked Adrián.

"Liberia," said Manuel. "But we could call a doctor to come here."

"That's okay," said Adrián. "I'll take her to Liberia." He put his arm around my waist and guided me down the steps.

Manuel waved. "I'm sorry you're sick." Did he buy it? Or was he playing along? "Feel free to come back when you're better."

There was zero chance of that. I didn't fancy learning more about his shotgun collection. As we walked down the dirt road, all I could think about was the little girl with the curly hair. She would probably be in the fifth grade, like my cousin Naomi. Naomi didn't have to pick coffee cherries in the hot sun for hours. She didn't even have to do her own laundry.

When we got to the Jeep, I flopped into my seat and Adrián turned on the radio. We were quiet for a few minutes while I tried to regain my composure.

"So much for cooperation," he said, finally. "What did the kids say to you?"

I turned the radio off and put my head on the dashboard. It was throbbing. "I only spoke to one. He said their mother went looking for their real dad and foisted them off on Manuel."

"That's terrible. It sounds like a telenovela." He looked uncharacteristically pensive. "I wish we could do something."

I was surprised. Free market Adrián wanted to intervene? Was this growth? Or had I not really understood him in the first place? We drove in silence. Adrián was chewing on the nail of his pinkie finger, which I had never seen him do. He had perfectly manicured nails.

"Hey," said Adrián. "Look." Sixty meters down the highway, two forms were flagging us down. As we got closer, I recognized them. *The teenagers.* Adrián pulled up alongside them and I unrolled my window.

Tomás came up to me. "Thanks for stopping." He leaned in through the car window, his forearm resting on the ledge. "I wanted to ask you for a favor. Could you give us a ride to San José?"

I was speechless. This boy had the balls of a mafioso.

"Now?" asked Adrián.

"Yes. If you take us to the city, Mario and I can make a report to an inspector." He gave me a sly smile. "Or *to you*. If *you're* an inspector."

"And then we'd take you back?"

"Well . . ." He looked at his brother. "Maybe we'd hitch another ride back."

There was no way they were returning to Café Alegre if they left. And they weren't going to the city to make a report, either. I turned to Adrián and spoke very softly. "Wouldn't that be kidnapping?"

Adrián looked at Tomás. "Are you eighteen? Answer carefully."

"I'm eighteen," said Tomás. "As is my brother."

Adrián turned to me. "To the best of our knowledge, this is not kidnapping."

"Please take us," said Tomás in rapid Spanish. "We need to find our mom. We're trapped here."

Adrián turned to me. "Let's do it."

"But . . ." Mixed emotions flooded me. What if Tomás had been exaggerating and only occasionally helped with the harvest? Wouldn't he be worse off penniless and unconnected in the city? I turned to Adrián. "What good is it going to do them to be on the streets?"

"These kids are here against their will," said Adrián. "And didn't you say yourself that they're illegal labor? I'm surprised by your hesitation, Dee. I thought your thing was justice."

Ouch. *Dee*. Not *Preciosa*.

"Look," said Tomás. "If you just happen to be driving, and we just happen to be walking down the road, and you just happen to give us a lift . . . where's the problem? That's not kidnapping. It's ridesharing."

"What about your younger brother and sister?" I asked.

"We'll come back for them when we have enough money."

Adrián unlocked the doors and the boys climbed in. Before I could protest again, Adrián hit the gas. The boys peppered Adrián with questions about the city until, high with excitement, they crashed like balloons with the helium sucked out. I looked in the rearview mirror. They were slumped together. Mario was snoring, and Tomás's eyes were flitting in REM.

I tried to sleep, too, but all I could do was imagine Tomás and Mario passed out on a dirty heap of rags with track marks running down their arms in an hourly motel in San José. Adrián noticed my tortured expression. He patted my stomach.

"Are you feeling better?" He put the back of his palm on my forehead. "Your temperature is normal." He put two fingers on my neck and felt for my pulse. I took his hand and squeezed it. Even if Adrián was a neoconservative, he was a really nice neoconservative.

"Thank you," I said.

"For what?"

"For coming to the bathroom to find me. For saving me."

"I didn't save you. You can take care of yourself."

I wasn't so sure about that. Completely exhausted, I put my head against the glass and passed out.

A few hours later, I awoke with a rude jolt at a traffic signal in downtown San José, near the Coca-Cola bus terminal. Young men and women in tight skirts and fishnets solicited men in cars. I turned to Adrián. "What are we doing here?"

"Dropping off the boys."

"Here? Are you out of your mind?!" A shirtless man came

up to my window and knocked on it. The Jeep lurched forward, and Adrián looked at me in genuine bewilderment.

"Where else am I going to leave them?" he asked.

"You should've thought of this before!" The traffic light changed, and Adrián drove through the intersection. Dozens of young men were lounging on the corners, waiting for work. "What are they going to do if you leave them here?"

"I don't know," said Adrián. "Work."

"Don't worry," said Tomás. "I don't want you guys to fight about us. We'll be fine, just drop us off here." Adrián nodded and pulled the Jeep to the side of the road.

"We can't leave them here!" I said, trying to lock the doors.

"Thanks!" the boys said, jumping out of the Jeep. "Bye!" They hit the pavement and ran around a corner.

"Adrián! Do something!"

"Do what?" He put the Jeep back in first and checked his side mirror. "They're gone."

"They're going to die! Starve! Turn into prostitutes!"

"They'll be fine." He made a U-turn, conscience completely unruffled.

Face pressed flat against the window, I searched for the boys as Adrián wound through the labyrinthine streets behind the bus station. "There they are!" I cried, pointing to a drug dealer surrounded by several teenagers.

Adrián peered over my shoulder. "That's not them."

"Oh."

Adrián continued to drive through downtown. "*Tranquila, Preciosa*. They'll find jobs."

"I guess," I said, glumly. *Having sex with strangers.*

"You know, Dee, it's not your job to fix every single problem."

He was right. The thing was—I wasn't sure if I could fix any of them.

# CHAPTER THIRTEEN

The next morning I went into a deep funk. Even Abuelita couldn't cheer me up with freshly baked *cocadas* and an extremely detailed accounting of the Colombian telenovela I'd missed yesterday. It was pretty salacious—apparently Lolita and Esteban could never be together, because Esteban was her hair stylist and her new boss, but also maybe her estranged half brother. But I wasn't invested. I was in ideological crisis. How to reconcile the fact that Cooperative Heaven was essentially the same as Corporate Hell? In Café Bavaria, an impersonal, large plantation owned by a German exploited Nicaraguan immigrants for low pay and no benefits. In Café Alegre, a cooperative owned by Costa Ricans exploited Costa Rican children and Nicaraguan immigrants for low pay and no benefits. They both used pesticides. Which was worse?

This disillusion shook me to the foundation of my being because for me, people are their beliefs. If cooperation was just a beautiful impractical dream, then who was I now? And what was I doing here in Costa Rica? I might as well go home and be that divorce lawyer my family wanted me to be. Before I could fully fall into a pit of despair, my phone buzzed. So I took leave of Abuelita and promised to buy her some lotto tickets.

I ran across the street and sat at the bus stop outside the Chinese-owned market. There was a young man painting over some fresh graffiti. A lot of it was already gone, but it appeared to be a xenophobic message. The universality of racism was a shocking lesson.

My phone buzzed again. I opened my email.

TO: Dee Blum
FROM: Matías Khalil
SUBJECT: Making fans

I got a call from Eugenio and he loves you. You know, he isn't an easy nut to crack. He was very impressed by your optimism and passion. He even said you'll be sharing research. What a vote of confidence!

By the way, I went back to your website—looking for clues about your identity—and I stumbled across your essay about cooperation and the fundamental goodness of humanity. You're quite an idealist. So if humans are fundamentally good, how do you explain greed? Violence? Deception?

Speaking of deception, faceless "Dee." Come on, give me *one* clue!

♥ ◐ *

TO: Matías Khalil
FROM: Dee Blum
SUBJECT: Re: Making fans

That's great to hear about Professor Ramírez, I'm so excited to be working with him. So, normally, I view violence and greed as a default from the norm. It's what happens when things break down. Evil is not part of our *essential* nature. But sometimes I have my doubts. Like right now. I went to a supposedly ethical farm yesterday and saw some very shady practices. That really rocked me. What am I supposed to think when the good guys are as bad as the bad guys? How do you reconcile that? Because I'm having a really hard time.

As per my identity, okay, fine, *one* hint: blue.

It was unusual to discuss something as profound as human nature with someone I'd never met, but somehow, it felt natural with Matías. So many conversations did. I couldn't pinpoint why.

An alarm started going off on my phone. Time to call Suzanne. I dreaded telling her about my site visit. My first real assignment was a fail, and that was *before* I committed a felony. Maybe I wouldn't tell her that part.

"I'm afraid Café Alegre is a bust," I told her. "They're not actually organic."

"What do you mean? They're Ethical Coffee International certified."

"I saw the pesticides myself."

"Wow," she said, surprise and concern seeping into her voice. I could almost see her at her desk, sitting up straighter.

"That's so strange." She paused, evidently needing a moment to process it. Just like I had. "Did you see them use it?"

"No."

"Hmm." I heard a clicking sound, like a pen against teeth. "Is it possible you misinterpreted something? It's just that this is *so* unusual. We've never had a reason to doubt the credibility of certified farms. Ethical Coffee International does very thorough evaluations. It would be shocking if anything got past them."

"I got a soil sample."

"Oh!" She sounded impressed. I puffed up. *I* had impressed Suzanne Lyon. "How? What did you put it in?"

"A Ziploc."

She laughed. She was no longer impressed. "We can't use that. Certainly you must realize that." Now that she said it, I did. "The bag could be contaminated."

A preteen boy sat next to me on the bench and said in Spanish, "I've had sex before."

"What was that?" asked Suzanne.

"Nothing." I scooted to the very end of the bench.

"Look, I'm impressed with your initiative, but if you'll permit me to mentor you for a moment, I think you need a reality check. You're new to this industry and don't have the lay of the land. It's likely that what you saw was a fungicide. Some are permitted."

"I guess that's possible."

"No, it's *probable*. Dee, it's easy for us to level accusations from our position, but how would you feel if you were struggling to make ends meet in a middle-income country and some inexperienced American came and slandered your farm without really understanding it?"

Oh god. Was I just a privileged and naive do-gooder who was making things worse by not understanding the complexity?

And how could I tell her about the child labor now? She already thought I was naive and overzealous. And what if she was right? What if those chemicals were approved? And what if Tomás was just a disaffected teenager, mad at his parents and making up stories? Kids help their families with work all around the world. I had spent countless hours of my childhood separating yarn knots for my mother's Etsy tea cozies.

"I hadn't thought of it that way," I said.

"Look, Dee, I don't want to completely dismiss it, either. If you have serious doubts, you should go back. Take a more extensive tour and see if they allay your concerns."

"I mean, I could." *No way.* I was not going back there. I had kidnapped Manuel's stepson. "But there are so many other farms to visit. Maybe we just take them off the list and focus on some other farms?"

"Café Alegre just got written up in *Condé Nast Traveler.* That translates into a lot of interest from our potential clients. So let's keep them in the mix. Anyhow, I've got to get to a meeting, so we need to wrap this up." I heard her chair creak and then the click of heels against the ground. "Visit some more farms so we have choices. But don't forget we need to get this trip up and running by June. Which means your work needs to be done by February."

Uh-oh. February did not seem like a realistic due date given my complete lack of forward progress.

"Once I had sex with an American," the preteen said. "A blond."

"*No hablo español,*" I said.

"What? Will this be a problem?" Suzanne asked.

"Nope," I said. "I'm on it." I hung up, more anxious than before the call. So far, I had failed at finding a farm for the trip, I'd failed at reporting Café Alegre, and I'd made myself look bad to my boss. Not a brilliant start to my career.

"I'm very advanced for my age," said the preteen.

I got up and walked to the *mercado* entrance. I did not need to add statutory rape to my list of crimes. I called my dad under the awning.

"Dee?" His voice was hopeful.

"I miss you, Dad." There was an echo. *I miss you, Dad.*

"We miss you, too, honey." I could hear him turning down the music in his office. "Do you need anything? Are you safe?"

"I'm fine." I struggled to make my voice normal. "I'm great."

"Thanks for that email. It's good to hear from you now and then. Even if the content is you reprimanding me." I pinched my fingers together, hard. He was quiet for a moment and I could hear the low buzz of his computer. "I'm sorry for impersonating you and making your website."

This was the first time my dad had ever apologized to me. I think my brain short-circuited. "I'm sorry I got so mad," I said. "The stuff you put on there was actually kind of useful. Also, I'm impressed you figured out how to hack my external hard drive."

He laughed. "Yeah, I had help with that."

"Nicole?"

"Yup."

"She's such a traitor."

"But a tech-savvy one, you must admit."

I couldn't help but smile. "Anything new?"

"Well, your mom's Etsy store has seen a big drop in orders. I guess the tea cozy market is saturated. She's also been getting into an unusual number of fights on Nextdoor. Causation or correlation?"

"Causation, definitely."

"Agree. And the Dodgers got a new pitching coach. I'll forward you the article."

"Yeah, do that."

I heard my mom calling my dad in the background. "Jacob, Coldwell's calling on the house line. Said you won't pick up your cell!"

"Look, honey, I gotta go. But please call again soon."

I hung up, my chest heavy with an unidentifiable emotion. *Baby steps*, I whispered to myself. You don't fix a broken relationship with one apology. I felt the cool gold snakes against my skin. I saw my grandfather picking me up from the Jewish Community Center the day I got into a fight with my cousin Nicole. *Always say you're sorry first*, he told me. *Love is a lot more important than pride.* Well, Dad said sorry first this time. Next time it would be me.

I headed into the market and perused the lotto selection—would Abuelita want to play *La Lotería Nacional*, *La Lotería Instantánea*, *Lotto*, *Pitazo*, *Nuevos Tiempos*, or *Los Chances*? I decided to get one of each to be safe. As I handed the clerk some money, my phone buzzed. Adrián.

"*Hola, Preciosa*. How's your existential dread today?"

"Somewhere between not great and tossing myself into a river. Like, not *all* the way to *The Sorrows of Young Werther*, but getting there."

"Stay away from all bodies of water! I'm about to pick you up."

"Really? Where are you?" I went outside the market.

"I'm approaching the greatest engineering marvel in all of Carmen del Guadalupe."

I looked toward the water tanks. Yup, there he was in his silver Jeep, racing through the blind intersection, scattering roosters, chickens, and an annoyed-looking dog. He screeched to a halt in front of the market.

I decided that opposites definitely attract as he got out of his seat, walked around to the other side, took my hand to help me in, and closed the door for me. There was a take-out coffee in the cup holder. He gestured toward it as he slid into his seat.

"*Para ti.* It's fair trade and organic."

"Are you messing with me?"

"No, I actually went to three different cafés to find it. I didn't want you to compromise your ethics for me."

"You mean compromise them *further.*" I gave him a kiss. "So kidnapping's okay, but commodity coffee is too far?"

"Exactly," he said with a devilish grin.

"Where are you taking me? Do you have some land to buy?" I teased. "Tenants to kick out so your dad can build a new hotel?"

"No, that's on Thursday. I'm taking you to my house."

This was new. Adrián lived with his parents, as most people did here until marriage. I wondered what the rules were regarding bringing girls home. I mean, we were adults. But barely.

"I know you were really disappointed by Café Alegre," he said. "So I thought we could research some other cooperative farms for you to visit. Maybe we can find one that lives up to your extremely high ideals." I looked at him, surprised. Adrián didn't care about cooperative farms. I guess that meant . . . he cared about me?

Thirty minutes later we were at the front door of his family's two-story home. It was in the posh neighborhood of Santa Ana, where the yards were manicured, the paint jobs were fresh, and even the palms felt stately. As soon as we got out of the Jeep, Adrián started acting very shady. He told me to wait by the front door, then entered the house by himself. I heard doors slamming. Satisfied that the house was empty, he came back to retrieve me.

"Wow," I said, as I stepped into the foyer. His house was a lot bigger than my host family's house, and more stylish, too.

They had utilized more than one color in their decor. I looked at some framed still lifes. "Nice prints."

"They're not prints."

"Ah," I said, reeling as I calculated their worth. The hotel business must be good.

"Come upstairs." Adrián led me up a central staircase to the top floor. He ushered me through a door and closed it.

"Why are we doing research here?" I surveyed the room. A large window, a twin bed with a maroon cover, and a computer. And, oh, Jesus on the cross hanging over the bed.

"Because the internet is very fast up here."

So that's how I found myself on Adrián's lap in front of his computer, surfing through coffee co-op sites. While I was busy writing a note in my phone, Adrián took the mouse and navigated to my Instagram page. It was clear he'd been there before. He immediately clicked on a picture of Cody at a picket in Oakland. Cody was staring straight into the camera in a flirty way.

"Who's that?" asked Adrián. "Your boyfriend?"

"Ex-boyfriend."

"Oh." Adrián shifted under me, and I could feel his eyes boring into my back. "He liked some of your photos."

"It was a friendly breakup." *Sort of.*

"Do you still love him?"

"I don't think I ever did."

Adrián let out a sigh. Then in one swift move, he turned my body so I was straddling him. He put his hands on either side of my face. "I like you," he said, with his lips one centimeter from mine. "A lot."

"Oh," I mumbled. My no-relationship resolution was fading faster than clothing left to dry in the sun.

"Do you like me?"

"I guess so," I said.

He moved one arm to my waist, pulling me in even tighter. "You guess so? Or you do?"

"Uh," I said. His body was pressing into mine. My brain was losing oxygen. "Okay. Yes."

Adrián kissed me. Fire surged upward from my torso. My lungs refused to push out more air, and I completely forgot about everything in the world except the fever raging all over my body. His hands were spreading like wildfire. Just as he was standing up and trying to lift me to his bed, we heard the front door open. "*Mierda*," he said. "Fix your hair."

"My hair?"

He licked his palms and slid them over my hair. It was futile.

"*¿Mijito?*" called his mother. "Where are you?"

"Quick." Adrián sat me in the chair in front of his computer. Then he opened his bedroom door and came back to the computer. "*Aquí arriba, mamá*," he said toward the door. "Helping Dee with her homework." He pulled a stray hair of mine behind my ears.

"Homework?" I whispered.

"Trust me," he said. "Oh my god, your neck."

And before he could pull up my collar to hide my erupting hickey, Doña Teresa entered the room. "Oh," she said, putting a palm over her chest.

"You remember Dee," said Adrián, gliding across the room and kissing his horrified mother on the cheek. "She has a project due for her Costa Rican politics class. I'm helping her with some translations."

"So nice to see you again," said Doña Teresa, with a becoming mix of shock and wrath. Her skin tone matched the platinum color of her dress.

"Likewise," I said, rising for the air kiss. I twitched my head to the right in a desperate effort to hide the swelling redness.

"What a surprise," she said, pulling back from our perfunctory embrace. "I wasn't expecting company this afternoon."

"I tried calling but you didn't answer," said Adrián.

"You could've texted," she said sweetly, but not sweetly at all. "But it's not a problem." Doña Teresa turned back to me. Her eyes widened. Oh Jesus Christ! A *new* hickey was forming on the other side of my neck. *Curse my extreme iron deficiency!* I tried to pull some hair out from behind my ears without her noticing. Her eyes immediately followed the trajectory of my hands. Why did I feel like I was in high school?!

"You're always welcome here," she said, her eyes moving shamelessly from my hands to my neck. I wondered what else was developing. Can you get shingles from kissing? "It's just a pity I didn't know you were coming. If I had, I would've prepared a nice dinner for you."

"You're too kind," I said, willing my neck to turn one color.

Her eyes responded, *I am.* "I just feel horrible that I don't have anything to offer you. In the future I'd appreciate it if you'd let me know before you come over."

"Of course," I said. It was a clever way to humiliate someone. She and my mom would get along.

"It kills me to not have anything to offer guests. I am so embarrassed."

Would she stop it already? Could she just get on with it and call me a filthy whore? I guess she was saving that for Adrián, because she gave my neck one last perusal, then turned on him. "I'll see you downstairs." And with that she flounced out of the room and down the stairs, trailing perfume and displeasure.

"She likes you," said Adrián, straightening his shirt. I looked at him with what must have been very poorly disguised incredulity. "No, really," he said, "She didn't kick you out." He hurried to the door. "I'll be right back."

And so I sat at Adrián's desk trying to distract myself with Instagram while Teresa had a stern chat with Adrián downstairs. He came sheepishly back to the room ten minutes later. "She's making us coffee." And without another word he left, went to his sister's bedroom, and snagged a foundation that was three times too dark for my skin.

"Does she hate me?" I asked.

"Not at all." Adrián was blending the foundation on my neck with a makeup sponge. He seemed way too practiced at this. "She's a little peeved with me, but I explained that it was crucial you complete this assignment by today or you'd fail the class."

"Fail the class for one assignment?"

"Very strict professor." He threw the sponge away and pulled me toward the door. "Come on."

So that's how I found myself having coffee and empanadas with Adrián's perfect mother, with Ping-Pong ball–sized bruises on my neck. Adrián had done a good job blending the color, but he couldn't do much with the size. Since when did hickeys come in relief?

"It's such a disgrace," she said. I wanted to jump under the table and embalm myself with coffee. "And she's only seventeen."

"Terrible," agreed Adrián.

Wait. *Who were we talking about?*

"And he left. Just like that. Dee," she turned to me. "Are all American men like that?"

Uh. "No?"

"Thank God. I don't know what her parents are going to do with her. She's talking about . . . *termination*. Is that normal, Dee? Do you think her American boyfriend is pressuring her?"

And then it all clicked. Adrián had mentioned in passing that one of his cousins had gotten pregnant by some American study-abroad kid, and obviously, I was the authority on sexually loose Americans.

"I don't know," I said. Teresa was smiling at me with so much saccharine that I knew I'd never see the inside of this house again if I didn't achieve a dramatic reversal. "I honestly can't imagine being in that situation."

"Oh?" Some of the saccharine left her collagen-enhanced lips.

"Premarital sex is strictly forbidden by my religion," I said. *Was that true?* I had no idea.

She nodded, pleased. "By ours, too." She gave Adrián a cold look. "Which some young people have forgotten."

It occurred to me that now was the moment to wrest this conversation into more favorable lands. "You know, our cultures have a lot in common. Pulling your own weight is very important in my community, and especially in my family. For example, we put a high value on being an entrepreneur. My mother has her own small business."

"Ooh." Teresa was impressed. "What kind?"

"Textiles." No need to get more specific. "And my father sells real estate."

"Really?" she asked, perking up even more. "Houses or commercial buildings?"

"Malls and office buildings, mainly. He just got into development."

"How lovely." She poured more coffee into my still half-full cup. "Developing's the way to go."

"Yes. That, or the legal profession."

"That's right," she said. "You're studying law."

And that settled it. Teresa didn't really want to believe that her son was with a harlot, so she was going to forget all about the hickeys. She was going to remember that my father was a developer, my mom was an entrepreneur, and I was industrious, dedicated, and celibate.

"You're considering working here after you graduate law school?" she asked. "You mentioned a particular interest in coffee."

I swirled my spoon in little circles in my coffee cup. "Yes. All options are open at this point."

"Ah," she said, with a smile that could eat the whole world. She placed another golden empanada on my plate. "Costa Rica is such a lovely country, Dee. If you stay here, I'm sure you'll love it."

I looked at Adrián, who was spooning Salsa Lizano onto my plate for me. "I already do."

# CHAPTER FOURTEEN

That night I holed myself up in my bedroom surfing through Costa Rican travel sites. Teresa's suggestion about finding long-term work here was intriguing. Maybe after I finished arranging the Truth Trip, I could get a job organizing other kinds of eco-tours. That had to be better for the world than being a divorce lawyer. Or maybe I could get another project with Justice Alliance. That seemed like a long shot though. After all, I hadn't accomplished even *one* of the tasks I'd been sent to do.

That realization made me sweat. So I stopped looking for new jobs and concentrated on the one I had. I had just finished making a list of proposed homestays for the Truth Trip when I heard Eva calling to me from her bedroom. "Dee! I forgot to tell you something."

"*Voy.*" I walked into their room. Eva was stretched out in sweats on her queen bed, surrounded by dozens of well-worn stuffed animals. To her right was a vanity table with a lavender organza ruffle. I wondered what sort of negotiations she and Luis had engaged in over the interior decor.

"What were you doing?" she asked, rubbing her eyes until

mascara formed dark rings under her eyes. "Where have you been all day?"

"Working."

She looked at me closer. "Are those hickeys?"

I blushed. "I have an iron deficiency."

"You weren't working!" But she didn't look mad. She looked amused. "So things are going well with Adrián." I nodded. "I'm glad. But do *not* have sex with him." She looked at me intently. "You haven't?"

"No!"

"Good. Remember, your body is a temple. You can't let just anyone in." That was an interesting way to look at it. Could you be sex-positive and also think of your body as a restricted area? How did I think of mine?

"Got it. Anyhow. You wanted to see me?"

"You got some mail." She pointed to a manila envelope in the corner of her room. I picked it up. FedEx. "You know," she said. "If you want to watch TV, you can come in here with me."

"Thanks." I looked at her petite frame lost in the large bed. I wondered if she was lonely. "Maybe later." I noticed she had a hot water bottle on her torso and prescription pain pills next to the bed. "Are you okay?"

She nodded, resigned. "It's my feminine time. I have a lot of trouble with it."

"I'm sorry. Let me know if you need anything."

She smiled wanly, lay back into her embroidered pillows, and returned to gazing at the intertwined bodies on-screen. I wondered if her painful "feminine time" was connected to their lack of children. And I wondered how it made her feel in a marriage that was clearly designed for procreation.

I returned to my room, making sure to leave the door partially open. Earlier, Eva had told me that it made her feel blocked out if I shut it completely. I had trouble understanding why until I remembered what she had said to me in the airport. *I hope you will be like a real daughter to me.* I wasn't exactly nailing it as an ideal surrogate daughter. I spent most of my time out of the house, and when I was home, I locked myself in my room. I sighed. I couldn't even be a good real daughter, so how was I supposed to be a good host one?

I ripped open the FedEx envelope. It was an (opened) letter from UC Berkeley inquiring if I intended to reenroll for the fall semester. Dad had written an accompanying note urging me to apply *RIGHT AWAY as my place was NOT GUARANTEED and I had to REAPPLY for admission*. I sighed. It was always like this with him—one step forward, two steps back. We were stuck in an endless pattern, destined to always circle each other, never connect.

I tossed it into the corner, rubbed my temples, and stood up. A clap of thunder shook my room. I looked toward the window and saw that it had grown dark. Clouds were coming in, hanging thick and heavy over the valley of San José. Lightning crackled far away in Cartago, on the other side of the mountain. I could see it hit like thin fingers striking a piano. As I watched the nearest clouds drop lower, large drops of water started to beat against the windowpane. Soon torrential rain was turning the backyard into a whirlpool. I walked away from the window and sat at my desk.

I tried writing my dad an email:

> *Dad, thanks for forwarding the letter, but I told you I have no immediate plans to go back.*
>
> *Dad, I know you really want me to graduate, but I'm a big girl and I can make my own decisions.*

*Dad. Why can't you understand that I can't be who you want me to be?*

My fingers became heavy as I remembered a big fight we had last summer. My mom was on vacation with Aunt Jackie at some "wellness" camp up in Ojai, torturing herself to lose the five pounds she didn't need to lose. The body positivity movement hadn't made it to her generation. To be fair, I had a hard time with it, too. It would be a lot easier to be body positive in a world that wasn't so negative about our bodies.

So it was just me and my dad in the house for one awkward, silent week. On the last night before Mom came home, I wandered into his office to borrow a charger. He was listening to a baseball game on internet radio. My dad was funny. He preferred listening to baseball games. He said he could see them better that way.

He was looking for the charger and I told him I wanted to quit working at Uncle Aaron's law firm. The next thing I knew, we were full-on yelling at each other.

"Why would you do that? You know you need that on your resume to get into law school!"

"Maybe I don't want to go to law school! Maybe I don't want to be like Aaron! And I certainly don't want to be like you!"

Everything had stopped after that, everything except the announcer. *And the deuces are wild, folks! Two out, two on, two strikes!* At first, I thought Dad would rage, yell, make the room shake with his anger. But all he did was sit down and look at me in complete silence.

*. . . he starts his windup. The runners are going!*

"I don't want you to be like me, either," he said.

*It's a fastball in for a strike! Ninety-four miles per hour!*

"I'm sorry," I said, wishing I could take those words back.

"You think I want my daughter to be like me?" His eyes filled with a rawness that terrified me. "How do you think it feels knowing I can't pay for my kid's school? How do you think it feels telling your mom she can't paint the house, or buy supplies for her store? How do you think it feels knowing we're one medical emergency away from bankruptcy?" I looked down. "Every time I see the paint chipping, all I can think is, 'I am a failure.' I can't support my family."

I looked back and saw his face twisted into a sick approximation of a smile.

"No, Dee. I don't want you to be anything like me. That's why I want you to study law. That's why I want you to work for your uncle."

"I'm sorry," I said, regret and pity and anger welling up in my throat.

My dad looked right at me, handed me the charger, sat back down, and turned up the radio.

*It's the bottom of the ninth and the heart of the lineup's coming to the plate.*

I looked at my computer screen and erased the message I was writing. I shut my laptop, lay on my bed, and listened to rain drown the valley of San José.

♥ ● *

The next day, the sun had dried out all the puddles, but I was still feeling melancholy. Had I made a mistake by coming here? I'd worsened my relationship with my father, jeopardized my future by dropping out of college, and accomplished zilch. They say the antidote to anxiety is action, so I started making calls to arrange the homestays. Once I had ticked an item off my to-do list, I started to feel better. Maybe I did have a handle on things! Maybe I wasn't an utter disaster of a person! That feeling lasted a whole five minutes before my mom called.

"Sweetheart, we have to make this quick because your dad's going to be home in ten minutes."

"What is it?"

"He was fired."

"God." Pity welled up inside me like rough water.

"He won't talk to me about what we're going to do. And as you may have heard, my tea cozy sales aren't meeting expectations. It's been an abnormally warm winter."

"Hmm, yeah. I can see how that would drive down demand."

"Yes. Global warming is affecting so many industries. Of course, we could borrow money from Aaron, but your dad would never hear of it. He's too proud." I swallowed the lump in my throat. Did she not know how many times we'd borrowed from Aaron? Did she really think her cozies paid for anything more than the gas bill? "Anyway, I just wanted you to hear it from me, because he's not going to tell you. And I know he's concerned about your financial situation—are you okay over there?"

"I'm fine. It's a job. They pay me."

"That's what I told him. He thinks you won't reapply to school because of money."

"That's not why."

"That's what I told him! Gap years are very common among your generation. Anyhow, don't you worry about us. I'm sure he'll find work for another brokerage soon. And I may expand my business into sweatbands so I can really have a four seasons shop."

"That's a great idea, Mom."

"Thanks, honey." I could hear the pride in her voice. "By the way, are you taking care of your eyebrows? Do they have waxing salons there?" *And there it was.*

"All under control!" I chirped.

"Good. It's important to take pride in your appearance." I heard her take a sip of coffee. "Sweetie, I hear his car in the drive. Next time you talk to him, act like you don't know, okay?"

I said goodbye and hung up. Mom didn't realize just *how* devastated Dad would be. I was the only person in the world that could be there for him, and I wasn't even supposed to know. I opened my email.

TO: Jacob Blum
FROM: Dee Blum
SUBJECT: Hello!

Hey Dad. I saw a Winter League game last night and thought of you. It looks like that rookie shortstop we're going to platoon next season is really something! After I get back from Costa Rica I'll probably be in LA for a while so we should definitely go to some games. Try to snag some dates from Uncle Stephen's box. Everything's good here. My bosses are happy with me and the pay isn't bad at all. I miss you, and I sort of miss Mom (Ha. Just send her my love).

I love you, Dee

I hit send with a heavy feeling. I couldn't stop experiencing my dad's feelings as if they were my own. Some people's boundaries were like a drawbridge; they just pulled them right up. But mine were like a river that was always overflowing its banks.

As I headed to the university to meet the Professor, I tried to compartmentalize thoughts about my dad. My mom excelled at compartmentalizing. Any unwanted thoughts were mercilessly stuffed into a remote corner of her brain, locked in by Xanax and Chardonnay. I didn't have either on me, but I did my best. I was less successful pushing away thoughts of Café Alegre.

When I got to campus, I dragged myself up the three stories to the Professor's office. His assistant waved me straight in, and I was surprised to find that the room was empty—except for the poster of Che. I could swear Che was staring at me with disapproval; his left eyebrow arched, his mouth a tight, thin line. Che wouldn't have taken Tomás and Mario out of Café Alegre. He would've killed Don Manuel and installed a dictatorship of the proletariat.

The Professor entered his office. He sat gracefully in his chair. "Did you go to Café Alegre? How was it?"

I fidgeted for a moment while I tried to muster the courage to tell him. "Not so good."

"Disorganized?"

"Not really."

"Excessive infighting?"

"Sort of."

"Not in the cooperative spirit?"

How could I tell the truth with Che giving me the evil eye? "They're frauds!" There, it was out.

"How so?"

I shoved the plastic bag of soil across the Professor's desk, and my iPad, open to the camera roll. He looked at the pictures of pesticides for several moments, surprise flitting through his strong features. He put the iPad down. "Strange." He wiped his hands across his tired forehead and wrote something down on a legal pad. "Well, let's move on."

I stared at him.

"Is there more?" he asked.

I pulled at my thumbs. "They use child labor."

"How old?"

"The youngest was seven or eight. The oldest was maybe fifteen. He said they got pulled out of school routinely."

"What a pity." He pushed errant strands of hair out of his face. "I'll try to get a Ministry of Labor inspector to go out there." He jotted something else on his legal pad. "We'll continue with our work. It was a fluke."

A fluke? That's it? Faced with the destruction of a dream, he says, *a fluke*? I couldn't move.

"What's wrong?" asked the Professor. "Are you sick?" *Why did everyone always ask me that?!* "Ah," he said, leaning back into his chair, making the diagnosis. "Look, if you let it, activist work can get you down. But you're not going to let one disappointment sink you, are you?"

I shook my head no, but without conviction.

"Good," he continued. "Because if you do, you aren't the person I think you are."

*But who did he think I was?* Someone stronger and wiser than the real me? "It's not just that," I said. "When I told Suzanne about Alegre, I was hoping she could pass the info on to Ethical Coffee International. But she said this wasn't proof and that my Ziploc bag was useless."

"She's right about the Ziploc. It's not sterile." He handed the bag back to me. "I would defer to her on this one, she's extremely experienced and knows the rules better than I do. It's a shame, but I think the best thing for us to do is concentrate on elevating farms that are actually walking the walk."

"I get that. But Suzanne doesn't want to take Alegre off the list for the Truth Trip. She says they have a lot of heat right now and will excite donors."

"Then you need to convince her that other farms are better.

I have just the thing." He stood up and started pacing around the room. "You are familiar with Las Nubes?" I shook my head. "They're one of the oldest coffee co-ops in Costa Rica, and until lately, the most successful. But they're going through a very rough time."

"Why?"

"That's part of what I'd like to find out. The coffee industry throughout Central America is suffering from a fungus called the Rust, causing widespread disruption. But due to altitude, Las Nubes has been spared the Rust. Something else is negatively impacting them." He put his wild hair back in a ponytail. "I'm going there tomorrow to investigate. Perhaps you could join me."

"I'd love to," I said, with equal parts hope and concern. What was this other factor causing disruption? I had hoped my days of armed guards were behind me.

"You will find them interesting; they operate more like a commune than a cooperative. There is no individual ownership; profits are shared equally. Definitely the real deal, politically speaking. Perhaps you can convince them to be on your Truth Trip. Until now they've been resistant to tourists."

"Why?"

"They feel like it's selling out."

"If they're ideologically opposed, how would I get them to consider it?"

"It's called persuasion, my dear." He sat back down at his desk and looked at me. "I have a feeling you can master it."

♥ ⬮ ✱

There was someone I knew who *was* good at persuasion. And he was currently trying to persuade me to take off all my clothes.

"I need you," he said, his breath hot against my neck.

"We're at a party, Adrián. I'm not going to have sex with you in public." To be fair, it was really dark in his friend's backyard, and other couples were undoubtedly taking some liberties.

"But you want to? If I can find somewhere else?" Finding somewhere else was no small feat, as he lived with his parents and I lived with the Purity Police. His hand traveled further up my thigh. "I really, really like you, *Preciosa*." Dammit, why was he so sexy? Why was I even contemplating going to third base in public? *What was happening to me?!*

"I like you, too."

"This isn't just a vacation romance for me," he said. He pulled back to look me in the eyes. Did he mean that? And if I said it too, would *I* mean it? "I want to be with you."

I answered with a kiss. I was still uncertain what our shelf life as a couple would be, but I could no longer deny that I was in a romantic entanglement. A very, very hot romantic entanglement. He led me to a bean bag chair that was covered in dirt. His very persuasive hand kept going higher up my skirt and I was quickly losing whatever willpower I had left when a voice interrupted.

"Adrián?"

I looked up. A young woman glared at Adrián. He looked like he'd swallowed a lime. He discreetly tried to remove his hand from under my skirt. "Hola, Lucía."

Lucía promptly burst into tears and fled, followed by two girlfriends who stared daggers at us. As they left, one of the friends cursed Adrián so quickly and colorfully that I couldn't quite catch it all. Something about dogs, shit, and pig genitalia. Adrián's face drained of color.

"What was that about?" I asked. "Who is Lucía?"

"An old friend."

"Mm-hmm."

He looked at me, debating. "We dated. A while ago. It was a messy breakup."

"How messy?"

"You know."

I did not. "How long ago?"

"*Un rato.*"

"A while? How long is a while?"

"I can't remember exactly." He pushed some hair out of my face. "Look, I feel bad for her, but that's in the past. I'm with you. Let's live in the present." He began to kiss me again, pushing me more deeply into the bean bag. My body shifted and I felt something damp under my butt. I tentatively touched the wet spot and smelled it. *Ugghhhh.*

"I just sat in a puddle of someone else's vomit," I said. "So presently, I'd like to go home."

♥ ◐ ✱

I took a steaming hot shower. At first, all I could think about was, *What diseases could I get from another person's vomit?* Could they spread via skin contact, or did they need oral transmission? What was the incubation period?

Then I started wondering what happened with Lucía—she seemed much more upset than one would expect for something that was "in the past." Adrián seemed so honest to me—but how well did I know him, really? We were communicating in my second language, in a culture still foreign to me. And his politics were confusing—was he conservative, or centrist? But what did political labels even mean in a totally different geographical context? And he was quick with endearments, but how deep did those feelings go? How deep did *mine* go?

My thoughts were too muddy and things were moving too fast. I needed to pump the brakes until I had more clarity. But I didn't know how to tell him that. Fortunately, I would be at Las Nubes tomorrow, which would buy me some time.

Competing visions of Las Nubes whirled in my head as I gave my body one last scrub. Las Nubes as a true Cooperative Heaven. Las Nubes as a Café Alegre–type scam. As the water in my shower turned lukewarm, I became more and more pessimistic. *Las Nubes was going to be a fraud.* I would never finish organizing the Truth Trip. I would go home in defeat and manage Aaron's legal office for the rest of my life while Nicole became a super-famous hacker.

I toweled off and went straight to my computer. I needed to talk to Matías. I vaguely noted that I was becoming somewhat obsessive about checking my email, but then again, who isn't? I opened my laptop and there his message was. It was as if he were reading my mind.

TO: Dee Blum
FROM: Matías Khalil
SUBJECT: Human Nature

So Dee, about your disillusionment—I see you, because I've been there. Every activist goes through it, because part of our job is seeing exactly what you don't want to see. It's not easy fighting the good fight. It means you have to get down in the dirt and see the darker sides of humanity. We don't get the luxury of clicking past the article or turning off the TV. We have to actively seek out the bad and then turn it into good. And I know that's exactly what you're going to do. You're going to pick yourself up, dust yourself off, and emerge even stronger. You're a fighter, Dee. *Una combatiente*. Keep the faith, don't get discouraged, and continue taking photos! You've got this.

So, *blue*. What the hell is blue? The people in Avatar. A gray alien with a bluish undertone. Maybe you're a Smurf? Dee, a color is not a hint!

♥ ● *

TO: Matías Khalil
FROM: Dee Blum
SUBJECT: Re: Human Nature

A color is most certainly a hint! Haven't you seen *Clue*? And I can't decide if you're a cheerleader or a coach, but either way, you always make my day. How do you know what's happening in my head? It's like you know exactly what I need to hear. Thank you. Really.

The good news is tomorrow I'm going to Las Nubes, and Ramírez assures me they're legit. This time (knock on wood) the photos will be usable, the farm will be a suitable candidate, and your faith will be validated. 🤞

As I closed my laptop, my phone buzzed. A text! From Matías!

It's the listening device.

What?

That's how I know what you need to hear. I planted a listening device in your brain. You know I'm the AI guy, right?

LOL. But, like . . . really. It's kinda weird you're inside my brain?

Maybe it's just because we're so similar? Or . . . maybe it's the listening device?

I'm not sure it's totally ethical to implant a listening device in your coworker's brain?

You're not just my coworker, you're my compañera. Despite the fact I have no idea who you are.

You have an entire website of info about me!

But no pics! Haven't you heard, eyes are the window to the soul?

Fine.

I snapped a pic of *just my eyes* and sent it to him.

Wow. There's something so intimate about just seeing the eyes.

∘ ∘ ∘

Can you send a pic of your chin? Maybe also your forehead?

No chance.

That's okay. I'll reverse search your eyes and find you. Newb mistake, Dee.

How do you know I sent you a pic of MY eyes? Maybe the pic was a red herring.

Dang it! You've outsmarted me. But at least you seem to be out of your existential funk?

Maybe? I'm excited about Las Nubes.

I'm excited for you. But if it's not all you
hoped for, please don't get too down.
The world is full of all things, good, bad,
but mostly a combo of both.

How do you know when you have
too many ups and downs?

Are you talking about mental
health?

I think so.

I think it's part of growing into
yourself. Especially for a person like
you or me. It's easy to be an idealist
when you're very young. The more
you see of the world, the harder
it is. Getting to a Zen space is the
ideal—but, well, I'm not 100% there
myself.

Do you think we will ever get there?

I hope so. Let's help each other.

🙂

Get some sleep, compañera. I
want to hear all about Las Nubes
tomorrow. I know you're going to
do great.

I turned off my phone and smiled. I didn't know why, but Matías believed in me. Maybe one day I'd be able to believe in myself?

# CHAPTER FIFTEEN

Matías's pep talk worked subliminally in my sleep. It was incredible that he could change my outlook with just a few sentences. By the time I showed up at Professor Ramírez's outer office early that morning, I was cautiously optimistic. Fingers crossed, Las Nubes would be suitable for the Truth Trip, and I would make my February deadline.

"*Buenos días, joven*," said the Professor, from his inner office. "I'll be right out."

I sat at his assistant's desk and wrestled with the screwed-up straps on my wide-brimmed adventurer hat. As I tried to untangle them, they appeared to recoil from my touch. I would have to stop taking my allergy medications; they were making me hallucinate. Goddamn that strap on my cap; it was actually *trying* to get *more* twisted. "Cooperate, here!"

"What?" asked the Professor, exiting his office. "Let's go. We're late."

*Right*, I thought. *Late.*

We ran down the stairs of the Social Science building and went to his Jeep. Did everyone have a Jeep in this country? The

Professor's was a lot older than Adrián's, which didn't seem fair. The cloth interior was separating from the plastic roof, and the whole thing reeked of cigarettes. I unrolled my window.

"Sorry," he said. "I quit six months ago, but I can't get the damn stench out." He peeled out of the parking lot and onto the road out of San Pedro. "So," he said, passing three cars from the right shoulder. "It's a bit unusual for a young North American to come to Central America for work. Why Costa Rica?"

"To learn about cooperatives."

"Please." The three cars were honking at him, but by the time I looked in the passenger mirror, they were dust. "You have co-ops in North America. What's the real reason?"

The last thing I wanted to talk about today was my family. I tried thinking of a credible explanation, but one look in those Neptune eyes and I knew half truths weren't going to cut it. "To escape my family."

"So you had to go to a different country?"

"You don't know my family."

"They're that bad?"

"Not *bad* . . . Controlling. Suffocating."

"Is that another way to say loving?" There was an edge to his voice.

"I mean, sure, they love me. Like I'm a possession."

We hit a speed bump. "It's hard not to," he said.

"What do you mean?"

His harsh features softened a little. "When your kid is born, they *are* yours. You do everything for them; they're completely dependent on you. Then one day, they get older, and you realize they're not yours anymore. Maybe they don't want to do the things you want them to do. Maybe they don't even want to talk to you. And, well, as a parent, it's hard to make that transition."

I looked at the Professor. He was a *parent*? It was hard to think of him as an actual human being and not a living legend.

"Okay. But it's kind of the parent's job to be the adult about it, don't you think?"

"Yes," he said, tersely. "But if they're having a hard time with it, that's not a reason to abandon them."

"I didn't *abandon* them."

The Professor was silent. In the quiet, I realized we had both raised our voices. We came up to the Pan-American Highway and he put his coins in the bucket. "My daughter won't speak to me."

*Oh.* I could see he was struggling to control his emotions. "I'm sorry. I didn't know you had a daughter."

"I used to." He stopped looking at the road and looked straight at me. "Don't let a small crack grow into a gorge." He shifted into a lower gear. "You'll regret it."

I leaned back into my headrest. If only he knew. Regret was my most familiar emotion.

"Look," he said, relenting just a little. "I don't know what happened between you and your parents, but I do know this. If you were my daughter, I'd do everything I could to fix it. And I bet your parents would, too. You just have to try and see it. Have pity on us old folks. We have a hard time expressing ourselves."

So do us young people, I thought, looking out the window. The Professor had just turned off the main highway and we were going up a one-lane road. He was concentrating on driving, and I was grateful for a few moments of silence. It was tragic, really. People try so hard to understand each other, but despite their best intentions, they keep failing. Were my parents trying to communicate something important to me? Was I just missing it?

"By the way," he said after a while, his voice much lighter. "There's going to be a community meeting tonight at Las Nubes," he said. "I have to make a speech. Can you help me with it?"

"*You* want *me* to help you with your speech?"

"I need a closer. Something generic, but also inspiring. Don't worry about being trite; people love that stuff. Lean in."

I thought for a few moments. "Tell them they are a shining example of cooperative values."

"Perfect." He smiled and looked into my eyes. I smiled back, touched, but only briefly, because I really wanted him to pay attention to the road. He drove even crazier than Adrián. Was it the testosterone? Was that what made them all insane?

Two hours and several thousand feet in elevation later, we reached the center of town. There was a plaza with a church on one end and a general store on the other. It was colder up here than I had expected; I drew my cardigan closer. We walked to the co-op's central office, where a compact, muscular woman was painting the eaves from a ladder. When she heard us approach, she climbed down. She had little specks of yellow paint in her hair and a Gen X attitude.

"Clara," said the Professor. "So wonderful to see you again. This is my friend, Dee. She's organizing eco-tours for Justice Alliance. She isn't your typical North American dilettante; she's a true ally."

Clara looked at me skeptically but didn't say anything.

"Nice paint color," I said. She just stared at me. I began sweating despite the chill.

"Would you mind showing Dee around?" he asked.

She nodded. Did the nod mean *yes, she'd show me*, or *yes, she minded*? The Professor was unbothered and headed toward the wet mill down the road. "See you in a few hours!" he shouted over his shoulder.

Clara scrutinized me for a moment. Her body language said: *You're wasting your time, interloper.* I sure wasn't getting any attendance trophies from her. She put her paintbrush on top of her paint bucket and wiped off her hands on a wet rag, which she tucked into the back pocket of her overalls.

"*Venga*," she said, entering the community center. I scurried after her like a chastened child.

In the main room, there were sofas, a TV, and board games. It sounded like there was a daycare happening in some of the other rooms, because I could hear bright peals of toddler laughter coming from underneath the doors. Clara went into the open kitchen and started making coffee.

"Is the community center open for all members?" I asked.

"Yes," she said, in Spanish. "We have game nights, movie nights . . . We even do yoga and meditation classes." I lifted my eyebrows. "The meditation classes haven't been wildly popular," she confessed. "Yet."

This was *perfect*. The tourists would go apeshit for this place. We could work in some coffee-themed guided visualizations. I couldn't wait to tell Suzanne! But first I needed to convince Clara to let the Truth Trip come here. "Professor Ramírez mentioned you haven't allowed tours here, but I think people would love to learn about Las Nubes. What's stopping you?"

Clara put the drinks on a tray. I followed her to a large veranda that overlooked the rolling fields. Shiny coffee leaves glinted in the midmorning sun, and hummingbirds darted from plant to plant. We sat in rocking chairs. She finally spoke.

"Tourists have expectations. Because they're paying, we feel obliged to fulfill them. Next thing you know, I'm wearing a ruffled blouse and full skirt while I hand-hull the dried beans." She made jazz hands. "I'm dancing for the Americans."

"There must be a way to do the tours that doesn't commodify your culture."

She looked me directly in the eyes. "Professor Ramírez didn't mention you were naive."

I paused. "Maybe I am. But we would work with you to make sure the tours were on *your* terms. And they would bring in a lot of revenue. Professor Ramírez said you guys are struggling a bit."

"A bit?" she scoffed.

"What's going on?"

Clara blew on her steaming coffee. "For the last decade, we've been a major player in the organic and fair trade space. But over the last two years, our market share has been reduced by 50 percent."

"Wow."

She nodded, grim. "There's a new co-op that's taken over one of our biggest contracts."

"How?"

"We don't know. We dropped our prices to the Ethical Coffee International floor, so they can't be underselling us." She rocked methodically in her chair. "And it isn't higher quality."

"What's the name of the co-op?"

"Café Alegre."

My heart began to race. *Was Alegre illegally selling their coffee at a price below the Ethical Coffee International minimum to steal clients from the competition?*

Clara looked in my face as if searching for a lost item. "You know them?"

"I've been there." I looked at my coffee, wondering how much to share. "I'm not sure they're playing fair."

"Neither are we."

I took a sip of the coffee. An explosion of chocolate and honey, a whole universe in a cup. Café Alegre's coffee was good, but this was better. There had to be something underhanded going on for Café Alegre to take over their contracts.

"We can't sustain production without buyers," she said.

"We'll have to sell land soon. People will have to move out." Her aloof facade cracked for a moment, and I saw how scared she was. "Our community is going to fall apart."

Suddenly, ten preschoolers ran by, all giggles and curls and scraped knees. They raced down the steps to a nearby play structure, followed by a teacher. Clara watched them wistfully.

"You know," I said gently. "If the Truth Trip came here, that publicity could result in new contracts. I understand your concerns, but on balance, this could be a good thing for Las Nubes."

She gazed into the distance, struggling with her options. "I'll bring it up to the council." She abruptly stood and left, leaving the chair rocking violently in her wake.

♥ ● *

I spent the next few hours wandering around Las Nubes taking photos. But I wasn't just photographing; I was poking around. And I went *everywhere.* There were no pesticides to be found. No children picking berries. No shotguns to scare off organizers. Las Nubes was the real deal. Maybe cooperation wasn't a fairytale, and humanity wasn't destined to remain in a race to the bottom. Sure, Las Nubes was in a bad spot at the moment, but like Matías had said—the role of activists was to find the bad and turn it into good. Justice Alliance could help Las Nubes—if they would let us.

I wished Matías was here; he would know what to say to Clara. A great organizer was persuasive but also compassionate. They had to *see you* and make you know that they saw you. That's how you got people to take risks. Matías made me feel seen. I knew he could do it with Clara, too. But it was just me here, and I had to hope I was enough.

I went to the drying platform to learn more about how

it worked. Two chatty co-opers in their twenties, Ramón and Héctor, showed me the ropes. They asked if I would like to try raking the beans. Why not? They handed me a rake, and I went to town.

"*¡Muy bien, Macha!*" said Ramón, the skinny one.

"*¡Con fuerza, joven!*" said Héctor, the brawny one. "Put some back into it!"

There was something hugely satisfying about the physical labor—probably because in my case it was infrequent and not compulsory. But after an hour, my back was beginning to ache. When my phone buzzed, I was relieved to have an excuse for a break. I put the rake down and sat on a bench. It was Adrián.

Hola, Preciosa.

Hi.

∘ ∘ ∘

∘ ∘ ∘

Last night was a little weird, huh?

∘ ∘ ∘

∘ ∘ ∘

Yes

∘ ∘ ∘

∘ ∘ ∘

There were some more bubbles, but they disappeared. Guess he found this as awkward as I did. I knew there was something fishy going on with Lucía, but I didn't know what. I wanted to believe he was telling me the truth, but something about her reaction just didn't compute. And what if he *were* completely blameless in the situation? He was still a magnate in training. I was still a radical. How would we reconcile that?

The bubbles came back. Then:

How's Cooperative Heaven?

Pretty great, actually. There's a really strong sense of community.

Have they jumped you in yet?

It's not a gang!

Right. Did you do blood rites? Or is it more of a branding-with-an-iron thing?

It's not a cult!

Sure, of course not. By the way, are you into pain? I'm not, but if you want to explore it, I'm open. Within limits 😉

I started giggling. How could he offend me and make me laugh at the same time? Ramón and Héctor heard my laughter and came to investigate. I stuffed my phone in my back pocket.

"Looks like someone has a boyfriend," said Ramón.

"Not exactly. Sort of."

"'Not exactly' sounds like no," said Ramón.

"But 'sort of' sounds like yes," said Héctor.

"It's complicated," I said. "Sort of."

After some more raking, and a lot of razzing about my "sort of boyfriend," Ramón and Héctor showed me how to change the shade nets hanging over the drying platform. The first three days, the coffee dried under a zinc cover. It was now time to switch to polyethylene netting. I don't think I'd ever done so much physical labor in my life, and I'd only been helping them for about two hours.

Later that evening, I met the Professor outside the church, where the meeting was taking place. "Were you successful in your persuasion campaign?" he asked.

"TBD. But I'm hopeful."

"Never lose your optimism, Dee. Many people renounce it as they age, but that's a mistake. The difference between people who can and people who can't is in what they believe they can achieve."

"So, *The Secret*?"

"Ha!" he scoffed. "No, I don't believe in that nonsense. Optimism isn't magic. It's common sense. It's what keeps you going when things get hard."

I envied him; common sense was not something I had in spades. He opened the door for me and we entered the church. The pews were lined with candles, and red-and-blue light flickered across the room from the stained-glass windows. Clara spotted us and ushered us to seats in the front.

Several co-op members spoke about their current issues. The cost of organic fertilizer. What to do with the unsold yield. Converting some of the fields to vegetables for community consumption . . . because they were getting to the point where they couldn't afford groceries. It was grim.

After a few speeches, Clara went to the pulpit and waved her hands for silence. The group hushed. The only sound was that of the wind beating against the windows. The heat of several hundred bodies and candles filled the large space and made it feel smaller.

"We came tonight not only to discuss our worries or our failures," she said. "We came tonight to celebrate our hopes and successes. So please join me in welcoming our guest and dear friend, Professor Eugenio Ramírez."

Expectation swelled through the air at the mention of the Professor's name. He proceeded to the front of the room. Candles cast dancing shadows onto the craggy nooks of his cheeks, making him look more imposing than ever. He waited until the audience was absolutely silent.

"I come to you today not as a co-oper nor as a scholar, but as a man." The crowd gazed at him with reverence. "As a man living in a world that poisons him. As a man trapped in a world that strips a person of his dignity and essence. I speak to you as a man who suffers in his world and longs to live in one like yours." He gestured toward the crowd.

"In this world, people work *for and with* each other. They examine every aspect of their life to make it more beautiful."

*To make it more beautiful.* The combination of his words and the light and the heat transported me into an interior world. *Look at your life like a work of art,* my grandfather had told Sadie, *so when it's over, you've created something.* Maybe that's what the Professor was saying. That here in Las Nubes, people made their lives works of art. They approached their lives with intention: examining their beliefs, challenging them, making them part of their lives. Was I capable of such a high level of intention?

I looked back at the Professor. I must have missed some

comments because he was closing his speech. His face was flushed and he was standing at his tallest. The people in my pew were straining forward to hear him better, even though his voice filled every space.

". . . Las Nubes is a world that celebrates the essence of humanity, the productive and cooperative nature of man and woman. It is a world that uplifts humanity to its highest spiritual expression. A world that brings us closer to God." Light from the windows quivered and sprayed the room. "You are a gift to our world. You are a prediction for our world." He stopped, scanned the audience, and found my eyes. "You are a shining example of cooperative values."

After the meeting, an army of admirers surrounded the Professor and took him to the plaza. The town was having a feast as part of the Christmas festivities that began earlier in December. Here, Christmas was a month-long affair. The sound of *villancicos*, traditional Christmas carols, filled the night; the smell of roasting pigs saturated the air; and alcohol rained down in a deluge. I sat on a curb with Ramón and Héctor, drinking *guaro*, the national alcohol, which was distilled from sugar cane. It was a type of *aguardiente*—literally, water that burns—and I was feeling the effects. I tried following the conversation, which was about *fútbol*, of course, but I couldn't stop thinking about Clara. Finally, she approached and signaled for me to follow her. I joined her by a small bonfire.

"I've been thinking about the Truth Trip," she said. "And I've discussed it with the council." The flames cast shadows onto her face. "We want to do it."

"I'm glad. I think this will be beneficial for both Las Nubes and Justice Alliance."

"As long as it fits our parameters, we do, too. Some of my *compañeros* pointed out that I am genetically resistant to change. I won't listen to music produced after 1999." She gave me a wry smile. But suddenly anxiety creased her brow. "The thing is, I'm not sure if Las Nubes would qualify."

"Of course you would," I said. "I just have to run it by my supervisor."

She bit her lower lip. "We're about to lose our Ethical Coffee International certification."

"What?"

"It lapses in a month."

"But . . ." I grappled with the implications. "You're still organic? And you're still abiding by Ethical Coffee International standards?"

"Of course. But it costs money to stay accredited. Money we don't have."

I looked at the fire, thinking. "Maybe we can turn this into a selling point. People who go on these tours are do-gooders. They would love to know that by coming here, they were helping you renew your Ethical Coffee International status."

"Do you think your supervisor will agree?"

"I do."

Clara looked relieved. But still defiant. "You can't Disneyfy us."

"You're in charge. *You* set the terms."

"There will be no dancing."

"We wouldn't dream of it."

She smiled at me as she stood and shook my hand. "Okay, *compañera*. We have a deal."

I was elated and overtired as the Professor drove us back to San José in total darkness. We had a farm for the tour—a *great* farm. And Justice Alliance could meaningfully help a truly special community during a rough time. I tried to sleep as the Professor sang along with Silvio Rodríguez protest music, but it was useless. I was too wound up, and also, the drive was terrifying. I could feel the hairpin turns but not see them.

The Professor dropped me off at home just before dawn. I crept past Eva and Luis's bedroom and went straight to my laptop. My phone had gone flat and I was dying to check my email. It was now impossible to deceive myself regarding the depth of my obsession with Matías's emails, but it was easy to rationalize. I was in a foreign land; I needed something familiar. The fact that Matías was only familiar to me in a virtual sense was something better left unanalyzed. Besides, I thought, better a harmless addiction like email than a sinister one like crack. I opened my browser, and as usual, there was an email from him:

> TO: Dee Blum
> FROM: Matías Khalil
> SUBJECT: Chestnuts roasting on an open fire
>
> I tried reverse searching your eyes and it didn't work. Was that an AI generated image? Ooh, I never considered *you* may be an AI. How do I know you're even real? Maybe you projected a hologram when you met with Suzanne?
>
> So, AI Dee, how was Las Nubes? Sorry for being impatient, but I like reading your emails. More and more, I catch myself looking forward to them. There's something so direct and vulnerable about them. Plus they bear a suspicious resemblance to full stockings on Christmas morning. Wait—are

you an agent of Santa? Is that why you hide your identity?!

I hope Las Nubes was everything you wanted it to be. Can't wait to hear all about it.

*Tu amigo en la lucha,* Matías

♥ ◐ ✱

TO: Matías Khalil
FROM: Dee Blum
SUBJECT: Re: Chestnuts roasting on an open fire

If my messages are full stockings, then yours are the present on the eighth day of Hanukkah. Batteries included.

Las Nubes was beyond description; I wish you could've been there with me. I can't tell you how relieved I feel on an existential level that a place like this really does exist. But they are in serious trouble, and I think we need to help them. I'd rather explain over the phone—that is, if you don't just download the info from my brain chip.

Covertly, Special Agent Vixen

I hit send and sucked in my breath. We were entering dangerous territory here. And I was loving it.

# CHAPTER SIXTEEN

Monday morning, I headed to my call spot outside the Chinese market, which I found covered in green wreaths for Christmas. I was surprised; the owners weren't Christian. But then I remembered my mom's not-Christmas Christmas lights and suddenly I understood. It was a way to assimilate. To stay safe. A sprig of holly to allay multigenerational fears.

I moved under some twinkling lights, feeling a sudden kinship with the shop owners, and checked my phone. I had a few texts from Adrián. I felt a pang of guilt for not responding, but I was still so confused. "Super busy with work," I wrote. "Call you in a few days!" How long could I push this off?

I mercilessly squashed that thought like a spider in the shower and called Suzanne. I was excited to tell her about Las Nubes. Finally I had achieved something! After very brief pleasantries, I made my pitch.

"I don't think Las Nubes is a good fit for us," she said. "If they're a sinking ship, what's the point?"

I paused. I had not anticipated resistance. "They're the oldest, most successful co-op in Costa Rica."

"We're not conducting historical tours. This is business." I could hear her typing in the background. "We're showing our customers the wave of the future. Think 'think outside the box.' Think 'cutting edge.'"

"Las Nubes is cutting edge! They have groundbreaking services for their members. Yoga and meditation, Suzanne. *Yoga.* Think about how much our customers would love that. We could do special sessions for them. We could even create a pose: The Finest Grind."

"I love that! *That* is creative thinking." Phew! I knew yoga would get through to her. Oh, wait, *would that be Disneyfication?* "But we could do yoga at any farm we choose," she said. "Look, Dee, you have to be practical. If Las Nubes is losing its certification, it doesn't qualify. And there are dozens of cooperatives in Costa Rica that do. By the way, Café Alegre is getting more buzz. The most recent US Barista Champion used an Alegre single-origin light roast."

I kicked the gravel with my sandal. "I still think Las Nubes is worth including. They have a super strong cooperative culture; they're an actual commune! And putting them on the trips will bring them the revenue they need to renew their status. Our customers will love feeling like they're part of the solution."

I heard the clackety-clack of her keyboard stop. "That's an interesting point." I could tell that I was now the sole recipient of her attention by the change in her voice. "I see that you are deeply invested in helping Las Nubes. And I love your passion." I sighed with relief. "I'll put in calls to some small roasters I know. Maybe I can get Las Nubes a direct trade relationship."

"As you've said yourself, there's no regulation with direct trade. We have no way of knowing if the roasters keep the promises they make."

"That's true on the macro scale. But some are very

transparent. I'm not going to call roasters I don't have faith in. Don't worry, Dee, we're going to try to help them."

*Try?*

"But now I need you to focus on *your* work," she said. "And you have a new assignment, on top of your old one, so you really need to dig in. I'm going to be in town next week for the People's Alternative World Economic Summit. Many of our donors will be there as well. So you need to set up a mini Truth Trip for the donors."

"In a week?!"

"It's not the full Truth Trip. It's just a proof of concept to excite the donors. One farm visit, one social activity, no homestays. I'll lead the tour, you just set it up."

"It's still going to be difficult to pull together that quickly."

"Fortunately, you've already made a great connection with Café Alegre. I'm sure they'd be delighted to be on our mini trip."

"But—"

"Not the Ziploc again."

"I wasn't going to mention it, because I can't verify it, but I spoke to someone at Las Nubes who thinks Café Alegre stole their biggest contract."

"*Thinks*?"

"Well, yeah, that's their theory, and I agree." As I said it, I realized I sounded insane.

"I think you need to cool it with the conspiracy theories. You're not in a Grisham novel. You know, after you brought it up the first time, I called someone at Ethical Coffee International."

"You did?"

"Of course! I don't want some farm masquerading as organic any more than you do. They said they had just recertified Alegre six months ago. What you saw was for mosquitoes."

"Oh!" *But was that true?*

"Again, *love* the passion, but let's direct it to the proper channels. And if you want to make allegations against another farm in the future, please make sure you have actual evidence. It makes *me* look foolish if I call Ethical Coffee International with nonsense. Do you get that?"

"I do."

"Okay, great chat. Report back soon." She hung up.

I held the phone to my ear like a conch shell, listening to the emptiness so many thousands of miles away, further from a solution than before the call. Not only had I not helped Las Nubes in a substantive way; now I was supposed to actively *help* Café Alegre. This was a big fail. So I did the only logical thing. I went into the market and bought two bars of chocolate, a small bottle of *guaro*, and six different kinds of lotto tickets.

I spent the next two days trying not to reply to Adrián's texts and looking for a compromise farm for the minitrip. I found one called Finca Atenas that was suitable, if a little pedestrian. But Suzanne was set on Café Alegre; they had the buzz. I hadn't made the arrangements yet. If I refused, I'd get fired for sure, and possibly blacklisted from all further employment in the nonprofit world. But if I did it, I'd be raking in more money for the evil Café Alegre. When I spoke to Suzanne again, I kept my deliberations to myself.

"So we're on the same page?" she asked.

"Yep."

"All set?"

"I'm going through a tunnel. I'll call you tomorrow." I made a whooshing noise and hung up. Not very professional, admittedly, but as far as Suzanne was concerned, the tour was green-lit.

I had also spent the last two days thinking of creative lies to tell my host family. They were expecting me to spend the holidays with them at Luis's sister's house in Liberia, but I couldn't think of anything more excruciating than watching the cold war between Pentecostal Eva and Catholic Luis. For Luis and his family, Christmas was the religious Super Bowl. But Eva's church didn't think Christmas should be celebrated *at all.* They said it was a pagan holiday. And they were right! Christmas was a rebranding of Saturnalia, the pagan celebration of the winter solstice. That Christmas tree? A symbol of the return to life as the days get longer. Holly? Sacred plant of the god Saturn. Santa Claus? A chubby, white-bearded deity named Odin. Honestly, Christmas couldn't be any more pagan if it had an orgy with Hanukkah and Mount Olympus.

I felt bad for Eva. It was her against everyone else. But I didn't think jumping in to defend her as a pagan-identifying Jew was going to deescalate anything. So I told her I was going to Tamarindo for Christmas with some work colleagues. As a kind of penance for my lie, I helped her pack for Liberia.

"Have you seen Adrián lately?" she asked, smoothing a white blouse.

"Not super lately."

"Everything okay there?" Wow. She had a mother's witchy instincts and she wasn't even my mother.

"We've hit a little bump."

"He's a catch, Dee. Respectful, sweet, successful."

"He has an ex situation."

"Ah," she said, carefully folding Luis's pants. "Well, remember, she's his ex for a reason. What happened with her?"

"I don't really know."

"Don't you think maybe you should ask him instead of avoiding him?"

"That would require conflict."

"You're American, Dee. Don't you excel at that?"

I laughed. How had I not realized she was funny? And she actually gave good advice. "You're right. I'll ask. Here," I pulled out a blue dress from her closet. "You look great in this dress. Pack this for church services. *Your* church services."

"They hate that I don't go with them to theirs."

"I really respect that you go to your own. Even though they hate it."

Her smile was so big and genuine, it made me smile, too.

I still had to figure out what I was actually going to do for Christmas. I couldn't hold off Adrián any longer, so I met him for coffee in a classic *soda* near the university. We sat on plastic chairs at a little table practically on the street, breathing in the fumes of gasoline and nearby ylang ylang trees. Instead of backing up and addressing the weirdness, Adrián was doubling down on the future. We skipped over talking about the party. No mention of the weird texts, no mention of Lucía, no mention of my confusion. Instead, he invited me to go with him to the beaches of Manuel Antonio.

"My parents are visiting my mom's sisters in Nicoya," Adrián said over his steaming cup. "I told them Christmas Eve Day was huge at El Río Bungee and that they needed me to work. My mom was really pissed, but my dad was impressed with my work ethic." Adrián added more sugar to the pre-sugared coffee. "What time should we leave?"

I knew I should decline, because my life was complicated enough as it was. I was considering disobeying my superior, sabotaging her trip, and probably my entire career. Now I was thinking of spending two nights in a hotel with Adrián, when I wasn't sure where our relationship was going, when I was starting to become obsessed with someone else—*who I hadn't even met*—and when I wasn't even sure how long I'd be in this country. These were the ingredients of a trashy reality show. Adrián was basically inviting me to The Fantasy Suite.

"You've never seen water like this. Absolutely crystal clear." Adrián grabbed my hands. "And warm." I was beginning to feel uncomfortably warm myself. Every time I was in Adrián's presence, my doubts started fading. It's like the heat of his body melted my reservations. "And we'll be alone." Was that a feature or a bug? Adrián leaned over the table and started kissing me. And kissing me. And kissing me. This option was sounding better. Goddamn hormones, they made everything so confusing.

So Christmas Eve morning, I threw caution to the wind and met Adrián at the water tanks, so my host family wouldn't see who I was going with. After all, they thought I was going on a chaste surfing trip to Tamarindo and I didn't want to disillusion them. Adrián was waiting for me in his Jeep, in shorts and a thin tee. It was strange to be going to the beach on Christmas, and I thought fondly of my mom's non-Christmas Christmas decorations.

After four hours of light banter and heavy sexual tension, we arrived in Manuel Antonio. Manuel Antonio was one of the most famous national parks in Costa Rica, consisting of hundreds of acres of rainforest meeting waves. Hotels lined the mountainside most of the way down to the park. The buildings looked like they were being swallowed alive by the encroaching greenery. Toucans were croaking at the tourists, and golf ball–sized mosquitoes swarmed near all pools of water. It was as if the entire ecosystem was making a coordinated attack against the invading humans. I was rooting for the ecosystem.

Adrián's father's hotel was the first on the strip, which meant it was farthest away from the beach. Adrián parked by the *Paraíso Tropical* sign, and I waited for him in the Jeep while he got the room keys, so no one would know he was potentially having illicit relations with someone he wasn't married to. The smell of guanabanas in varying stages of decomposition hit me when I rolled down the window, so I rolled it back up and almost passed out from the heat.

Adrián came back with the keys, and twenty minutes later we were in our bathing suits and flip-flops, traipsing down the hill toward the beach. It was approaching three, and the air felt like a melting block of cheddar cheese. The humidity was much worse than in San José. By the time we got into the park, my coverup was soaked through with sweat and bug repellant. We were in the rainforest now, and scary-looking red wasps followed us while howler monkeys shrieked in the treetops. The trees here were dense, but occasionally there would be a break where we could see the turquoise waves rolling in, framed by palm leaves. Finally, the vista opened up and we found a secluded blue lagoon buffeted by cliffs on two sides.

The landscape was almost painfully beautiful. A thin crescent of white sand was backed by rainforest, and the cliffs on both sides kept the lagoon private and tranquil. Small waves rolled in and out with a gentle rumbling. This was my personal definition of heaven.

It was also my personal definition of acceptably safe ocean conditions. The water was light blue and clear, just like a heavily chlorinated pool, which is the only kind of water I'll enter, because you can see the creepy crawly things before they get you. Adrián and I waded out to a sandbar and dug ourselves seats in the sand. Looking toward the shore, I could see the wildlife: capuchin monkeys, crabs, and Italian guys in banana hammocks. I turned my back toward the shore and looked out toward the open sea. Adrián closed his eyes, but I kept a vigilant eye on the water, on the lookout for pernicious fish. Which in my opinion, was *all* fish.

He opened his eyes. "You're so quiet, *Preciosa*."

I was thinking about Café Alegre and Las Nubes. Even in the midst of all this beauty, it was hard to push them from my mind. I hadn't mentioned my dilemma to Adrián. I was afraid to hear what he thought about it. "It's just, I have a lot of decisions to make, and it's making me a little anxious. Maybe even depressed."

"I've been reading a book about that, actually. *Being and Nothingness*."

I stared at him. Genial, even-tempered Adrián read Sartre *for fun*? What other depths was he hiding? "Tell me about it."

"Sartre says that life is a futile passion, because we have no immutable essence. So you can think of yourself as an amorphous blob."

Adrián traced an amoeba on my shoulder. I wasn't fond of picturing myself as a blob. Especially not when I was wearing a bikini.

"Since we have no essence," he said, "we have to *choose* who we want to be. Which means we are responsible for who we are."

"Choosing *is* horrible," I said. "But why does it make us depressed?"

"Because we feel anguish at the responsibility." Adrián started to float on his back, turning his hands into paddles. I got on my back, too. Water filled my ears. "What if you choose wrong? If you fail, then it's *your fault*."

It sounded like Adrián had been talking to my dad. I stood up, tilted my head to the side, and started pounding—to get out the water, and the thought demons.

"And if *you* are the one responsible for your choices, that means there's no higher authority. So you start to feel abandoned. Like why isn't there a god out there helping you?"

I could already feel the nightmares forming. *There is no God, Dee. You are alone! Totally alone! And responsible!*

"So," said Adrián. "You're not adequately equipped to make your life choices, and no one is coming to help you. What are you supposed to do? Flip a coin?"

A wave crashed over me. I sat up choking.

"Normal people don't feel comfortable flipping a coin about something as important as who they are. We want a rational basis for our lives, but we can't find one. So—" He stopped looking at the sky and looked at me. "Life is a futile passion of always wanting answers and not being able to get them."

"Wow." I sunk my head under the water and stayed there for a moment. If I never surfaced, I'd never have to make any decisions. I wouldn't have to decide if I should set up the mini-trip, sleep with Adrián, finish my degree, stay in Costa Rica, or go to law school. It was very appealing.

But I couldn't hold my breath for that long. So I surfaced. "That's very depressing." I buried my face into Adrián's shoulder. "Let me know when you've discovered a higher power. Because until then, I'm checking out."

♥ ◖◗ *

The thing is, you can't check out, not for very long anyway. You are forced to make decision after decision, even though you have no road map. I was forced to consider one of them that very evening when Adrián and I returned to our room after dinner.

We were standing on the small balcony of our room. Directly

below us was a large canopy of trees stretching down the hillside toward the Pacific. Monkeys were shaking the trees, and the night was alive with insect sounds. It was just after sunset, and the horizon was covered with orange and pink streaks. Above the colored bands, the sky was a deep blue, and stars and planets were beginning to twinkle.

I knew I should have just been enjoying this live theater of the cosmos, but I wasn't. I was thinking about what Adrián had said on the beach. Who designed all this beauty if there was no higher power? What was I supposed to do if there was no rational basis for choice?

Adrián slipped his arm around me and began kissing my neck, leading me back into the room. I had been both excited and anxious about this precise moment. This was the first time that Adrián and I were truly alone.

"I'm dying for you, Dee," he said into my ear, as he lifted me onto the bed. His hands were gently caressing my waist, and slowly moving south. It was simultaneously so tender and so passionate, and I was flooded with the craziest mix of desire and trepidation. What did I want? *Why didn't I know?*

Adrián noticed my ambivalence right away. "What's wrong?"

I said nothing. When it mattered the most, I was able to communicate the least.

"Speak to me."

I wanted to, I really, really did. It's just that I couldn't.

"We don't have to do this." Adrián sat up. "Tell me what's wrong."

I took a deep breath. "I'm just really stressed out."

"About what?"

I sat up. How do you tell someone that you care for them, but you're not sure if they're right for you? We were so different, and while he was okay with that, I wasn't sure I was. The one thing I did know is that if we took this step together tonight, it would be a lot harder to turn back.

But I didn't know how to tell him that. So I told him something else. "It's work."

Adrián put a warm hand on top of my cold one. "Tell me about it." I caught him up on Café Alegre and Las Nubes.

"That's rough," he said, wrapping his arms tightly around me. The sky was completely dark now and it was getting cooler.

"I don't know what to do. I don't want to set up the mini-trip there."

Adrián didn't hesitate. "You have to."

I was startled by his response. Was it that clear-cut to him? "Why?"

"It's your job. They're paying you."

"So I'm supposed to do whatever they tell me? Even if it's immoral?"

Adrián moved back a little so he could look at me in the dim light. "We're talking about a contractual relationship that you entered willingly. If you don't want to fulfill your part of the obligation, you should quit."

"Are you serious?"

"Yes." His face was in deep shadow, but I could see moonlight reflecting in his eyes. He had no idea how painful his words were to me. The curtains rustled, momentarily blocking out the moon.

"It's about a lot more than me, Adrián. Café Alegre is stealing business from Las Nubes. There are a lot of people suffering and I'm in a position to help."

"This is the way business works, Dee. Café Alegre is just like every other corporation in my country and yours. You can refuse to put them on the trip, but it isn't going to make a difference."

I bit the knuckle of my second finger. "It will to the farmers in Las Nubes."

Adrián took my finger out of my mouth and pressed it into his hands. "How? Suzanne will fire you. Then she'll set up the trip herself. Look, she doesn't believe Café Alegre is violating the rules, because we didn't have enough proof."

"Then I need more proof."

Adrián's mouth twitched. "Dee, you can't attack a whole system, because you're going to fail. If you want to help people, there are much better ways. Start with individuals. Start with battles you can win."

"We can win this one."

He let go of my hand and wrapped both his arms around my waist, trying to squeeze his logic into me. "I doubt it."

"Thanks for the vote of confidence."

"Let's not fight, *Preciosa*. You know I hate politics."

"We're not fighting." I closed my eyes. This couldn't work. I would never understand him. He would never understand me.

"Can we talk about something else?" He lifted my hair and kissed the nape of my neck.

"Sure. Yeah." I sat up straighter. "There's something I've been wanting to talk about anyway." He looked relieved until he saw my expression. "Let's talk about Lucía. I want to know the truth."

He stopped trying to touch me. "You know the truth. She's my ex."

"In the past? *Way* in the past? That's why her friends looked at you like you killed a puppy?"

Adrián bit his lip, uncertain. Finally, he spoke. "Okay, maybe it's not the whole truth. I didn't tell you everything because I thought you wouldn't understand."

"Try me."

"I was seeing her when I met you."

How goddamned typical. "So you cheated on her?"

"Cheated? Dee, you and I haven't even had sex."

"So that's what defines a relationship for you? It's only cheating if there's a penis in a vagina?"

"No! Obviously not, or I wouldn't be here."

"Oh cool, cool, thanks for being so patient about sex. You win a prize."

"That's not what I'm saying! I'm saying I care about you." He looked at me, pain and passion competing for dominance. "How many ways do I have to show you?"

"Like you cared about Lucía?"

"I did care about her. But not the way I care about you." He fiddled with the bed sheet. "I broke up with her right after my cousin's wedding."

"Were you supposed to take her as your date?"

"Yes."

"Classy."

"It's complicated," he said, wounded. "Haven't you ever had feelings for two people at once?"

I gulped. Did he know? "I've never acted on it."

"I'm not proud that I hurt Lucía. But Lucía isn't the person for me. You are."

I stared at him. What was he saying?

"But I'm obviously not the person for you," he said, a hint of bitterness seeping in. "I'm just your vacation romance." He looked at me, not even attempting to hide the hurt. "You know, I have a question for you, Dee."

"Okay."

"If I'm not good enough for you, why do you spend so much time with me?"

"I never said you weren't good enough."

"You've said it plenty. Just not with words." Jesus. Had I really been that cruel? "If I'm not radical enough for you," he said, "not a committed enough comrade in the fight, then why don't you just break up with me? Because if we keep going on like this, you're going to break my heart."

"It's late," I said, fuzzy, confused, sad. "We're not making sense. Let's finish this in the morning."

I lay down on the bed. Adrián lay behind me, with six inches between us, maybe six miles. But I couldn't sleep. I just lay there silently staring out the window, counting the shooting stars and the fallen moments.

♥ ● *

The next morning my whole body felt sore, like I had spent the night physically fighting. Adrián's eyes were puffy and his neck seemed stiff. There were so many bruises, and so few were visible. It was clear to me now that Adrián's feelings were deeper than I had realized. I couldn't keep leading him on like this. My feelings were too ambiguous, too fluctuating.

So I asked Adrián to take me back to San José. I told him I had to go research other farms. He didn't believe me. He told me how much he cared about me, he told me that he would help me find another farm tomorrow, he told me to just forget about last night. I told him I needed to go home.

He called me about an hour after he dropped me off at my house. I was alone, because my host family was in Liberia celebrating Christmas. Oh yeah, Christmas. Classic day for a breakup.

"I'm going to Panamá tomorrow," he said, his voice heavy. "For five days. My dad wants me to check out some hotels to buy."

"Oh." I closed my eyes.

"Are you mad at me?"

I squeezed my forefingers against my thumbs. "No."

"You sound mad."

"I'm just confused."

"Don't you know how much I care about you? Don't you know I . . ." His voice trailed off.

I turned my head toward the wall, trying to keep the tears in check. I clenched my fists and bit hard on my lips. Adrián waited for an answer. I didn't have one.

"I'll be thinking about you the whole time," he said. "Can I call you?"

I took my hair tie and doubled it around my wrist. I wanted to cut off my circulation. I wanted to be numb. "Maybe it's better if we just take some time off." I wrapped the tie tighter around my wrist. "It's just five days."

After I hung up, I looked at my wrist. Purple lines encircled it. I wondered if I had said the right thing. It certainly didn't feel like it. I lay face down on my bed. I didn't know if there was a possible future with Adrián. I did know I had never been this sad. I refused to think any more about him. I refused to think about Café Alegre. I refused everything.

# CHAPTER SEVENTEEN

You can't refuse the morning. Even if you sleep in, the afternoon will get you, and even if you manage to escape that, too, there's the night. And while I was depressed, I didn't have the luxury of bed rotting; I needed to finish organizing the minitrip.

First, I had to push all thoughts of Adrián out of my mind. I did this by listing all the reasons it couldn't work. We were politically incompatible, we didn't share the same values, and *we didn't live in the same country*. Why hadn't I focused on that one? That was huge! Okay, I was hanging onto that.

I went to work on arranging the social activity. Costa Rica was known for its outdoor adventures, but we couldn't have older donors keeling over from heart attacks. That would be tragic, and of course, bad for donations. So I chose ziplining. It seemed adventurous, but was actually pretty tame. As I was finalizing things, my phone buzzed with an email: Matías. My pulse quickened. I hated myself for being excited, but it is a universal truth: there is nothing to take your mind off a failing romance like the hint of a new one.

TO: Dee Blum
FROM: Matías Khalil
SUBJECT: Let's get serious

Hoping you had a magical Christmas. Or Hanukkah . . . or Festivus? We haven't discussed religion yet. I feel like we should. Where are you on the Big Guy/Lady? I think it's useless trying to figure out the unknowable. So I try to focus on what I can do *here*. I'm a humanist.

Actually, that's something I admire about you. Your commitment to humanity is so intense; that's why you feel the ups and downs so much.

Anyhow, these conversations are better had in person, don't you think? I look forward to a time when we can chat about this, about everything.

He *admired* me?

♥ ● ✱

TO: Matías Khalil
FROM: Dee Blum
SUBJECT: Higher Powers

I guess you could say I'm a pagan Jew. I converted to Christianity on the plane to Costa Rica, but I converted back to Judaism pretty quickly. There was chocolate involved, which is a condition that is true for most of my decisions. But truthfully, no

> religion really fits me. I guess it's the problem of evil. I know this isn't a groundbreaking thought, but it's just so hard to reconcile a kind god with all the suffering in the world. I can't wrap my head around it. But then there are these times—these times when I *feel* something divine—and even though it continues to not make "sense"—I know it's there. But maybe I'm just hoping? Wow, I'm rambling. I should just delete this. But somehow, I don't want to?

I hit send before I could overanalyze it. It was terrifying to be so vulnerable—but also exhilarating. Somehow communicating via email made it easier to open up. However, I knew on some level, this was crazy. I didn't even know him!

But was it true that I didn't know him? Sure, we'd never met *in person*. But we had shared our deepest values with each other. Maybe I didn't know if he took sugar in his coffee, maybe he didn't know if I liked my eggs runny or hard, but *he understood me*. That was something I had never experienced. This sense of really being known—it felt like flying.

I couldn't bear to examine my feelings too deeply; I was hurtling down a highway with my eyes closed. And there was the inconvenient fact that I hadn't completely let go of Adrián. I was a mess; torn between two versions of how I wanted my life to look. A life of revolutionary adventure with someone like Matías, who would know my thoughts before I even had them. Or a life of fun with Adrián, who would always watch my heart but might never understand it. Which world did I belong in? Until I figured that out, how could I figure out with who?

But those were future problems. I had current, urgent problems that needed addressing. I needed to find enough evidence to get Café Alegre off the minitrip, and hopefully enough to also get them decertified. Suzanne had made it clear that we needed concrete, *irrefutable* proof. At first I had been upset, but now I was glad she had pushed me to be better. We needed to make our case *undeniable.*

I knew one person who might have that evidence: Tomás. Problem was, I had no idea where he was. The last time I had seen him was when Adrián and I had dropped him off at the bus station downtown. So I took the bus downtown and got off near the Central Market. I figured Tomás and Mario would still be looking for work, and downtown was fairly small.

I had been wandering the market and surrounding area for a few hours when I heard, "*Macha!*"

I jumped, surprised to hear the Costa Rican equivalent of *gringa*. I turned to find two teenage boys on a corner selling plastic chickens that lit up and cried, "Kikiriki!" which is how Spanish-speaking roosters say, "Cock-a-doodle-doo!" I couldn't believe I had actually found them!

"Do you remember me, *Macha*?" Tomás asked, giving me the effusive hello-goodbye kiss. "Thanks for giving us that ride." Already his Spanish had changed. He'd adopted a city accent and seemed to have aged ten years. "We're doing great here. In a few months, we'll have enough money to get our brother and sister, and maybe in a year we'll have enough money to go to the US."

"Really?" I studied his clothing. He did have very nice Nikes.

"Yes. And we owe it to you. Let me give you a chicken." He reached into the tray of kikirikiing chickens and handed me one.

"No, really, I—"

"Please."

"But I—"

"We wouldn't be here if it weren't for you. We'd still be picking coffee." A shadow passed over his face as he remembered.

But he shook it off quickly. "We're much happier now. We're entrepreneurs." He placed the chicken in my hand. "You have to take it."

"Thank you."

Energy infused his wiry body, and he leaned in closer to me. "Do you think I could sell these in the US? Is there a good market?"

I almost started to laugh, but when I saw the earnestness in his face, I gulped. "Yes."

"Really? Show it to your friends when you get home. Start a buzz, so when I arrive, there's a demand." I saw him collecting three more chickens. "Please take them." He thrust them at me. "Give them to your friends."

"But you should sell them."

"They're a present."

I didn't have the heart to refuse him. He clearly believed in his business venture 100 percent, and what did I know about sales anyway? What he lacked in product, he made up for in chutzpah. He started wrapping the cooing chickens in newspaper.

"Did you find your mom?" I asked.

Tomás didn't look up from his wrapping; he just pulled the ends of the strings tighter. The package began to buckle at the ends. After a moment he spoke. "No." He handed me the package.

I felt a pang in my chest. Tomás had been forced to become a man before sixteen, selling plastic chickens to make enough money to raise his siblings. What a contrast to Cody. At sixteen he'd received his first luxury car.

"But I will," he said. Tomás's optimism was inspiring. I would not bet against him.

"I believe you. Hey," I said, in a lighter tone, "do you think I could ask you some questions about Café Alegre?"

"Well, I am hungry."

"Great. I'll take you and Mario to lunch."

"Somewhere with beer?"

I hesitated. What the heck. This was surely a lesser crime than kidnapping.

Twenty minutes later the three of us were sitting in La Joya, a mariachi gathering place and restaurant. While a Mexican institution, mariachis were still popular in Costa Rica. It was afternoon, so it was pretty empty, but occasionally a white-and-gold suited man would wander by with a violin. The tables were made of thick, dark wood, and the ceilings were high. We ordered three Imperials and some nachos—a rarity in Costa Rica—from a waitress in a full skirt and petticoat. The nachos came smothered in sour cream.

"You mentioned Café Alegre violated Ethical Coffee International regulations," I said to Tomás. "Could you elaborate?"

Tomás took a swig of his beer and leaned over the table. "They don't pay minimum wage to the pickers. They fire people who complain. They make kids work. But other than that, I guess they're okay." A mixture of sweat and condensation from the beer bottle formed a mustache of droplets above his mouth. "Like, in comparison to working for sugarcane harvesters."

Mario nodded as he crammed his mouth with nachos.

"And what about the organic regulations?"

Tomás laughed. "There are more loopholes in the list of approved chemicals than there are prostitutes outside the bus terminal. And your shade-grown coffee? You have one tree in the fields? That's shade. It's greenwashing."

I twirled my beer around; maybe the pesticides I had seen were just the tip of it. "I heard that over the last two years Café Alegre won a lot of new contracts. Do you know anything about that?"

"Oh yeah. Two years ago a bald dude with a handlebar mustache came from Portland. We got a huge contract with him."

"Was it an Ethical Coffee International sale?"

"Sure. In name."

"You think Alegre accepted less than Ethical Coffee International price minimums to get the contracts?"

"Yes. I overheard Manuel talking to my mom."

My suspicions were correct. I watched Tomás proudly sipping his beer. This kid was extremely bright and had a deep knowledge of business practices. Maybe he *would* do well selling his chickens in the US.

I peeled the label off my beer. "So Alegre is definitely violating a few regulations."

"Not a few. Several. Manuel also buys conventionally produced coffee from other farms. It's their surplus, so he gets it cheap. Then he slaps a Café Alegre label on it and sells it as 'organic' and 'fair trade' for an Ethical Coffee International premium."

I paused, taking it in. "Wow, that's so brilliantly evil. Do you know which conventional farms he buys from?"

"There's a few. The biggest one is owned by some gringo with a weird accent," said Tomás. "Not American."

I felt a gnawing in my stomach. "German?"

"Yes! You're totally psychic!"

*Dieter. Ugh.* "Is it Café Bavaria?"

"Doesn't ring a bell."

Huh. How many German-owned coffee plantations could there be in Costa Rica? Then I remembered all those hundred-pound bags I saw in the mill. "Fuerte?"

"That's it!"

I let the chip I was holding fall into the sea of white. "Fuerte must be the name of a shell company for Bavaria's surplus."

Tomás nodded and reached for his matches. I wondered if he had just started smoking since he got to the city. The way he held his cigarette was awkward.

"So," I said, "Alegre is taking their ill-begotten gains from the surplus conventional coffee and using that money to stay afloat while they illegally undersell the ethically produced competition. It's a loss leader strategy to achieve market dominance."

Tomás took a deep puff on his cigarette and coughed. "I never thought about the big picture, but yeah."

"But how do they get away with the pesticides and labor abuses? Isn't anyone checking on the farms?"

"They can't police all the farms. The inspectors come out, like, once every three years?"

"Do any of the other co-ops know?"

He shrugged. "If they did, what could they do?"

I set my beer bottle on the table. I realized what they could do. What *we* could do. "They could take the proof to Ethical Coffee International. So Café Alegre could be decertified."

Tomás looked dubious. "Maybe." Tomás tried to blow a smoke ring. "If they had the guts." He blew two more fuzzy rings and lowered his cigarette. "There's a lot of money in this. Which means there's a lot of people that would be really pissed if Alegre got decertified." He put out his cigarette violently. "A lot of people who would do whatever it took to stop it."

"Then why did you want me to make a report? If nothing can be done?"

"I don't really care if you make the report. I'm already out." He leaned back in his chair and signaled the waitress for another beer. "But I didn't say nothing could be done." He leaned back over the nachos and tapped my beer bottle. "I just said I didn't know anyone who had the guts to do it."

# CHAPTER EIGHTEEN

Tomás had hinted at violent repercussions if someone blew the whistle on Café Alegre, but would that really happen here? Sometimes I just felt so hopelessly lost in Costa Rica. Being in a foreign country was like having everything you thought you knew stripped from you, washed in the laundry with a red shirt in hot water, and returned to you. The same clothes, but tighter, and pink.

But even though I didn't know exactly what I was getting into, I knew I had to do something. If I didn't follow through on my beliefs, who would I be but an armchair intellectual with the added dubious distinction of being a college dropout?

I went to my call spot outside the Chinese market. As usual, the employee was painting over some graffiti: *Chinos Go Home.* But this *was* their home now. Their relatives in China probably thought they spoke horrible Mandarin and liked weird food. I felt for him. I had never fully belonged anywhere, either. I hadn't had my bat mitzvah—there was no money for that. I was never Jewish enough, but not goy, either.

I stood under the Christmas lights they still hadn't taken

down and called Matías, feeling a little hesitant. We had never actually spoken, and somehow crossing the email-and-text barrier seemed more perilous than traversing the Siberian land bridge. I couldn't believe the things I had written in my emails. There should be a mandatory twenty-four-hour consideration period before you send those things.

After a ridiculously painful ten seconds, an intern answered and put me through.

"Dee," he said, warmly. "*Mi compañera en la lucha*. We speak at last."

"Hi," I said, suddenly forgetting both English and Spanish.

"Why didn't you Facetime me? You're really very mysterious, you know."

"It's part of being a covert special agent."

"I see. You know, I did finally find a photo of you. On one of your friend's Instagram accounts."

"You Insta-stalked me?"

"Of course. I had to make sure you weren't a Russian spy."

"How'd you figure out which one I was?"

"The one of you dressed entirely in blue, standing in front of a painting from Picasso's Blue Period. Very erudite. You know, Dee, you're . . . not unpleasant to look at. Why do you hide yourself?"

I blushed. "Not unpleasant to look at" was now the most wonderful compliment I'd ever been paid. "Uh, you know, privacy, etcetera."

"Uh-huh. Do you think it's weird this is the first time we've spoken? Since we know each other so well?"

"Mm-hmm."

"Have you noticed we're basically ideological twins?"

"I . . . have."

"We need a better analogy. I don't really think of you as a sister."

This was accelerating fast.

*"Five minutes,"* I heard the intern say in the background.

"Okay, looks like we only have a few." His voice became slightly more businesslike. "What's up?"

"Something terrible is going on here," I said, forcing my vocal cords to work. "There's a giant conspiracy with one of the Ethical Coffee International cooperatives."

"That's disturbing."

"I know it isn't totally relevant to the Truth Trip, but I think Justice Alliance needs to do something about it."

"Listen, I want to hear all about it, but our intern is threatening to cut us off, and she has a very sharp letter opener. Here's what we're going to do. You sit tight, and we'll discuss it in person in a few days."

"In person?"

"Yes. I'm going to Colombia to do some work with the oil pipeline. So why don't I stop by for the summit?" Jesus. I was talking to a man who thought nothing of stopping by *internationally*.

"Uh, yeah, that would be great."

"Good." His voice became softer and more intimate. "Also, I'd love to talk to you more about your higher power. Because it sounds from your last email like it might be chocolate?"

"That's a fair interpretation."

"Mine's whiskey."

"Whiskey and chocolate go great together."

"They do," he said, with more than a hint of double entendre, "they really do." My heart thudded against my ribs. "Maybe when we see each other we can do a taste test. You know, to confirm that hypothesis."

*Oh. My. God.* "Scientifically."

"Of course," he said. "But seriously. I'm really looking forward to meeting you properly. The old-fashioned way."

My heart shot straight out of my mouth. I think it hit a Starlink satellite. Fortunately, before I had to respond, I heard the intern again: *"They need you in the conference room. Eco Alliance is here."*

"Gotta go," he said. "But I'll see you soon, Chocolate. Tuesday, three o'clock, the café at the Gran Hotel."

I hung up, my head spinning. *I was going to meet Matías.* We were finally taking this thing offline.

♥ ⚬ *

But before I met with Matías or Suzanne, I needed to find *physical* proof of Alegre's misdeeds. After all, I still only had Tomás's word and an inconclusive photo. But how to actually get this proof? And in just a few days? This is where the Professor came in: he was the saint of impossible battles. Where others might become discouraged, he only became more resolved.

I climbed the steps to his office. It was a Sunday, and just two days after Christmas, but I knew he'd be there. This was a man who didn't understand the word *leisure*. I decided to be a person who didn't understand the word *pain*. My calf muscles would be springs that propelled me up the stairs. My biceps would be lean, mean fighting machines. I stepped into his office with one long stride, my fists pumping at my sides.

"The triumphant warrior returns," said the Professor, putting down his newspaper. "How many did you kill?"

"What are you talking about?"

"You look like you just came back from battle. What did you do? Slay Christmas presents?"

"Only the bad ones." I sat in the chair opposite his desk. My nerves were tingling. I couldn't keep my decision to myself one minute longer. "I know why Las Nubes lost their market share. Café Alegre stole their contract. And they did it by bypassing Ethical Coffee International price minimums."

"What takes you to that conclusion?"

"Do you remember I told you that Café Alegre used child labor?" The Professor nodded. "Well, I spoke to one of the kids again." No need to mention the kidnapping. "His name's Tomás. He confirmed that Café Alegre cuts their production costs by using illegal labor and pesticides. Then they make themselves more attractive to buyers than the other co-ops, by selling at an illegally lower price. They also sell surplus conventional coffee from other farms as organic and fair trade. So we're going to make a case for decertification to Ethical Coffee International."

The Professor stared at me for a second. I was vibrating, waiting for his response. "How?" he asked. "You have one kid's testimony."

"I'm going back to Café Alegre to interview the pickers."

"You're going to need more than interviews." He started ticking items off on his weathered fingers. "You're going to need receipts, contracts, bank transactions. How are you going to do this?"

"Tomás will help me." I crossed my fingers in my lap. Tomás didn't exactly know this yet. "And I've been in the offices. I have an idea where they keep their documents."

The Professor chuckled. "You're so naive."

My heart sank. How would I do this without him?

The Professor opened a pocket calendar. "When are we going?"

"You're coming with me?"

"Of course."

I sighed with relief.

"There's no way I'd let you go there by yourself. Revolution is a team sport."

"Thank you." I pulled a gift out of my purse. "I brought something for you."

The Professor didn't look at me as he unwrapped it. I knew he must have been remembering his daughter. All the gifts he never received, the Christmases he didn't celebrate, the years he'd lost. All of them were right there on that table sitting between the two of us. He peeled away the last layer of newsprint and tossed it to the ground.

"Hughes." His face lit up when he saw the title of the book. "*Good Morning Revolution*. How did you know I love him?"

"I didn't. These poems just remind me of you." It was an out-of-print collection of his later poetry, all fire and revolution. I didn't know how to tell the Professor what I really thought. That he *was* these poems. The words turned into action.

The Professor looked straight at me, and I felt he understood. "I have something for you, too." He handed me a neatly wrapped package. Now it was my turn to remember. That presents from my parents had never been gifts; they had been a way to control me. I unwrapped the package and saw a silver flask engraved with the words *La Comefuego*.

"Do you know what that means?" he asked.

"The Fire Eater?"

"Yes. It's slang for *revolutionary*."

I traced the engraving, unable to speak. The Professor had put me in his category and that was better than ten thousand words. When I looked up, I saw that he was standing at his file cabinet, staring out the window. He stayed there for a moment. When he turned back, his face was softer. He sat down at his desk and his voice was uneven. "I have to make some calls, but I'll pick you up tomorrow."

I nodded and started walking toward the door. The Professor motioned for me to stop. "Try not to murder any innocent presents on the way, *Comefuego*." He swiveled in his chair and picked up his phone. "Not all gifts are the henchmen of the evil capitalist economy."

♥ ⦶ ✱

Five minutes later I was sitting under a tree across from the Noxious Brook, with my blended guanabana drink from the *soda*, calling Clara from Las Nubes.

"So, I haven't been able to arrange Las Nubes being on the Truth Trips yet, but I'm still working on it. My boss is calling around to see if she could make an intro for you with an ethical roaster."

"That would be great."

"But I'm calling for another reason. You were right about Café Alegre. They did steal your contract."

"*¡Hijueputas!*" I heard her bang her coffee mug on a table.

"I think we should present a case to Ethical Coffee International to decertify them."

"We'll help."

"Great. First I have to interview the laborers. I'll disguise their faces, but I'm still a little worried about their safety."

"We can give them sanctuary here," she said. "Look, Dee, I know this goes without saying, but you shouldn't tell anyone what we're doing. Until you've delivered the evidence to Ethical Coffee International, you're vulnerable. We all are."

*Vulnerable.* That word had a strange effect on me. It made it feel true. I knew the fewer people who knew, the better, but it still freaked me out. We were vulnerable, but to what, exactly?

"So, there's something I have to tell you," she said, dread filling her voice.

"What?"

"The Rust is here. I found it on a bush yesterday."

"Shit. What are you going to do?"

"I killed the plant. And all the plants surrounding it."

"Hopefully that's enough."

"*Ojalá*."

But we both knew it might not be. I tried to shake off my concern as I rode the bus to downtown. The Rust was a foe that had no morals, no reason, and no easy answers. I jumped off the bus near the Central Market and headed toward the corner where I had last seen Tomás. He was in the exact same spot, except this time, he was selling a collection of plastic mooing cows. Mario must've been on break.

"*¡Macha!*" he said, giving me the hello-goodbye air kiss. "Did you come for more chickens?"

I looked around. We were surrounded, but no one seemed to be paying attention to us. There was a major commotion in the street because a disheveled young man was standing on top of a taxi, whipping his shirt around in the air, crying, "*¡Yo soy Che! ¡Yo soy Che!*"

"We're going to get Café Alegre decertified," I said, looking around to make sure no one was listening. "I need you to come with me tomorrow. We're going to record interviews with the laborers, and we need to secure some documents."

"We?" Tomás was smiling, but his eyes were distant. "I told you. I'm already out. I don't care what happens to them."

"What about your brother and sister? They're still there."

"I'm going back for them. I just need to save a little bit more money."

"What about the other pickers?"

"It's too late for them this season. Next season, they'll work somewhere else."

"Tomás, I need your help." He was startled by my directness.

I could see him struggling with his desire to help and his unwillingness to go back. He was so smart for someone so young, but he was still a teenager. I decided to appeal to his worse half. "I need your help to give Manuel what he deserves."

I watched the battle play itself out in his eyes. Revenge. Getting caught. *Revenge.*

"Do you think Manuel would get in a lot of trouble?" he asked.

"*So* much trouble."

"Jail?"

"He'd definitely lose the farm."

"But you don't think jail?"

"I don't know the ins and outs of the Costa Rican legal system, but it's a distinct possibility."

"What would happen to my brother and sister?"

"I know a wonderful co-op that will foster them. Until you have the money to get them yourself, of course."

"What about the people we interview?"

"I'm going to distort their faces when I edit the film."

Tomás watched police approach the man on top of the taxi. Then he studied my eyes. "You aren't scared?"

"As soon as we have the evidence, we'll give it to Ethical Coffee International. Then it's out of our hands. It'd be pointless for anyone to come after us after we turn in the evidence."

"*After.* But what about before? What if we get caught?"

I hesitated. "We won't get caught."

Tomás smiled. "You're brave for a *macha.*" The police began to handcuff the man and drag him to their car. "And you know what?"

"What?"

"I always knew you were the inspector."

"I'll pick you up here at five a.m." And before he or I could change our minds, I lost myself in the crowd. I *was* scared. But I was doing it anyway.

# PART THREE:
# THE ROASTING

# CHAPTER NINETEEN

The next day, I woke up groggy and uneasy, my windowpane still a square of black. I had slept maybe four hours the entire night, and they weren't contiguous. I had taken some herbal sleeping pills from the Central Market, which turned out to be a mistake. They were clearly hallucinogenic. When I tried counting sheep, they morphed into sheep-guards chasing me with shotguns as I leaped over bloody spears. When I tried to focus on something comforting, like my childhood dog, I saw a horned Dieter-and-Manuel conjoined twin trying to drown me in a vat of scalding hot coffee—single origin, of course.

At three a.m. I gave up and got dressed. I needed to get a grip on reality. Café Alegre was huge; no one was going to catch us. If someone came near us, we'd hop in the Jeep and go. And even if we did get caught, would Manuel *really* shoot an internationally famous professor, a young female American, and his own stepson? Wouldn't that be more trouble than it was worth?

The Professor came for me at four-thirty and we headed into the city to pick up Tomás. It was still dark, and vendors were just starting to unload their pickup trucks. Men with wide-brimmed hats lifted crates of mangos onto folding tables while women unpacked cardboard boxes full of beaded necklaces. Tomás was waiting on his corner, wearing old blue jeans and carrying a small backpack. The Professor held out his hand to Tomás through the window.

"*Eugenio Ramírez. Un placer.*"

Tomás's eyes widened. "*The* Professor Eugenio Ramírez?" The Professor nodded. "What an honor," said Tomás in Spanish as he climbed into the backseat of the Jeep. "Dee, why didn't you tell me he was coming? I would've said yes right away." He looked at the Professor in the rearview mirror with reverence. "You were a legend in our house. My mom said you single-handedly released two hundred indigenous prisoners in San Cristobal de las Casas during the Zapatista uprising."

"Well, it wasn't single-handed. And it was more like three hundred."

"You're such a badass," said Tomás. "Do you have a machete?"

"I do," he said. My eyes widened. "However, I only approve of violence as a last resort."

"But it's okay for self-defense?"

"Certainly. But guns work better for that." My eyes got even wider.

"Do you have a gun?" asked Tomás.

"Son, I have an armory."

The two talked about the Professor's exploits until we hit the Pan-American Highway, where the conversation grew more immediate and less murder-y. "So here's the plan," said Tomás in fast, colloquial Spanish, moving to the middle of the backseat. I was surprised to realize I understood it all, even the idioms. "When we get to the fields, I'm going to find the foreman, José. He'll select some people he knows we can trust to keep quiet.

Then he'll bring them to you guys for the interviews somewhere close to the highway." Tomás's fingers tapped against my headrest. "Then I'm going to find my little sister, Luisita, so she can get us the keys to the filing cabinets. That's where most of the documents are. Manuel keeps the keys in the urn with my grandmother's ashes."

"Eeew," I said.

"It's a very safe place. No one wants to disturb the dead."

"Or touch them."

"Good point. Once I have the keys, I'll sneak into the mill and get the documents."

"I should be the one to do it," I said. Tomás looked surprised. "I know what we're looking for. You can't just take every piece of paper in the place. Also, some of the information may be in his computer."

"It's too dangerous for you, *Macha*. If they catch me, at least I'm family." I gulped, considering the implications. "Also, no way it's computerized. Manuel is a dinosaur."

I put my head straight back against the headrest while Tomás and the Professor discussed logistics. I couldn't believe we were actually doing this. I thought back to when Adrián and I had hidden in the ditch in Café Bavaria. Trespassing—hah! That would be a mere misdemeanor. Now I was going to commit felonies. Images of me evading armed guards flitted across my eyelids until I sat up with a jolt. Looking out the window, I realized I'd been dreaming. Several hours had passed; it was now midmorning and we were in the Central Highlands. Branches hung over the highway and the smell of burning trash wafted into the Jeep.

Without warning, the Professor turned off the highway and plowed through some ferns, continuing until we couldn't see the road. After he was sure the Jeep was hidden, he turned off the engine and rolled down the windows. We all hopped out of the Jeep. As we followed Tomás through the forest, I thought of Adrián again. We had been here together, and he would be here now if I had let him. Had I made the right decision? Maybe I shouldn't have been so cold to him in Manuel Antonio. Maybe I was incapable of knowing myself.

"Are you okay, *Macha*?" asked Tomás.

"Fine," I said, trying to believe it.

Tomás gestured to a large cedar tree. "I'll send the pickers here. When you're finished, meet me back at the Jeep." I nodded and sat under the shade of the tree. The Professor sat next to me, and we went over our interview questions. But my mind wouldn't focus. It jumped from scared thought to sad thought, sad thought to scared, in an endless loop of no good. I tried concentrating on the shifting patterns that the sun cast on the ground. Maybe in the negative space I could lose myself.

After a few minutes, I heard a rustling and looked up. Standing before me was a thirtysomething woman with hazel eyes, dark curly hair, and a small scar near her ear. How did she get that scar? What combination of events had brought her here? I thought of a proverb that was common here: *Cada persona es un mundo.* It was the same as a Talmudic teaching: *Each person is a whole world.*

The Professor pulled out his phone and nodded at me to begin. I felt apprehensive, especially since he was watching, but this is what we were here for. So I attempted to draw her out while the Professor recorded. "What brought you to work at Café Alegre?"

"I came here because they told me it was a fair trade co-op," she said in lilting Spanish. I couldn't identify her accent, but I knew she wasn't from here. "I knew that was a lie after the first week because they didn't pay us. They say they're going to pay us at the end of the season. They also say they're going to pay us per basket, but they're lying about that, too." She dabbed at a drop of sweat that was trickling down her neck. "Another picker who worked here last season said they'll pay us one sum for the whole season. So now I don't kill myself trying to pick the most baskets. But we can't pick too few baskets, or we get punished."

"How?"

"They give us less food or they put more people in our bungalows, or they don't give us medicine if we are sick. Or they can fire you and never pay you anything. So it's better to just be quiet and get paid at the end of the summer."

"Where are you from?"

"Matagalpa, Nicaragua." Her voice was heavy with longing. "I used to work there, but the Rust took everything."

"I'm so sorry you had to leave your country, *compañera*," said the Professor. "Thank you for having the courage to tell your story."

José sent a few more laborers, and we continued the interviews. After the last one, we started walking back to the Jeep together. "We make a good team, I think," said the Professor.

"I agree." But wouldn't any team be great with him on it? He was a legend.

"Matías was right again. You know, he talks about you a lot. He even sent me your website. How long have you known each other?"

"Not that long. We've never actually met in person."

The Professor considered for a moment. "Sometimes it doesn't take long. It's like in your thesis about charismatic leaders helping people's class consciousness evolve during a moment of struggle. People form strong connections quickly when they go through something important together." He paused. "*Como nosotros.*"

*Like us.* I smiled at him, and we kept walking in silence. I was vibrating. *The Professor felt close to me. And Matías talked about me—a lot.* I couldn't believe the way my life had opened up since I'd come to Costa Rica. It was so much more expansive and vibrant. Everything felt so much more *real.*

When we got to the Jeep, we found Tomás pacing around it, distraught, and my happy feelings vanished. "The key wasn't in the urn!" he said. "It wasn't anywhere! We can't get the documents." My stomach started forming a knot. "I'm so sorry, Dee," said Tomás, anguished. "I failed."

"You didn't fail," said the Professor. "So far, *we* haven't succeeded."

We stood there in grim silence, processing. Had we come this far for nothing? But then I remembered something. "Oh!" They looked at me expectantly. "Last time I was here, I kinda, well, snooped around."

"Obviously," said Tomás. "That's how you found me and kidnapped me."

The Professor gave me a sideways glance. "Kidnapped?"

"Long story." I turned to Tomás. "I thought we determined it was ridesharing." Tomás smiled. "Anyhow, I snooped around Manuel's office in the mill. I found an armoire with a secret compartment, and I heard keys in there. I wonder if they open the file cabinets."

"It sounds like him to keep duplicates," said Tomás. "Now that I think about it, why would he want to dig around in his mother's ashes every time he needed to open a cabinet?"

"That would be a very weird fetish."

Tomás nodded. "Can you tell me where in the armoire the key ring is?"

"I'll get it."

"You will not," said the Professor. "We already settled this.

Tomás has a more plausible excuse for being caught on the premises. He is returning home after a small 'ridesharing' episode."

"But if they catch him, he'll have to stay here."

"You kidnapped him once, surely you can kidnap him again," said the Professor.

"Let's park the Jeep closer to the mill," said Tomás. "Dee, make a sketch for me of where the keys are in the armoire. Then I'll sneak in through a window, get the keys, and find the documents. You two wait in the Jeep and I'll return when I have everything."

"But what if you don't come back?" I asked. "How will we know if someone found you?"

"Give me half an hour. If it's longer than that . . ." He picked at his lip with his thumb and middle finger. "I don't know." He looked hopefully at the Professor. "You'll think of something."

Think of something? Who did we think we were? Freaking James Bond and Mata Hari? "If I don't come back, you should return to San José, and then come back in a few days when things have settled down."

"We're not going to leave you here!" I said.

"What are you going to do?" he asked. "Call the police on Manuel? You can't be kidnapped by your own family."

"Let's not worry about every possibility," said the Professor, starting the engine and backing out toward the highway. "Sometimes the cost of inaction is greater than making a mistake."

"Agreed." Tomás sank into his seat. The two of them were composed, but I was freaking out. Was this a gender difference? Cultural? Or were they also freaking out but just hiding it? I saw Tomás continue to pick at his lip through the rearview mirror, and the Professor was driving more maniacally than usual. They were suppressing their feelings; I was sure of it.

The Professor took us back onto the highway and drove

to the gate that marked the beginning of Café Alegre's property. About thirty feet from the gate, he veered off the highway and hid the Jeep in a bank of monkey tail ferns. Before I could really absorb what was happening, Tomás was out of the Jeep and running toward the mill. I watched the black laurels close back over him, branch after branch returning to place like a never-ending turnstile.

I turned to the Professor. "Do you think it's a good idea to let him go by himself?"

"Do you?" asked the Professor. He studied my face. Here was the second test! I knew it was coming!

"No." I grasped my snake necklace. "I'm going to follow him."

"I'll come, too."

"No, it's better if you keep the engine running. I'll call you if we need backup."

He nodded. "Do you want my machete?"

I blanched. "Not this time, thanks." I unbuckled my seatbelt and opened the door. I tried to keep my hands from shaking so he wouldn't know how nervous I was.

But he saw. He leaned over and put a hand on my shoulder. "You can do this, *Comefuego*."

*But could I?*

# CHAPTER TWENTY

I took off after Tomás. I couldn't see or hear him, but I could see the depressions he had caused in the grass. Branches of scarlet poró were still swaying ahead of me, and small leaves quivered on either side of the freshly cut path. As I tried to retrace his steps without sound, I kept reminding myself that even if I got caught, I'd likely just get arrested. Manuel wasn't going to risk going to jail for manslaughter over a few lousy interviews. He'd confiscate my camera and phone and turn me over to the police.

All my rationalizing dissipated like so much volcanic steam when I got close enough to see glimpses of the community center through the tree branches. In my mind I heard the Death Star theme music. I wrapped myself around the trunk of a large laurel negro tree and observed my surroundings. In front of me lay the soccer field, and beyond that, the community center and mill. The field was ringed by almendro and laurel negro trees.

I took a deep breath and leapfrogged to another tree that was closer to the soccer field. If I peeked around the trunk, I could see the community center perfectly. There were two people sipping coffee on the veranda. Their hideous Teva sandals heavily suggested that they were tourists, but how could I be sure? As I scanned the area, I saw Tomás run out from behind a different tree, heading toward the mill. I looked at the tourists: Had they noticed? No. They seemed to be having an animated discussion in French, perhaps about nihilism, or transit strikes, or the health benefits of drinking before noon. I recognized the word *fromage* and realized they were debating where to have lunch. Hopefully they would be so engrossed in Yelp reviews, they wouldn't notice us.

After a few minutes, Tomás sprinted toward me from the mill, carrying several manila folders. "What are you doing?!" He spoke softly. "I told you to wait in the Jeep."

"I was worried about you. I wanted to make sure you got in and out okay."

"Don't be stupid! Take these and wait for me in the Jeep. I forgot to put the keys back."

"Who cares about the keys! We need to leave before we spend the rest of our lives in jail hammering license plates with volcanoes!"

"I have to put them back," he said. "When Manuel notices they're missing, he'll know someone was here."

"So what?"

"He'll have time to cover his tracks. Write up new receipts, new invoices."

He pushed the folders into my hands and ran back toward the mill. I almost stopped breathing. Tomás was going to breach the Death Star *twice*. I couldn't return to the Jeep; I had to make sure he got out okay. I put the folders down, hugged the tree, and peered around the side. What I saw next sent my heart racing. The tourists had gone inside, and Manuel and Paula were taking their afternoon coffee onto the veranda. Tomás stopped in mid-sprint and flattened himself behind a tree twenty feet from the mill. He was perfectly still.

"Did you hear something?" said Manuel. "I heard footsteps."

"It was probably one of the kids," said Paula.

"They're supposed to be studying."

"Would you relax? Maybe it's some tourists who got lost on their way to the bathroom."

"Maybe it's that goddamned union organizer." Manuel scanned the forest. "If I catch him, I swear I'll slit his throat." He went into the community center and returned carrying his shotgun. Suddenly I felt very, very cold. "Pablo told me he was seen at Café Irazú on Friday. I'm telling you, Paula, I'm not letting that piece of shit steal my labor."

Jesus Effing Mary and Joseph. I flattened myself against the back of my tree, facing away from the center. What if Manuel saw me? What if he mistook me for the union organizer? What if he saw me move and thought I was a *bird*? My heart was beating so loudly I couldn't think; I was just one big throbbing mess of blood.

"Who's on my property?" shouted Manuel. I heard footsteps coming down the veranda steps, but I couldn't risk looking. I heard the footsteps stop, so I turned my head to the left. Out of the corner of my eye, I saw a blur of movement: Tomás darting toward the mill, while Manuel was looking in the other direction. *Was he insane?!* I whipped my head back and tried to pull out my phone to text the Professor, but I lost my grip and it fell to the ground with a thud. I dropped to the ground to retrieve it.

"*¿Qué carajo?*" said Manuel. His footsteps were now coming in my direction. I lay paralyzed on the ground, the blood pounding against my eardrums. But then the endorphins kicked in. I tucked the folders under my shirt and started crawling. There were tall ferns scattered among the trees. If I kept low to the ground, Manuel wouldn't see me . . . hopefully. I crept over poisonous red bugs and prickly plants, but I barely noticed because I was focused on one thing only: getting as far away as possible. Manuel was getting close to my original tree, but I was almost behind another.

Then I heard a *click*. Like a metal door closing.

I stopped moving. I turned my head and looked toward the mill. Tomás was running from the side of the mill toward the cover of the trees. Vomit rose from my stomach to my throat. I turned to look in Manuel's direction. I wasn't sure if he had seen Tomás.

"Paula?" Manuel shouted, now at my original tree. "What was that?"

"Leave me alone, you old bastard, I'm trying to meditate. The doctor said it would be good for my blood pressure."

"Did you go in or out of the center?"

"No. What's wrong with you?"

Manuel headed toward the clicking noise to investigate . . . which meant he was heading straight toward Tomás. *He was going to catch him.* I had no time to think. I stood up, took the manila folders out of my shirt, and placed them underneath a fern. I dusted the dirt off myself and stepped away from the protection of the tree.

"Don Manuel!" I said, waving in the sunlight, stepping into the soccer field. "*¡Saludos!*"

Manuel stopped right before he hit the cluster of trees where I thought Tomás was hiding, then turned around with his gun pointed. "Dee?"

I was reeling. You see a lot of guns on TV, but *nothing* prepares you for what it feels like when one is pointed at you. Waves of black muddled my vision and everything was much louder than normal.

But I had to shake it off. "I've come back." I swung my arms and walked quickly to keep myself from keeling over. "To finish the tour!"

Manuel's eyes narrowed. He took a few steps forward, lowering his gun. "What a pleasant surprise." I crossed the soccer field, counting each step so I would remember to breathe. "Why didn't you call first?" he said. His finger was still curled around the trigger.

"I did. Several times. No one answered. Well, finally, someone did, but to tell you the truth, I couldn't really understand her. My Spanish is terrible." I tried to keep my voice as light as possible. If I seemed stupid and cheery enough, he might put down his gun. "Did Suzanne call you? We want to stop here on our minitrip Wednesday."

"She mentioned it, yes." I saw his fingers relax. He was still holding the gun, but his fingers weren't on the trigger. "She said you'd be getting in contact with me. But you really should have made sure you spoke with me first." He let the gun hang loosely by his side. "I thought you were a snoop. I could've shot you by mistake." I clasped my hands together to keep them from shaking. "We've been having a lot of problems here." He led me toward the veranda.

"Oh?" I managed to squeak out.

"There's been a union organizer and an unofficial inspector," he said. "Some kid from an American nonprofit making unannounced visits to organic farms." Manuel led me up the steps of the veranda and sat me in one of the chairs. "Paula, bring Dee some coffee." He sat down next to me and put his gun down in front of his feet.

"It's got us all on edge," he continued. "It's like our boundaries don't count anymore. People are violating them left and right." He leaned back into his chair. "The worst of it is that it's totally pointless. Co-ops don't need unions and organic farms already get visited by Ethical Coffee International. Now, Ethical Coffee I welcome. Those inspectors go through rigorous training. But what does this nonprofit kid know? What kind of training does she have?" I shrugged. "Foolish, naive, well-meaning foreigner. She has no idea what she's getting into. Personally, I feel bad for her. If she finds what she's looking for, what then?" I swallowed the bubble of panic rising from my gut. *I was the foolish, naïve, well-meaning foreigner.* Paula came back with the coffee.

"Let's say she finds a farm not in compliance," he said. "And she wants to do something about it. What's going to happen to her if she does? She could get in a lot of trouble. People here protect their land." He tapped his gun with his foot. "She might get herself killed, and for what? It would be a tragedy for everyone. Aren't you going to taste the coffee?"

I swallowed a new, larger bubble of panic. "I'm just waiting for it to cool down."

"Why don't I give you a tour of the property while we wait?" he said. "I mean, that's why you're here, right?" I blinked. The longer I stayed, the more at risk we were of getting caught. But where was Tomás? Had he made it back to the Jeep?

"Come on," said Manuel, walking down the steps. He brought his gun with him. *Why, God, why?* I scampered after him, trying to decide what to do. He stepped onto a dirt path. "Let's go look at the fields."

"Can we make it quick?" I asked, looking at my watch. "I'm very sorry, but I got here a little later than anticipated, and I want to get back to San José before dark. And I know Suzanne wants to make a stop here on the trip, so seeing the fields is a formality. I just need to take a few pictures for her promotional materials."

"Of course," said Manuel. "I'll take you to the east fields. They're right here." Manuel veered to his right.

The forest closed in around us like dark green curtains, and my dread intensified. I felt the trees pressing against us, smothering. The only things alleviating the gloom were stigmata plants, with their green leaves and red centers. It looked like they were bleeding.

"We're very isolated here," said Manuel, walking more slowly. "Sometimes I feel like we're at the end of the world. Like anything could happen here, and no one would ever know. You know what I'm talking about?" I nodded. *You can kill me with impunity.*

We both heard a rustling sound.

"What was that?" I asked.

Manuel held a finger to his lips. He raised his shotgun and scanned the area. I turned my back to him and looked into the forest. There, peeking out from behind a large bush, was the tip of a tennis shoe. *Tomás.* Jesus Christ, he was following us.

"I see something!" I turned and pointed in the *opposite* direction. "There! A quetzal!" Manuel followed the trajectory of my finger. But behind me, Tomás rustled again. Manuel turned back around.

"That didn't sound like a bird." He lifted his gun and pointed it in Tomás's direction. Panic flooded me again. His finger released the trigger before I could stop him. A loud boom filled the air, then something heavy thudded to the ground with a short cry. My body shrieked in protest. Without thinking, I ran to where Manuel had aimed. When I saw a furry tail, I sank to my knees. A capuchin monkey.

"What is it?" he asked.

"I've never seen anything shot before," I said, sobbing. I put my head in my hands. Grateful Tomás was alive. Gutted for the monkey. Way out of my depth.

"You know what?" said Manuel, unnerved. Apparently even evil men hate to see women cry. "Why don't we just go back to the community center? You tell Suzanne you saw the fields, and I'll send you some photos. It will be our little secret, okay?" I nodded, wiping tears and snot from my face. "Come." Manuel put his gun down and helped me off the forest floor. Then he picked up the gun and walked me to the soccer field. I was still shaking. Where was Tomás? Was he still following us?

Manuel turned to me when we got to the path that led to the highway. "Let me walk you to your car."

A fresh wave of panic rolled over me. The Jeep was hidden behind ferns *with the Professor* at the wheel. How would I explain that?

"I'll be okay," I said.

"I can see you're shook up. I'm sorry for killing the monkey. I was just concerned that it might be the organizer. I wanted to scare him off." I started shaking uncontrollably all over again. "Where's your car?"

"I'm fine, really. Thank you so much for the tour."

"I'm accompanying you to your car. These are dangerous times. Who knows who's out there." Manuel started walking with me down the path. What the hell was I going to do? Should I walk in a different direction and pretend the car had been stolen?

"Is this yours?" he asked. I wrenched my head up. I had been so tormented I wasn't even seeing what was in front of me. There, parked next to the gate, was the Jeep. *Not* where we had left it hidden thirty feet down the road. *Not* with the Professor in it.

"Yes," I said, trying to hide my confusion. Manuel opened the front door and I slid into the driver's seat. The keys were in the ignition. Where were Tomás and the Professor?

"You shouldn't leave your keys in the car," he said.

"I know. Terrible habit." I started the engine. It was a stick! *How was I going to drive it?!* "Thanks, Don Manuel. I'm sorry I came unannounced."

He nodded. "Just remember what I said. You shouldn't be walking around these places unaccompanied. It's too dangerous. God knows what would've happened if I hadn't recognized your voice."

I nodded, then pressed down on the clutch because that's what I thought I was supposed to do. The gears squealed. "See you Wednesday."

"Looking forward to it," he said, backing up. "And Dee—" He made very intentional eye contact. "Don't go looking for trouble."

I gulped, then pressed the gas, and after a terrible crunching sound, the Jeep lurched forward. Manuel shook his head at my driving and turned back down the path.

Once he was out of sight, I resumed breathing. I drove slowly on the highway, looking for Tomás and the Professor. No sign of them. So I lurched back toward the gate in bursts and stops. On my third circuit, Tomás and the Professor leaped out of the bushes. The Professor opened my door and motioned for me to move to the passenger seat and Tomás hopped into the back. In less than ten seconds, the Professor was racing the Jeep down the open highway.

"Didn't need me to come, huh?" the Professor said.

"Where'd you learn to drive, *macha*?" asked Tomás. "School for the blind?"

I burst into tears. Both immediately tried to comfort me. "I was kidding about the blindness!" said Tomás.

"Also kidding!" said the Professor. "You would've been fine without me."

"Actually, it was you who saved me," said Tomás. "If you hadn't distracted Manuel, he would've found me for sure."

"I forgot the documents!" I wailed, too caught up in the post-adrenaline crash to be embarrassed.

"*Tranquila*," said the Professor, opening the glove box and revealing several manila folders. "I was following you the whole time."

"You were?" I asked, barely intelligible through my sobs. "Even in the forest?"

"Of course. You think I was going to let you go alone into the forest with some maniac with a shotgun?" I blinked away tears. "It's okay, *Comefuego*. You did great." He looked at me fondly. "Remember: Revolution is a team sport."

♥ ● ✱

By the time I got home, I wasn't hysterical anymore. We had gotten the interviews and most of the documents! The only thing we didn't have was physical proof that Bavaria was selling surplus coffee to Alegre—they did a good job hiding things in their shell business, Fuerte. Also, much of the terror had been washed away by the Imperial beers we consumed at a dive bar on the outskirts of San José. There, in the dim light of flickering candles and mosquito lamps, the Professor, Tomás, and I had taken turns rendering our own versions of the adventure. Each time we retold it, the dangers multiplied, and the heroism was magnified. We hadn't merely broken into Café Alegre and stolen evidence; we had pulled off the greatest caper of all time.

*What would Matías think of it?*

I shivered in a light cotton shirt at my desk, even though the night was still humid and warm. I had been repressing my feelings the whole way through and now they were threatening to erupt. I never knew what I wanted until I was so far-gone reason wasn't invited to the party. I opened the flask the Professor had given me and took a sip. Whiskey. Of course. With a burning sensation coursing through my stomach, I opened my laptop. As I had hoped and feared and expected, there was a message from Matías. I took a long swig from my flask and opened my eyes to this:

TO: Dee Blum
FROM: Matías Khalil
SUBJECT: ramblings

It's very late at night or very early in the morning and I've just come back from a celebration with too many bottles of wine and a sky full of lights so you must excuse me if I ramble, but I needed to say goodnight to you before I could sleep. I can't believe we are finally going to have our reunion because I know that sometime somewhere someplace we've already met. Will you be the same person I've always known? And do you understand my strange words because you are feeling them too?

Sweet dreams,
Matías

I didn't know if it was the whiskey or his words that had gone to my head, but I felt woozy. My hands shook over the keyboard as I responded.

TO: Matías Khalil
FROM: Dee Blum
SUBJECT: the same ramblings

It's late here too and I am wondering if you are still awake. I understand your thoughts perfectly because they are mine as well. Thank you for your wishes of sweet dreams. I will be sure to have them now and I anxiously await our reunion because I think I missed you.

I hit send and lay sleeplessly in my bed, staring at the mysterious swirls of plaster on my ceiling. Matías liked me. I liked Matías. These two facts were so unbelievable.

# CHAPTER TWENTY-ONE

Putting on mascara was a real adventure that morning, because my hands would not stop trembling. Today I would meet Matías. Matías the human, not the amalgam of emails and fantasies. I had spent so much time imagining him and so little time knowing him—how could he live up to the ideal I had created? But what if he exceeded it? The possibility that reality could be even better than my imagination both terrified and titillated me.

But nagging thoughts of Adrián seeped into my daydreams, tempering my excitement with sadness. Was he in Panamá with his father? Was he doing okay? I attempted to push away these questions as I tried on clothes in Eva's room.

"What do you think?" I asked, tugging my jeans on. "Are they too tight?"

"There's no such thing as too tight." She felt the fabric of my tank. "But don't you think you're going to be a little cold?" She went to her closet and pulled out a beautiful silk blouse for me.

"I can't. It's too nice." It was ten times nicer than anything I owned.

"That's the point. You said you have an important work meeting."

"But what if I spill coffee on it?"

"Then we'll wash it."

"But what if it doesn't come out?"

"It's a thing, Dee. It doesn't matter." I looked at her. The proverb came back to me: *Each person is a whole world.* Eva valued things and appearances so much. But at the same time, she didn't.

"Thank you." I put it on and admired myself in the mirror. I looked good. I never thought I looked good.

Eva looked at me keenly. "It's just a work meeting?"

"Mm-hmm."

"What's happening with Adrián?"

"I think it's over."

She looked disappointed. "Is he still in love with his ex?"

I shook my head. "We just aren't the right fit."

She looked over my outfit. "I hope the new guy is."

Damn, she was good. How did she read me so easily when half the time I didn't even know what I was feeling? I thanked her again for the shirt and hustled out before she could see all my thoughts.

When I arrived at the outdoor café of the Gran Hotel, I was a nervous wreck. There were umbrellas over the tables to keep out the sun, a fountain sprayed mist to keep out the heat, and hundreds of little birds kept out the bugs. Tourists picked at baked goods while older Costa Rican men sipped espresso and smoked cigars. I sat back in my chair and tried to relax, concentrating on the sound of birds and traffic jumbling together to form a cosmo-tropical mix.

I had picked a prime location. My back was to the hotel and I was facing the plaza. Now I could scrutinize each passerby while I waited for Matías. It would have been perfect except for the fact that an unseasonably cold breeze raced across the plaza. So I sat there freezing, stomach rumbling. I hadn't eaten anything today. Why, why hadn't I eaten?

I rubbed my shoulders and checked my watch. Twenty after three. I looked at the mafiosos and thought about the exquisite sounds emanating from my stomach. I was so enthralled by my own misery that I ceased to scrutinize the newcomers. I didn't notice that someone had approached me until he was standing two feet away. I looked up.

There he was. Six-feet tall, or seven, who could say? The TED Talk video had not given a proper sense of scale. He was muscled but not beefy, with a fierce jaw, burnt amber skin, and hazel eyes that seemed to set off sparks. I stood up, feeling weak all over, not just in the knees. Whoever thought of that stupid, inaccurate expression?

"Dee?"

I nodded.

"You're real!" He smiled. "And even more beautiful in person. I love how you're three dimensional."

Me? *Beautiful?* I was dying. But I had to pull myself together. "Sure I'm not a hologram?"

I went for a handshake, but he pulled me in for a hug. I could feel the outline of his chest muscles against my body. Heat rolled over me in waves. When he finally let go, I sat down quickly to hide my trembling. He took off his jaunty brimmed hat and sat down, gracefully arranging his linen-clad limbs.

"So," he said, shifting in his chair. The sun was behind him, and his wavy hair glowed like a halo. As if the universe was saying, *"He is our chosen one."* I stared at him. I could tell he was struggling to say something, but I couldn't help him. I had immediate onset laryngitis. Finally, he gave me a shy, questioning smile. "We reunite at last."

I almost fell off my chair. Did he have to start with that? Was he going to *quote* me? I looked up for a moment to see what he was thinking, became terrified by his fond expression, and went back to rattling my ice cubes. We sat there in charged silence. You just can't have this kind of conversation in the daytime, especially without alcohol. Evidently, he came to the same conclusion.

"I've been looking forward to seeing your photos," he said in a more neutral voice. "Of the co-ops. You've been shockingly slow putting them on your website."

"Yeah, I don't really maintain that site, per se."

"Can I see them, per se?"

"Sure." I was relieved that he wasn't going to remind me that I had written, "I think I missed you." I was also relieved to have a prop. He wouldn't be looking at me if he was looking at the photos. I pushed my iPad bashfully across the table, open to the Las Nubes section. He took it every bit as bashfully, made uncomfortable by my discomfort. Shyness is a highly contagious disease.

He scrolled through the pictures, taking his time. We ordered coffee and I pretended I wasn't staring at him staring at my photos. His tranquil eyes focused on one image. I began to sweat despite the breeze. When he looked up, his eyes weren't tranquil anymore; they were passionate waters. "Have you ever thought of being a professional photographer?"

"No," I said, unhinged by his eyes. "It's just a hobby."

"If I were half as good as you were, I'd think seriously about it."

I hid my blush and extreme confusion in the coffee that had just arrived. "It's impossible to make a living as a photographer. It's a job for people with rich parents. Like being an architect. Or influencer."

"It *is* very difficult. But you know the saying, cream rises to the top. The best still find work."

"I'm not *the* best."

"With time, you could be. Your pictures are moving. It's one thing to learn the technical aspects, but who can teach you to have soul?"

I was both deeply flattered and deeply uncomfortable. "Don't we all come with one? Standard issue?"

He smiled. "We're often the last to see our own talents. And to recognize our own desires. People have a hard time understanding what they want. I know I did."

What a relief to hear my worries from his perfect lips. "You didn't always want to be an organizer?"

"Oh, no." He spooned sugar into his cup. "My parents are first generation immigrants. Dad is from Lebanon, Mom's from Mexico. They have typical immigrant mentality: Doctor and lawyer are the only options."

"My parents want me to be a lawyer, too!"

"Something is funny about that generation," he said. "Don't they realize there are other high-paying jobs? Like engineer or programmer? Or, if you really want to be rich, movie star or basketball player?"

"I don't think you're tall enough."

"Or handsome enough," he said.

"Disagree about that one."

We shared a dangerous smile. "Anyhow," he said. "I was more into writing emo folk songs. Then spray-painting guerrilla art on freeway underpasses. I changed paths about five times before I went to grad school. In fact, I didn't really start to feel comfortable with myself until last year." He must have noticed my downturned lips. "Don't worry," he said. "You're much smarter than I ever was. You're going to figure things out a lot faster."

"I hope so."

"I know so. You know, Justice Alliance hires photographers as independent contractors. After you finish the Truth Trip, we should talk about it. I'd hate to see your spying talents go to waste, but I think it would be criminal of me to keep you from your true calling."

I tried to hide my deepening blush, but it was taking over my face like shingles. Even my own family didn't say such nice things about me. I should say, *especially* my own family didn't say such nice things about me. But it occurred to me that I was playing my cards all wrong. I needed to take Eva's advice: play hard-to-get.

"What kind of projects do the Justice Alliance photographers work on?" I asked in a cool, detached voice, trying my best to project intense indifference. *Wait, was that an oxymoron?*

"They document the work on our social and environmental justice campaigns, and of course the Truth Trips. It involves a lot of travel, sometimes to dangerous places. It requires someone who has more than artistic talent. They need to be brave and resourceful. You'd be perfect." He turned his smile to full wattage and I felt unsteady again. Wish these seats had seatbelts. "We also hire videographers to make educational videos. You'd be great at that, too. You could combine your detective work with your artistry."

I would do anything he told me to. I was a goner. But I had to keep up appearances. "I'll think about it."

He stopped looking at me for a moment to sip his espresso and I resumed breathing. I hadn't realized I had stopped. He looked up again and said in a low, sultry voice, "So how are you doing with your disillusion?"

I couldn't breathe. It didn't even matter what he said. It was *how* he said it. Pure sex. "Okay. Better."

"Do you still think co-ops are the answer to inequality?"

I nodded, light in the head. "Alternative methods of economic production are the least violent form of cultural and economic revolution."

Matías leaned across the table and I lost what was left of my cool. "You think cooperative production is a form of revolution?"

"Yes." I fought to regain my composure. "As more and more people take up alternative forms of production, there will be less room for exploitative forms of production." I gave up. "Co-ops displace capitalism! It's a bloodless revolution!"

"Yes," he said. "A democratic one!"

"Right! The desire of the people!"

I think firecrackers were exploding over the café, but I wasn't sure. It's not every day that you meet someone who dreams the same revolution as you.

He placed his hand on mine, gently. "I can't believe we understand each other so well."

I can't even remember the rest of the conversation. The touch of his hand completely erased sound. My mind couldn't get over it. And then suddenly, my stomach made a high-pitched squeal, followed by a low rumbling. It wrenched me out of dreamland and back into the very real world of humiliation. Why was this happening to me? In the middle of *this* conversation? My stomach whined again. I wanted to die.

"Wow," he said, glancing at his watch. "I had no idea it had gotten so late. It's almost five o'clock."

"Wow," I said, not surprised at all. It could've been three days and I would've believed it. "I have to get going." This was a lie, but I had to create mystery. And get to a bathroom.

"And I have to get to that meeting," he said. Pangs of jealousy pricked me. Who was he meeting? I suddenly remembered that I had forgotten the main purpose of *our* meeting. Getting him on board to lobby for the decertification of Café Alegre.

"Matías, before you go. We were going to discuss the corrupt co-op."

"Ah, yes. You said there was a conspiracy?"

"They're evading Ethical Coffee International price floors, as well as violating environmental regulations." I scrolled through the camera roll on my iPad. "I have interviews with the laborers. I also have documentation about pricing."

He looked at two pictures. "This is terrible." His brow furrowed. "But it's incredible work on your part. I want to go over everything in detail." He handed me back the iPad and placed his hand over mine again. "I can't look at everything right now or I'll be late to my meeting. Obviously, I need to give something as serious as this my full attention. Can you bring this to me on Thursday? We can meet in my hotel in Alajuela." He squeezed my hand, turning my balmy temperature into outright sweltering heat. "You are coming to the conference?"

"Of course."

"Where are you staying? Did Suzanne arrange a room for you?"

"I don't need a room, it's not that far. I'll take the bus in from San José."

"That's nonsense." He released my hand. "I'll get you a room. You need to be close to . . ." He suddenly became self-conscious. "Close to me and Suzanne. For work."

My mouth became completely dry. "Yes. For work."

He stood up to hug me, and his lips brushed my cheek. "I'll see you Thursday, Chocolate," he said into my ear. "I can barely wait."

# CHAPTER TWENTY-TWO

I wasn't sure how I made it home without dying, because I certainly wasn't paying attention to where I was going. All I could think about was the fact that Matías had a) kissed my cheek, b) said he needed me to be close to him, and c) left without seeing most of the evidence. I was the biggest moron in the world, and I didn't even care. I wasn't just walking on air; I was doing cartwheels over the jet stream. I didn't even look across the street when I crossed by the fatal water tanks. I waved at the young Chinese man painting over the wall of his store. I kicked pebbles with my shoes and skipped over the little ditches on the side of the road. Matías liked my photos. Matías said I was beautiful. Matías wanted me to be in the same hotel as him, and if that's not code for sex, I don't know what is.

I spent the rest of the evening chatting away with Eva as we washed dishes. I had never shared anything truly intimate with her before, but I couldn't stop my mouth from moving. I repeated every comment Matías had made, analyzed every look, recalled every gesture. Eva seemed wary of my new crush.

"Be careful with this one. He's a man. Not a boy."

"He's like twenty-eight. I'm twenty-one."

She shrugged. "Even so." Then she began listing her dating rules. Don't call him—*ever*, wear something seductive but not slutty, and bat your eyelashes. I couldn't deny that those tactics would get you a man; but would they get you a man that you wanted?

As I was washing my face, I saw an unidentified number flash on my phone. I hit speakerphone.

"*Preciosa*." My stomach began to ache. "I know you told me not to call but I couldn't help it." It was unidentified because Adrián was calling from Panamá. I could hear street noises in the background: car engines, children, vendors. "I need you to understand something. I'm sorry about Lucía. I'm sorry I didn't tell you the truth."

"It's okay, Adrián. I'm not mad about that."

"But I should've been more honest. Right from the start. I can't lose you over this."

The ache in my stomach was unbearable. "It's not about her."

"I really miss you," he said. His vulnerability was like a physical presence. I felt salt water begin to collect in the corner of my eyes. "Do you miss me?"

*What could I say that wouldn't make this worse?*

"It's okay," he said. "You don't have to answer."

I sat there in silence, pricking crescent moons into my cheek with my fingernails.

"We drove down the Pan-American Highway," he said. "It wasn't the same without you."

Now the water was trickling out of my eyes and down my face, mixing with the water from my chin. There was nothing wrong with Adrián. There was nothing wrong with me. We were just so different. "I'm sorry," I said finally, my voice choked with dryness.

"Don't be sorry." I could hear the constriction in his voice. "I guess . . ." He stopped speaking. A car horn blared. "Do you want me to call you when I get back?" I could hear how much that question cost him. And he couldn't put it on a card.

"Maybe not." Now I was crying and I knew he could hear me and I knew that me crying made it harder for him and that just made me cry harder. "I'll call you."

♥ ⦸ *

The next morning I was still emotionally unbalanced. Excitement about Matías and sadness about Adrián competed for dominance. I put Salsa Lizano in my coffee instead of in my *gallo pinto*, which I quickly learned was *not* an improvement. Abuelita *tsk-tsk*ed but gave me fresh coffee and added the salsa herself to my rice and beans. I thanked her, then silently told myself to *get it together, Dee.* I had a meeting with Suzanne in two hours and I needed to be in top form.

She was staying at the Fantasía Resort in Alajuela. It didn't look like a conference hotel; it looked like the jungle brought to the city. It was a collection of bungalows and suites spread out among ponds and stones and trees, with brightly colored toucans flitting from tree to tree. Steam wafted from the fern-covered patios where delegates drank their morning coffee, and rotting leaves collected in deep green pools. The air was so dense you could feel beads of moisture on your arms and face.

I found Suzanne sitting by herself at the café, wearing a white button-down top and elegant gray pants. She was not dressed for the tropics. She was dressed for a business-casual runway. I sat across from her and signaled to a waiter.

"Is everything ready for the trip?" she asked, sipping her cappuccino. "The donors should be congregating in the lobby soon."

"Yes. But there's been a change of plans. You'll be visiting Finca Atenas instead of Café Alegre."

"What?!"

"There's emergency roadwork on Route 126," I said. "Something about a boulder falling into the road? Two trucks in the ravine. Multiple fatalities. It would take all day to get to Café Alegre. We're very lucky I was able to arrange something else so quickly."

Suzanne absorbed this. "Oh. So you just set it up this morning?"

"Yes," I lied. "But while we're discussing Café Alegre. You know how you told me that if I wanted to make allegations about a farm, I needed concrete, irrefutable proof? So that we could actually do something with it?"

She nodded.

"You're totally right."

"I'm glad you finally understand."

"Thank you for mentoring me. I was really naive about all this."

She gave me a sweet smile. "My pleasure. It's part of the job. You know, Dee, we all start out naive. Nothing to be ashamed of."

"Thank you." I smiled back. "So . . . I *did* get solid evidence."

She put down her coffee. "What kind?"

"Receipts. Contracts. Interviews. Pictures. *Everything.*"

Her eyes widened. "Wow." I beamed with pride. "Matías mentioned you were an excellent sleuth but I thought he was exaggerating."

"Well, I had a lot of help."

"I'm rather blown away."

"Can I show it all to you?"

"Yes, I can't wait to see it." She finished her cappuccino. "But we'll have to do it tonight. I have to meet the donors now and play shrink." She gave me a wry smile. "They use their donations to erase their carbon footprint and guilt about their nannies and housekeepers and house managers." She rose. "Meet me in bungalow sixteen at eight o'clock tonight." She headed toward the lobby, then said over her shoulder, "I'm really impressed, Dee."

♥ ☕ ✱

I was buzzing with pride and caffeine as I left the café. I had impressed my boss, and I would see Matías tomorrow. Soon both of them would officially be on board, and together with the Professor, Clara, and Tomás, we would decertify Café Alegre. Then hopefully Las Nubes would regain their contracts. Things were finally working out!

I checked into the bungalow Matías had arranged for me. I couldn't even think about that detail or I would completely lose my mind. I took out my laptop and reorganized my arguments for decertification in what I hoped was an ironclad brief. Working for Uncle Aaron had finally paid off.

When I'd finished the brief, it became a lot harder to push Matías out of my mind. So I gave up. I obsessed about his dreamy eyes. Then, for variety, I obsessed about Café Alegre's decertification. Then, because I'm a masochist, I obsessed about Adrián. Then I obsessed about whether or not I needed a hairstyle that more clearly conveyed my personality. An undershave was out, but what about some shaggy layers?

By eight p.m. I had consumed six cups of coffee, eaten two dozen oily *bizcochos*, and run through countless permutations about how the next two days (and the rest of my life) were going to go. So I was feeling both sick and excited when I showed up at Suzanne's bungalow. I knocked on her door.

"It's unlocked," she said.

I opened the door and surveyed the dimly lit room. Suzanne

was reclining in an upholstered chair by an open window, sipping what looked like a Cuba Libre. There was a Coke can and a mini rum bottle on the table. Unease filled me. It was well known that Suzanne was sober. It was part of her mystique. One day, she decided to stop drinking, and that was it. She was just that formidable. Thunder rumbled and lightning crackled over the mountains. Rain started to pelt the window.

"Come have a drink," she said. Her normal erect posture was relaxed. I tried to peek into the partly opened minibar to see how many bottles were missing. She followed my gaze. "I see you've heard. I don't drink." She lifted an empty glass from the table and mixed me a rum and Coke. "It's not what you're thinking. I was never an alcoholic. I just decided I didn't want to drink anymore." Alarm bells rang in my head. Non-alcoholics never said, *I was never an alcoholic.* "Today I decided I wanted a drink. So I'm having a drink. That's it."

I sat in the chair opposite her, a little wary. "Did the trip go okay?"

She handed me my drink. From my new vantage point, I noticed three empty rum bottles in the wastebasket. "Fine. Finca Atenas was unremarkable. They won't be on the full trips."

"But the donors were happy?"

"Yes. I'm very pleased." Her expression was grim. She poured more rum into her glass. The Coke was so diluted it was beige.

"Pardon me saying so, but you seem . . . not pleased."

"It's unrelated," she said, flatly. "I was up for a chief of staff job with my home senator. I didn't get it."

"I'm sorry."

She downed her drink. "Not as sorry as me."

It was so startling to see her out of control. This was a woman who didn't even let her linen wrinkle.

"It's okay, I'm not one to dwell on spilled milk. Let's brighten the mood." She clinked glasses with me. "After all, we're celebrating! You are a bona fide sleuth!"

Her demeanor was so chaotic I wasn't sure what to think.

"Bring out the evidence!"

I pulled out my iPad. She smiled back, encouraging.

"Right," I said. "Well, Café Alegre verifiably doesn't abide by Ethical Coffee International rules. For example, they aren't a hundred percent organic. Here are a few photos."

Suzanne glanced at them, nodded, then put down her drink. "Question, Dee. Do you think any farm is really, truly, a hundred percent organic?"

My jaw dropped. "What?"

"You know what the Rust is?"

"Of course."

"It's a plague. An existential threat to coffee farms. So do you think there's any farm that wouldn't fight it however they can?"

"I mean, some farms will use only organic or approved fungicides."

She smiled at me. "Darling. Those don't work. No one is using them. And if you believe that, I'm afraid you've been taken for a ride."

I stared at her in noncomprehension. "You're saying it's okay if they use toxic chemicals? Even at the expense of the Earth?"

"Dee, if they don't fight the Rust, they lose their farms. They won't be able to worry about the Earth then. Who would be helped in that scenario?"

I couldn't believe what I was hearing. Our *whole deal* was advocating for environmental and social justice.

"Okay. But it's not just pesticides to fight the Rust. There are other violations." I scrolled through the camera roll to show her pictures of kids. "Alegre is using child labor. Want to see a video?"

She shook her head no and took a sip of her drink. "I'm so sorry to tell you this, Dee, but all the farms use child labor."

My jaw dropped further. Why was she so blasé?! "That's totally abhorrent."

"If we're talking about actual children, ten hours a day, I completely agree. But teenagers? Or kids helping out for an hour or two a day? We're talking about middle- and low-income countries, Dee. Kids work. They have to."

"People pay premium prices so those kids *don't* have to."

"Yes. And the sad thing is, even those prices aren't high enough." She started rummaging through the minibar for snacks. Her tranquility was in marked contrast to my inner turmoil. "Dee, darling." She handed me a napkin with cheese and crackers. "Let me explain something to you." The rain was really coming down hard now, and some was coming in through the window. "When I was your age, I was just like you. Naive, idealistic, rigid. Then something happened." She shook some peanuts onto my napkin. "Life. You'll learn, too, Dee. It doesn't make a difference if Alegre follows all the rules, because either way millions of workers are getting screwed by the global economy. And the differences are marginal in the working conditions between the 'ethical' co-ops and the conventional farms anyway."

I was so stunned I could barely make my voice work. "You know that's not true."

"Not true?" She gave a brittle laugh. "The kids get to finish five years of school as opposed to four? The problem is so much bigger than what you're looking at. If Costa Rican farmers all organize into Ethical Coffee International or other fair trade co-ops, they'll flood the market with expensive coffee. Supply will far outstrip demand, and they'll have put themselves out of business. Labor's cheaper in Vietnam. In twenty years, there'd be no coffee coming out of Central America at all."

"That's not true! Many consumers are happy to pay higher prices for better-made coffee."

"No, Dee, they're happy to pay for better *tasting* coffee. That's why direct trade is on the rise. Direct trade companies focus on quality—and that's what the consumer *really* wants. They slap words on the bag like 'hummingbird friendly' and 'partnership' so the consumer feels good. The consumer doesn't bother to check if those labels mean anything. And they do not bother to check how much of the premium price goes to the laborers working on the farms."

"All the more reason to fight for coffee that's strongly regulated!" I said. "And if you don't believe in sustainable practices and regulation, then *why is this your job*? Why do you run a nonprofit?" I couldn't stop my voice from rising. The room was turning into a sauna and I was about to melt down. *How had my mentor turned into my enemy?*

She looked at me with temporarily clear eyes. "First of all, I do believe in fair working conditions and organic farming. But I recognize that the real world is complicated. And I can't help everyone."

"So to hell with them?"

"Please, Dee, you're being hyperbolic. After the Truth Trips bring in lots of money to Justice Alliance—which I fully expect they will, if we use Café Alegre—I'll use the enhanced stature to run for office. When I'm in Washington and can write legislation, I'll try to help the people left behind. But I can't change world economics with one nonprofit." She rattled her empty glass. "I can't even get a chief of staff job."

"But why are you actively *choosing* Alegre when a good alternative like Las Nubes exists?"

"Alegre gets a lot of press. They're a big draw. And the Truth Trips are to make money. Period."

As I stared at her, it suddenly clicked into place. "You *knew* about Café Alegre. You don't care about seeing the videos because you already knew."

She bent down to the minibar to retrieve another rum bottle. There weren't any. She grabbed a bottle of vodka. "When you brought up your concerns after your first visit," she said, "I did a little digging myself."

A flash of lightning illuminated the dim room, and pain started welling between my temples. The swoosh-swoosh of her drink sloshing around the ice cubes was magnified. Now it all made a strange sense. Suzanne's indifference. Manuel talking about the snoop. How could I have been so stupid?

"Of course I didn't love what I found out," she said. "But, on balance, considering their positive press, I still felt Alegre was our best option. Perception is more important than truth, which I hope you're starting to understand."

I blinked hard. "Does Matías know about Alegre?"

"Probably not consciously. But he's a realist, like me. We focus on the greater good. Make enough money to fund our campaigns. Make consumers aware so they buy fair trade coffee. When the demand for organic, fair trade coffee is strong enough, *then* you can strengthen the enforcement of regulations."

Whatever blood remained in my head drained right out. A thick feeling of dread replaced it.

"I know all of this is difficult for you to accept now, Dee, but one day you'll understand what I'm saying." Her eyelids were heavy with nostalgia. "You remind me so much of myself when I was younger. One day—" She gave me a smile. "You'll be just like me." And with that she slumped over in her chair, dead drunk. Her tousled red hair splayed across the upholstery.

Something started rising from my gut and I knew I was going to be sick. I ran straight to the bathroom and knelt at the toilet. Vomit came out of me in great choking waves, and when it finally stopped, I rested my head against the porcelain. Justice Alliance was the Bad Guy. And I worked for them. I gagged again and put my mouth over the toilet, but nothing would come out except sticky yellow bile. My stomach heaved with contractions and my head throbbed with the effort, but there was nothing to expunge. The contractions wouldn't stop. I kneeled there, retching nothing, losing everything.

# CHAPTER TWENTY-THREE

I grabbed my bag from my room and took the last bus back to San José; I couldn't bear staying anywhere near Suzanne. Two hours later, I was buried in my bed in with the sheets pulled up to my chin, clutching at the comforter as if it could save me. All I could think about was the emptiness that started in my body but ended nowhere. It stretched out from me, went through my window, and into the night sky.

When I woke up the next morning, I remembered I was unhappy before I remembered why. Cheery sunlight was streaming through my window, but it only made me wince. Memories from last night started attacking me and I wanted to hide under my sheets, but I knew they'd still find me. I opened my email. I needed to remember that there was more to my life than farms and Suzanne. That my life was something vast, and that if part of it were destroyed, other parts would stretch out to cover the hole. There was a message from my parents, and for once, that made me happy.

TO: Dee Blum

FROM: Jacob Blum

SUBJECT: Happy New Year!

> Happy New Year, honey. Don't stay out too late and watch out for the drunk drivers. Also be careful because I've heard that sometimes people shoot off their guns to celebrate New Year's.
>
> Love, Dad
>
> Hello sweetie I'm using your dad's email because I forgot the password to mine again and locked myself out. Just want to say happy new year! I miss you so much, don't ever leave home again, especially not on a holiday. I hope this year brings you everything you wish for. I know if you want it badly enough, it will. Love, Mom

I sat there staring at those words for so long they started to blur. *If you want it badly enough.* Is that all it took? What about all the people who spend their whole lives wishing but never receiving? Desire wasn't enough. That was a terrible lie the 1 percent sold to the rest of us, to keep us hoping instead of revolting.

I closed my email and got dressed. Today was the People's Alternative World Economic Summit. I was supposed to meet Matías before the conference to show him the evidence. I didn't believe what Suzanne had said—that Matías wouldn't care if he knew about Alegre. While I dreaded seeing Suzanne, I wasn't going to let that stop me.

When I got to the Fantasía Resort, I passed straight through the lobby and wandered through the meticulously landscaped grounds, searching for Matías's bungalow. It was hard to find, because the number was half covered by paradise vines. Lavender flowers littered the ground. I knocked, full of jittery anticipation.

Matías opened the door. I gave him a big smile, expecting the same from him.

But I didn't get it. Instead, I got a small, perfunctory smile; the kind you give to an acquaintance. "Dee. You're very early." Nowhere was the hint of the person who said, '*I can barely wait.*'

Matías had been replaced by a stranger. Why was he so distant? What had changed? I stood there staring at his face, waiting for him to invite me in. But he just stood in the doorway.

"Can I come in?"

He ran his hands through his wavy hair, turned straighter from dampness. "I'm just getting ready. Why don't we meet up later?"

I was completely thrown. But I pushed on. After all, I had a goal, and it wasn't just romantic. "I'd like to chat before the conference starts and we're too busy. It won't take long."

He gestured to some seats outside his bungalow. He perched on the edge of his chair, as if he were ready to get up at any minute. I pulled out my iPad, still mystified by his change in energy. "I want Justice Alliance to lobby to decertify Café Alegre," I said. "These videos are the testimony of the laborers."

"I don't have time to watch them all right now."

*But that was the point of the meeting.* What was going on? Then it dawned on me. "Have you talked to Suzanne?"

"Briefly." My heart fell right down through the ground, under the hotel, into some subterranean stream that flowed to Puntarenas.

"Look, I don't know what she said to you, but I didn't even get to tell her all of Café Alegre's violations. They're buying commercially produced coffee and selling it as certified organic and fair trade."

"Oh." He looked surprised. "That's not good."

I smiled, relieved. But his expression changed from surprised to resolute.

"Listen," he said. "I know this is really important to you, and it's important to me, too, but this isn't something we can deal with right now."

"What?! Why?"

He met my gaze. "Café Alegre is too big for Justice Alliance to take down." It was so hard to process the words, especially since my blood was seeping through the stones, feeding the waters of Costa Rica.

"We have to pick our battles," he said. "Once a farm gets certification, it's very hard to remove it. Ethical Coffee International, understandably, would rather work with the farms on improving conditions. Café Alegre would put on a big show, clean up their act for six months, then go back to business as usual. It's whack-a-mole for the certifying organizations—they really don't have the time, or staff, to make sure farms stay in compliance."

"So once a farm gets certification, they just keep rubber stamping them?"

"No, it's not that bad. They would remove certifications for egregious violations. But I'm sure the folks at Alegre are clever enough to hide their tracks."

"But these *are* egregious violations. There are kids there."

"So Alegre pays off someone inside Ethical Coffee International to tip them off when an auditor is coming. They make sure the kids aren't there for that visit."

"They can do that?!"

"It's not that hard to bribe the cousin of someone's assistant to look at their calendar. So we'd need to be there every step of the way, applying pressure, maybe even applying financial incentives ourselves." He was running his hands through his hair again and it was getting frizzy. "Justice Alliance is spread too thin for that."

I scrambled, looking for a solution. "What if I presented the evidence to Ethical Coffee International as an individual, with Eugenio? Not as representatives of Justice Alliance?"

"I don't suggest you do that without approval from Suzanne. And I doubt you'd be successful. Do you two personally have the resources to fight this when Café Alegre starts playing dirty?"

I just stared at him. Of course we didn't.

Matías stood up. "Look. I'll try to convince Suzanne that Alegre shouldn't be part of the Truth Trips, but that's the best I can do right now."

Matías wasn't looking at me anymore. He was looking at his phone. I couldn't believe this. All this excitement, promise, belief—it was all crumbling into nothing right in front of me. This man that I counted on, this man that I believed in, this man I had thought I was falling for—was he going to let me down, too?

I stood up and faced him. "You're saying this isn't your problem?"

"I'm saying we have a lot of priorities as an organization. This is not how we want to use our political capital at the moment." He looked regretful. Could this truly be how he felt? Or had Suzanne pulled rank on him? "I really have to go, now, Dee." He reached for his key card. Before he could swipe it, I heard a sound *from inside the bungalow.* We both looked toward the door. Matías's face reddened as it swung open.

"Where's the hair dryer?" And there was Suzanne, in the doorway, dripping wet, in nothing but a towel. Bile came up my throat. *This* is what had changed.

"It's under the sink," he said, trying not to look at me. "I'll see you at lunch, Dee. We can talk more then." He grabbed his computer bag from inside the door and left.

Dazed, I watched him head toward the conference rooms.

Suzanne opened the door wider. "I can't stand here half naked. Come in, Dee." She rubbed water out of her eyes and crossed the room as I followed. She pulled on a robe and took in my crestfallen expression. "Are you still upset about Café Alegre?" She sat on the couch across from me. "I know how difficult this is for you, but I promise, you'll get over it. Politics is the art of compromise." When I didn't respond, she looked at me closer. "This isn't all about Café Alegre, is it?"

I averted my eyes and looked at the door. As Suzanne followed my gaze, her face went through a series of ah-has. She leaned back into the couch and wrapped her hair up in a hand towel she was holding. "It's about Matías."

My cheeks were burning and my eyes were stinging, but I didn't say anything.

"You'll get the next one." She tied her robe tighter. Her skin was absolutely perfect. "This wasn't a fair contest. You're too young for him. He's not one of those disgusting jerks who goes after college girls. He's an actual gentleman. In five years you can catch your own Matías. Now you need to settle for boys your own age."

My head sank into the chair cushion. Why had he slept with her when he cared for me? How had his feelings changed so quickly? Or had I been wrong about everything?

"I know what you're thinking," she said, peering into my brain, seeing my most intimate fantasies, defiling my most private hopes. "He did seem to have a thing for you." She rubbed moisturizer on her arms. "When he got in last night, he called me and woke me up. I was so drunk. What the hell did you and I do last night? My memories are so hazy." She touched her temples. "So I came over. He wanted us to call you and have a nightcap all together." Jesus. "I told him you were otherwise occupied." She smiled. "Amorously occupied."

Amorously? All oxygen fled my brain.

"Dee, here's some free advice. If you want something, take it. Don't worry about the details. And never underestimate the fragility of the male ego." She started walking toward the closet. "One more thing. If they don't fight for you—they're not worth it."

♥ ● *

I didn't go to the conference that morning. I went straight back to San José. Everything I believed in had turned out to be false. The man I had thought Matías was wouldn't give up on someone if he cared for them. The man I thought he was wouldn't give up on a political fight because his opponents were powerful. The man I thought he was . . . wasn't.

It was all too much for me. Disillusion at Café Alegre, deception from Suzanne, and now disappointment in Matías. And worst of all, my inability to help Clara and Las Nubes. I took one of the Central Market sleeping pills and slept for hours. When I woke up that evening, someone was knocking on my door. I picked up my phone from the tiles next to my bed to see the time. Nine o'clock. And I had fifteen missed calls and thirty-three texts. I heard another tentative knock and saw a thin strip of light come into my room from the crack beneath my door.

"Dee?" It was Eva. The concern in her voice brought hot tears to my eyes. Why hadn't I let her in more? She wanted a daughter. I needed a parent. "Can I come in?"

"Yes," I said. My throat was dry and my head was pounding. I looked around to see if I had a glass of water in the room. Eva opened the door slightly. She was carrying a glass of water. She came and sat on the side of my bed, then turned on the light on my nightstand. The lone bulb cast a rectangular shadow against the wall. Eva felt my hot forehead with the back of her cool hand.

"Are you okay?" Her eyes were shiny and wide with worry. She smoothed the hair away from my forehead as I sat up. "Here." She handed me the glass of water with Tabcin in it. I almost choked on the fizzy water. "Do you want to talk about it?"

I saw the genuine concern in her eyes and I thought about saying yes, but only for her. I didn't want to talk about it, to anyone, ever. I shook my head.

"You got a phone call on the house line an hour ago, but I didn't want to wake you. Should I have woken you?"

"No, that's okay." I tried to sit up straighter. "Who was it?"

"Clara Pérez."

A little bit of water escaped from my mouth. "Did she say what it was about?"

"No. She just said it was important." Eva wiped the corner of my mouth with the sleeve of her robe, just like I was her baby. "But I told her you were ill."

"I should call her back."

"You should rest." She pushed me back into my pillows. I had the feeling that she was happy I was sick. Not in an ungenerous way, but just because, finally, she got to take care of me.

"Could you do something for me?" I asked.

"Of course," she lit up.

"Could you make me some tea?"

"Right away." As she walked out of the room, I saw her mouth stretched into a smile. I resolved to ask her for more favors. Once I heard her fussing about downstairs, I picked up my phone. I tried calling Clara. The phone just kept ringing and ringing. When she finally answered on my fifth attempt, she sounded breathless and tense.

"Someone threw a Molotov cocktail into one of our warehouses," she said.

*A firebomb?* My breathing stopped.

"No one was seriously injured."

I let out a long breath. "Who was there?"

"Ramón and Héctor were unloading some berries, but they escaped the fire. Ramón was scratched by some flying debris. Héctor inhaled a little smoke. That's it."

My honorary big brothers. I shuddered with what might have been. "What happened to the warehouse?"

"Half of it burned to the ground. We lost some coffee."

I closed my eyes, trying to digest this information. Eva came up the stairs with tea. When she saw my face, she put the cup on my night table and went to her bedroom. She left the door open.

"We think it was Alegre," said Clara. My body filled with dread. "Does anyone know about the plan to decertify?"

"Suzanne and Matías from Justice Alliance."

"I told you not to tell anyone!"

Fear and guilt choked me. "I needed their support to take the evidence to Ethical Coffee International. No one is going to listen to Dee, college dropout from California, or Tomás, alienated and angry stepson."

"And they're not going to listen to me, the competition," she said, the anger draining out of her voice.

"Exactly. We need a neutral, respected body. Unfortunately, they said no. But I don't think Suzanne or Matías would've said anything to Alegre. They're not going to help us, but I don't think they would act *against* us."

"Did they see the footage?" she asked.

"They've seen a few photos. Why do you think it was Alegre?"

"Who else could it be, Dee?" she said. "And Héctor recognized the pickup truck."

"How would he know their truck?"

"The same truck was spotted here a few days ago, driving around the fields. Right when, well . . . when I discovered the Rust."

*Holy shit.* "You think they sabotaged your fields?"

"I know they did."

Jesus. But it made sense. The Rust rarely grew at that altitude. It must have been planted there. Alegre was ensuring Las Nubes didn't win the contract back.

"Dee, you need to get the evidence to Ethical Coffee International, *now*. As long as you're holding the evidence, we're all targets."

But wouldn't we still be targets? As long as Ethical Coffee International was investigating? *If* they investigated?

"This was just a warning, Dee. If they wanted to hurt someone, they could. Next time might not be so 'subtle.'"

I hung up the phone and stared at my cooling tea. A freaking *Molotov cocktail*? I was in way over my head. Was I making things better . . . *or worse*? Without Justice Alliance, I had no clear path to getting the evidence a fair hearing at Ethical Coffee International. What if I had opened up a whistleblowing can of worms, but instead of helping anyone, I had just put them in danger?

Maybe I should just return the evidence to Alegre, tell them we were dropping it, and return home. At least that way no one would get hurt.

I didn't know what to do. And unlike almost every other decision I'd had to make in my life, this one had serious consequences for other people. I paced my room, vacillating like the pendulum of a grandfather clock. Was discretion the better part of valor here? Or was it *just valor*?

My cell buzzed. It was a link from my father. *My website?*

I clicked the link and saw my bio had been completely rewritten. There was no mention of law school now.

*"Dee Blum, photographer, organizer, activist. Proudly fighting for social and environmental justice."*

Wow. My dad had finally found a way to tell me he supported me. Sure, he had impersonated me *again* to do it, but he had also given me my answer.

I went to Eva's room. She was in bed reading a romance novel. She put a bookmark in it, then looked up at me, expectant.

"Would you mind doing me another favor?"

# CHAPTER TWENTY-FOUR

Eva dropped me off at the Professor's front yard. His house was a small concrete block in desperate need of a paint job. Plaster was flaking off in three-foot sections, highlighting the political slogans the Professor had let kids spray paint on the walls. There were no bars on any of the windows, and the garden was an untended tropical mess. The steps creaked under my weight as I peered through the open front door.

"Dee!" said the Professor, coming to the door. "I couldn't understand your text. My generation doesn't use absurd abbreviations. Are you okay?" I nodded, waved at Eva, and shut the door behind me. I flopped down on a murky brown couch that was bleeding feathers. Just being in the Professor's house made me feel a little better, because somehow, it felt like home. Rugs from Guatemala mixed with pottery from Nicaragua and carved wooden statues from Cuba. On one faded red wall hung a full-length poster of Che, exactly like the one in his office.

"What's going on?" he asked, pouring me a cup of coffee.

"Someone threw a Molotov cocktail into one of the

warehouses at Las Nubes. No one was seriously hurt. Clara thinks someone at Justice Alliance tipped off Alegre."

The Professor just stared at me, with the coffeepot at a diagonal angle to the mug. Coffee spilled over the sides. "Why would she think someone at Justice Alliance tipped them off?"

"Because no one else knows."

The Professor put the coffee pot down. "Many people could know. We interviewed several people, and people talk." My hands shook as I tried to pick up the mug. "Don't worry, Dee. Alegre is bluffing." He picked up a dish towel and wiped the table. "I can't tell you how many times I've had someone try to scare me off with an explosion. But it's all show. Think of the problems it would create for them if they actually killed someone."

"Yeah, but 'accidents' happen."

He busied himself with cleaning so I couldn't read his expression. But he knew better than I did that people can and do get hurt over these things. He'd been in danger. He'd lost friends. He just didn't want me to be scared.

"We just need to get the decertification process started," he said, brightly. "Did you speak to Suzanne?"

"She's not going to help."

"Wow. That woman really likes to play things safe. But Matías will?"

"No."

The Professor dropped his teaspoon. "Of course he will."

I felt phlegm collect in the back of my throat. "Suzanne got to him. He said it's too risky for Justice Alliance. He said they have other priorities."

"*Matías* said that?"

I nodded. The Professor's fist curled so tightly against the saucer he was holding that he dropped it. It shattered, little pieces of clay spreading out on the hardwood floor like dirty snowflakes. Cream dripped down the wall.

"I'm sorry, Dee." He ran his hand across his forehead. "It's just that I'm close to Matías, and I thought I knew him better than that." The Professor put his great white head in his hands, and let his emotions pass through his face in private. I looked beyond him to the small table behind the couch. It was full of old pictures of a girl at different ages. The pictures stopped abruptly when she looked sixteen. *His daughter.* When the Professor looked up, his face was troubled. "It's hard being disappointed by people you care about. But everyone doesn't disappoint, Dee. I want you to know that."

The Professor looked at me quietly. And in the negative space of the words he didn't say, I heard his meaning. He stood up and walked back into the kitchen, hiding his feelings in the cabinets.

"So, it's you and me and Tomás," he said from the kitchen doorway, his voice once again even. "But we're not going to be successful without organizational support." He came back into the living room with a dustpan and rag. He gave the floor and wall a cursory cleaning, and then leaned back into his armchair. "It's too bad about Suzanne," he said. "It confirms my belief that the vast majority of Americans are self-centered. I remember when I was in Paris during the Spring of '68, coordinating actions between the students and the trade unionists. There was an American organizer from Massachusetts that . . ."

My mind drifted. It seemed like an interesting story, but it was unrelated to our present problem. I needed to figure out a way to get Justice Alliance behind us, despite Suzanne and Matías. I was deep in thought when I noticed something very odd was occurring. The Che poster was looking at me. Like, *really looking* at me.

*"Strike while the iron is hot!"* Che cried, ostensibly just in my mind. *"Smite Suzanne now! She's a bourgeois pig!"*

*What* was in that tea Eva gave me? Did it interact with the sleeping pills?

*"Kill her now, while conditions are favorable!"* cried a meticulously groomed Lenin, from a poster hanging right next to Che.

*"I'm not going to kill Suzanne,"* I answered, also just in my mind. I hoped. *"You two need to settle down."*

*"Don't think she wouldn't kill you if she were in your position,"* said Che.

*"Okay, no one is killing anyone,"* I said in my mind. *"We work at a nonprofit. We fight with words and innuendo."*

*"Naive, feckless American. If you want to be sovereign, you must exterminate all sources that limit your sovereignty,"* said Lenin. *"Justice is ruthless."*

Che and Lenin both glared at me. The Professor was still talking about Paris. Was I finally losing my mind?

*"Your duty is obvious,"* said Che, focusing his famously penetrating eyes on my own rather meek ones. *"Don't disappoint me."* And just like that, he was an inanimate poster again.

"Dennis, I believe his name was," said the Professor. I looked at him with a start. "Dee?"

"Sorry." I blinked my eyes. "I was just thinking about what to do." *And having a short break with reality.* "We have to find a way to force Suzanne and Matías to help us." *Without killing them.*

"Do you have anything on them?"

"No. But what if we told everyone at the summit tomorrow about the corruption at Café Alegre? The social pressure would be enormous. Justice Alliance would have to help us."

"You'd humiliate the organization," he said. "That would be counterproductive."

"What if we presented the information as sponsored *by* Justice Alliance?"

"How would we do that?"

"I know." I got up, suddenly energized, and headed to the door. The Professor followed me. So did Che and Lenin.

*"Don't forget what we said,"* said Lenin. *"Smash in her bourgeois skull!"*

*"Be a New Man!"* said Che, swinging his machete above his head. *"Smite the opponent of the people!"*

"What are you looking at, *Comefuego*?" asked the Professor, following my line of sight.

"Nothing." *Definitely not imaginary bloodthirsty revolutionary friends.* "Let's go." I looked at Che and Lenin. "Not you two."

♥ ☕ *

Thirty minutes later, the Professor and I were sitting in his office at the university, trying to become proficient filmmakers. I had remembered that Justice Alliance was going to show a promotional video for the Truth Trip tomorrow at the People's Alternative World Economic Summit. So the Professor and I were going to hijack the original and show *our* version to three hundred attendees, plus whomever was watching on the livestream. This public airing of Café Alegre's crimes would put Justice Alliance in a position where they *had* to help with the decertification of Alegre. I wished we could out Alegre's dirty deal with Café Bavaria, but this was the one piece we didn't have solid evidence for.

It was humid and warm, so we had all the windows open. I looked at the outline of palm trees against the dark-blue sky, and the soft orange glow above San Pedro. It was strange to be in a school building right now; heat and night weren't things I associated with academics.

"This is how you spend your evenings?" asked the Professor, as I downloaded all my footage onto his computer. "Don't you have a boyfriend? Where is he?"

"I don't have a boyfriend anymore. I was kind of cruel to him."

"People have a way of forgiving cruel behavior when there's infatuation involved," said the Professor. "It helps you forget a lot of things."

"That's true."

And then it hit me. What I had felt for Matías wasn't true affection; it was infatuation. He was a fantasy I had concocted; a cipher, the perfect revolutionary knight.

But Adrián. He was real. And he had consistently been there for me. Joining me on political adventures he had no interest in—or even flat-out disagreed with. Pushing me to be brave, but also accepting me as I was. Maybe he didn't fully understand me, but he *valued* me.

"Could you excuse me for a minute?" I asked the Professor.

The Professor graciously pretended our conversation and my request were unrelated. I went into the hallway to coax food out of the vending machine, then picked up my phone. I wasn't sure what I was going to say. I didn't know exactly *how* things had changed for me. I only knew that they had.

"*Preciosa.*" Relief flooded Adrián's voice when he heard mine. "I've been looking for you everywhere. You wouldn't answer your cell, so I kept calling the house. Eva insisted she didn't know where you were until I told her it was an emergency." Sweet Eva, doing her best to keep up with my complicated love life. "She finally told me you were at the Professor's, so I went there, but the house was dark."

"We're at the university."

"Can I come there?"

I closed my eyes, considering. The air was so heavy with consequences. "We're in his office."

Thirty minutes later there was a knock on the door. I exited the office and stood in the hallway with Adrián. When he saw my bloodshot eyes, his eyes widened with worry. "What happened to you?"

"I'm okay," I said, even though that wasn't a hundred percent true. "Let's go outside."

Adrián reached out for my arm, but then remembered everything that wasn't, and drew back. I wished he hadn't. He opened the door for me and followed me into the courtyard. There was a crescent moon hanging low in the sky. We sat down on the steps that surrounded the fountain. Moonlight glinted off the thin palm leaves, casting shifting shadows over us. It was like we were in a silver mine. And he looked at me like I was the most precious nugget there.

"I want to apologize again," he said. "About not being totally truthful."

"No, Adrián, I need to apologize to you."

"About what?"

"It wasn't fair of me to be with you while I was so confused. It was selfish. And maybe its own kind of untruthfulness."

"What? No. Everyone has the right to take a relationship at their own pace. I shouldn't have pressured you for more than you were ready for."

"You didn't pressure me."

"I did. I knew you weren't all in. I just didn't want to believe it." He sat straighter and took a deep breath. "Look, I've been thinking about us a lot. I know we're different, but honestly, I think that's what makes it great. I learn things from you. And hopefully you learn things from me." One of his hands hovered in the air by my cheek. But he didn't touch me. "But I thought about something else. You were right about Alegre. You can fight these battles and you should." The wind changed direction and he was bathed in moving silver light. "I want to help you."

The muscles in my jaw went slack. These were not words I expected to come out of his mouth. "But you said I couldn't change the world. That I should start with individuals."

"The people at Las Nubes are individuals. Start with them."

"I don't want you to do this for me."

"Don't flatter yourself." He smiled, both tender and teasing. "I'm doing it because it's right."

And at that moment, the disillusion I was harboring about the world dissipated and floated off into the night. The Professor was right. Everybody doesn't disappoint you. And sometimes they surprise you. I leaned over and hugged Adrián. At first, his arms were tentative, resting lightly on my back. But I drew him in closer.

"I want to testify against them," he said.

"But Café Bavaria is involved," I said, pulling back to look at him. "This implicates your cousin."

"Only by marriage. And he's a Nazi—I am *not* owning that relationship." I laughed, a welcome release. He gave me an adorable lopsided smile. "Look, when you go to Ethical Coffee International, I'll tell them everything I know about Café Bavaria." He pulled out his phone and showed me his Google Drive. "These documents prove the under-the-table deal between Alegre and Bavaria. I stole them from Dieter."

"What?! How?"

"I went there yesterday, after I got back from Panamá. His laptop passcode was his birthday."

"Wow, so boomer." I stared at Adrián. I couldn't believe he had gotten the final evidence for us! But then I thought about his future. "Isn't it going to piss off your family if you testify against your *cousin*?"

"Probably."

"But you work for your dad."

"Not anymore. I quit."

"What?!"

"I never wanted to work in the hotel business. I was just going with the flow. I always go with the flow. That's the same reason I didn't tell you about Lucía. Because it was easier. But watching you leave your family, your country, and take on Alegre. Well, it inspired me."

"*I* inspired *you*?"

"Yes. Because you don't go with the flow, Dee. You swim upstream."

I couldn't speak. I never felt like I was good enough or brave enough. But Adrián did. He took my hand. "I want you to know something," he said. With his other hand, he softly brushed back the stray hairs from my forehead. "This isn't about us." His eyelashes were heavy with moisture. "You know how much I care about you. You know I want this to work." He looked down and I saw one perfect, shining tear in his lashes. "But I respect your decision. If you don't want . . ." He couldn't finish that sentence. I could feel his body trembling. I could feel mine trembling. I didn't want him to let go of my hand.

"Whatever you decide about us is fine," he said. "But we're going to do this thing together. We're going to get Alegre. And either way," he paused again, "I'm your ally." I could see more than one perfect tear now. "And your friend."

I felt so many emotions: relief, affection, desire, uncertainty. Part of me wanted to say: *Forget everything I said in Manuel Antonio! Let's get back together! I made a mistake!* But another part of me said: *Wait. Be sure this time.*

Adrián watched the kaleidoscope of emotions flit across my face. "Is there a chance for us, *Preciosa*?"

I looked at his beautiful, open, vulnerable face. Yes. There was a chance.

But I couldn't hurt him again. "I need to be sure before I answer that. Can I sleep on it?"

He smiled, hope beating out fear. "Take all the time you need."

We stood up and walked back to the steps, our arms touching, my mind whirling.

♥ ☕ ✱

The Professor was hard at work editing. I tried to put romance out of my mind and focus on the task at hand. We had my stills from all the farms, as well as the video footage from Alegre and Doña Belén's testimony at Café Bavaria. I called Clara and recorded an interview over the phone. After a few hours of splicing, we had a rough cut. I also had a raging headache.

"I can't look at this anymore. I can't tell what's good and what's terrible."

"Go home," said the Professor. "I'll finish it up."

"But—"

"But nothing. Adrián will take you home. All the content is done. It's just a matter of editing it more cleanly. Don't you trust me?"

Only one right answer to that question. "Of course."

"Then goodnight." He rose and pushed us out the door. "Meet me here at six a.m."

Adrián and I walked to the parking lot. This was the most awkward moment yet. I didn't know how to be with him without holding his hand or kissing him, and I knew that it was even stranger for him. Just when the tension of all that was missing became unbearable, we heard a loud explosion. I jumped into his arms. "What was that?"

"Fireworks."

"Why?"

"It's New Year's Eve." As he spoke, three giant pink mums exploded above us. I looked up and laughed; I had forgotten. The sky was crackling with purple and pink and green. I caught my breath. Fireworks always make me a little teary. We create these complicated things, then blow them up. All that work, just to feel something for a moment.

Adrián took out his handkerchief, an old-fashioned touch that delighted me. He dabbed at the corner of my eyes. There was an enormous *Pop! Pop! Pop!* as the entire sky ignited.

"What time is it?" I asked, watching the lights fizzle out as they fell to Earth.

Adrián pulled out his phone. "One minute till midnight." We looked at each other, painfully aware of a certain tradition that was sixty seconds away. "Have you made a resolution?"

I thought for a moment. "Yes." *Many.* "Have you?"

He nodded. A bell tower began to ring. I was still in his arms, with my mouth very close to his. Our mouths moved closer, like magnets outside of our control. He kissed me gently on the lips. "Just for New Year's."

"Just for New Year's." And then I put my cheek next to his, and I held him very tight.

# CHAPTER TWENTY-FIVE

Early the next morning, Adrián picked me up. As we drove to the university, we passed people still celebrating New Year's. It gave me the sensation that I had never slept and that yesterday just hadn't ended. It hadn't for the Professor; we found him slumped over his desk. After we roused him, we hopped into his Jeep and went downtown to pick up Tomás and Mario. I knew Tomás would want to be at the conference when we showed the video. I also knew he would look at it as a business opportunity.

"There's going to be lots of people there, right?" he asked, holding a bag full of rubber cows and chickens. "With disposable income?"

It was nearing eight a.m. by the time we got to Alajuela. The Justice Alliance video wasn't scheduled to show until noon, but we still had to get to the hotel, scout out the area, and figure out a way to show the video the whole way through without Suzanne stopping it.

When we got to the Fantasía Resort, we fanned out. Tomás and Mario went to secure the goodwill of the hotel employees, Adrián went to find out who the manager was, and I went to assess the tech situation. The Professor was going to locate representatives from Ethical Coffee International and give them copies of our video.

I was apprehensive about my mission. What if there wasn't a separate area we could secure to upload our video? What if it was just a laptop in the back of the conference room? I finally found the empty Esmeralda Ballroom, where disco balls and fake trees coexisted in uneasy harmony. There was a bar on one side and a small stage with a screen and a podium. There were no windows, the ceiling was high, and the floor was smooth linoleum. It reminded me of a high school multipurpose room. Completing the effect were hundreds of folding chairs set out on the floor, facing the stage.

I scanned the room and saw an enclosed control booth in the back, about twenty feet up, right above the crowns of some plastic palm trees. I couldn't see any doors leading to it, so I decided to look backstage. To get to the control booth in my high school theater, you went up a backstage stairwell, then crossed the length of the theater in a second-story hallway. This layout was similar. I found the door that led to a staircase and went up.

The control booth was also just like my high school control booth, without the marijuana butts or used condoms. There was a laptop on a desk and a control panel. Now I would just have to figure out how to keep Suzanne out of the booth.

Reconnaissance completed, I left the ballroom and met up with Adrián, Tomás, and Mario in one of the smaller hotel bars. It felt like midnight in there, with maroon plastic booths and dark purple walls, candles in the middle of tables, and Mexican ballads coming from the stereos. It was only ten a.m., but people were already knocking back drinks, in denial that last night had ended and a new year had begun. The four of us took a booth and ordered Bloody Marys. I was way beyond policing

Tomás and Mario's alcohol consumption; as far as I was concerned, they were adults now.

"We need a way to secure the door to the control booth," I said, batting the celery stick around my tomato juice, wondering if the antioxidants from the vegetables counteracted the toxins from the booze. I mean, they had to be doing *something*.

"We've figured it out," said Adrián, sipping his drink like it was water. "Tomás is going to pose as a hotel employee and Mario will be a lookout. They'll hang around the door to the staircase and make sure Suzanne can't get into the control booth."

"No way she's getting past me," Tomás said smugly, enjoying his role as "the muscle." Mario's eyes widened with concern. Perhaps he was not as enthusiastic about the plan.

"But what if she causes a commotion?" I asked.

"I'll pretend to call the manager," said Tomás.

"Then I'll take over," said Adrián.

"Why would she believe you're the manager?" I fiddled with my straw. "And what if the real hotel employees hear her complaining?"

Adrián pulled out a name tag from his pocket. *José Rivera, Assistant Manager*. "We had a little 'chat' with the staff." He rubbed his fingers together in the gesture of a bribe. "No one's going to bother us."

"She's going to freak out when she sees the video. She's going to bust through that door if she has to."

"I'm taking care of it." He put his arm around me. Little thrills traveled from my waist to my head. "*Tranquila*."

I tried to relax, but I couldn't stop thinking of all the things that could go wrong. The tech person could refuse to swap videos. Suzanne could find out that the Professor was distributing videos to Ethical Coffee International reps and cancel the presentation. If we didn't have the audience as witnesses, we'd lose the crucial social pressure aspect. I was so nervous, I decided to order a coffee to balance out the Bloody Mary. It was steaming, but I took a sip anyway.

"How is it?" asked Adrián.

"Nice," I said. "It has a full, creamy body. Hazelnut and . . . hmm, nectarine."

He looked at me, amused. "You're like a professional taster now."

"You're right!" I looked at the cup, amazed. "I am!"

"So, have you decided, do you like single origins better, or blends?"

"Both."

"But he asked which was *better*," said Tomás.

I placed my hand on Adrián's and looked at him. "I decided that maybe what you like doesn't have to be your whole identity. Maybe you can be multiple things."

Adrián smiled so tenderly. He understood. "*Cada persona es un mundo.*"

I nodded. "*Cada persona es un mundo.*"

"Well, I like Bloody Marys better," said Tomás.

The guys ordered another round while I enjoyed my hazelnut-nectarine coffee. Adrián left his arm around my waist the whole time, and amid my anxiety, I had to admit I was happy. When I was near Adrián, my whole body just felt *good*. Did that mean this was right? Was my body telling me something my mind was too stubborn to hear?

The Professor slid into the booth next to Tomás and Mario. "Ethical Coffee International will be at the Justice Alliance presentation at noon. And they will have a meeting with Justice Alliance at two."

"What if Suzanne finds out between now and when we show the video?" I asked.

"I told them you were the point person. Besides, they're all in different meetings right now. They're not going to see Suzanne."

"So we're all ready?"

"Yes." The Professor picked up a glass. "To our first collective revolutionary act." We all clinked glasses. "May it be the first of many. No machetes required."

♥ ◐ ✱

At eleven forty-five the five of us sailed through the open double doors of the Esmeralda Ballroom. Well, the Professor and Adrián sailed, and Tomás, Mario, and I staggered. The Professor took up a position near the front. He was in charge of keeping an eye on Suzanne and Matías during the showing of the video to make sure they didn't take over the microphone. Tomás and Mario went backstage to man the door to the control booth, and Adrián stood in the wings. I scanned the room. My penultimate task was personal. I wanted to see Suzanne and Matías one last time. I needed to show Suzanne that she hadn't beaten me, and show Matías that he hadn't diminished me.

Finding them was difficult. The Esmeralda Ballroom was packed to the gills with people dressed in black and charcoal, in accordance with the rules of protestor chic. I had chosen today to sport a new red dress Eva had helped me pick out. This was a new year, I was a new person, and also, I wanted Matías to be sorry. The assembled used-clothing couture crowd gasped as I walked by. I was so unfashionably fashionable.

After traversing the length of the ballroom several times, and eliciting more than one judgy look, I spotted Suzanne at the far end of the bar, sipping mineral water. As usual, she managed to look elegant without looking out of place. Matías was by her side. I stopped to watch them. When she laughed, she leaned in closer to him. Waves of ill-defined emotions crashed over me. I didn't know if I was jealous; I only knew that I hurt. And that I had had a reason for going to see them, but I'd forgotten it.

I was about to go backstage, but then Suzanne turned to Matías and pecked his lips. And for some reason, I had to go forward. I pushed my way through the tipsy bullshitting multitudes, ignoring anyone who said anything like "Ow," or "Hi," or, "What do you think of American hegemony?"

Suzanne and Matías were talking with two people I didn't know. The woman had bleached, spiky hair; a black denim miniskirt from the eighties; and a hand-sewn blouse from Mexico. The man was tall and painfully skinny, with a scruffy goatee and a green ski cap.

"But the Roman Empire fell," he said.

"It was overextended," the woman replied.

"Are you really defending the present expression of Manifest Destiny?" he asked.

I came from behind and tapped Matías on the shoulder. When he turned around, his eyes filled with heat. Maybe he regretted his choice; maybe it was my dress. Suzanne didn't notice me. She was too busy discussing American Imperialism.

"You made it," he said softly. "I was so worried when you left yesterday. I felt bad about our conversation. I felt bad about . . . everything." The kindness in his voice came at me like a lifeline. But I wasn't sure if I should take it.

"Matías." I leaned in close. "Are you sure you won't reconsider? Please just think about it for a minute. The people at Las Nubes need Justice Alliance's help."

Matías's forehead creased. "You know I want to."

"Then why don't you?" He looked into my eyes, then across the room, and finally to the floor. And then I realized. *Because he didn't have the guts.* This wasn't the man I had started to fall for. That man only existed for moments. But the moments didn't string together. By themselves they were nothing.

"Dee!" said Suzanne, just spotting me. "I'm so glad you came." She gave me an air kiss.

"I just wanted to ask you one more time," I said. "Will you help me blow the whistle on Café Alegre?"

Suzanne gave me a condescending smile. "Honey, you know how much I want to get those bastards." She put down her mineral water, leaned into the bar, and asked the bartender for a "special water." "But we just can't right now."

And suddenly their collective hypocrisy was more than I could bear. "That's not the reason you gave me the other night. Why don't you tell Matías what you told me?"

"I don't know what you're thinking of," she said in a light voice. "Honestly, Dee, you need to relax. You've been working hard and we're so proud of you. Why don't you get a drink and then join us for the screening? We'll be sitting in front." And with that, Suzanne took her vodka tonic from the bartender and headed off into the crowd.

Matías started to follow her, then stopped to look at me. Was it wistfully? It may have been wistfully. "Maybe we can do it later, Dee," he said. "It's just not the time."

"I'm begging you."

He hesitated. But he let go of the line. "I can't."

I turned around without another word and looked for a way out. People surged at me like waves, and I knew they would sink me. I had nothing to hold on to. I spotted a door and went toward it. I found an empty hallway and leaned against the rose wallpaper. I still couldn't accept Matías's capitulation to Suzanne. If the people leading the fight weren't fighting—what hope was there for change? It all felt so pointless.

As I wrestled with that horrible feeling, I heard footsteps come around the corner. I straightened up and tried to look composed. Had I been crying? My face was wet.

"*Preciosa.*" It was Adrián, in his white shirt and José nametag. When he saw my wild eyes, he became concerned. He knew he wasn't meant to witness this. "I'm sorry. Do you want me to leave?"

"No." I wiped some of the tears off my cheek. I could taste salt in the corner of my mouth. Adrián took a tentative step forward. He took my hand, and when I smiled at him through my mist, he took me into his arms. I pressed my head against his chest. He held me closer.

"It's okay. Whatever it is, it's going to be okay." He stroked the back of my head. "I'm sure of it."

"You were right. About Sartre. About life being a futile passion."

"Oh, I've moved on from that," he said, cheerily. "Now I'm reading *The Plague*."

I blanched. "That sounds worse."

"On the surface, yes. Most people would say it's also about futility. That Camus believes there's no intrinsic moral or rational meaning in life."

"Great."

"But I actually think it's uplifting."

"Weird take. But I could use some uplifting."

"Well. There's no God. There's no meaning." He wiped a tear from the corner of my eye. "And the plague is killing everyone."

"Do you know what uplifting means?"

He smiled and caressed my cheek. "But even though it is futile, the doctors and nurses keep showing up to fight it. Even though they're in danger of dying themselves. If there's no meaning, why do they do it?"

"You tell me."

"Because we are beings that love. Beings that can't help but care. It doesn't matter if there 'is' meaning. Where there is no meaning, we make it."

The tears came back. But they were of a different kind. "Adrián," I said. "You give me meaning."

His face filled with so much light, I had to kiss him. So I did. And everything that had been so unclear was finally clear. Different didn't mean wrong; it just meant different. I could finally make a choice. I was choosing him.

# CHAPTER TWENTY-SIX

I went back to the Esmeralda Ballroom and slipped backstage. Mario was pacing nearby, wishing he were anywhere but here. Tomás, chest puffed up with importance, gave me a thumbs-up and let me through the door to the stairwell. I went up the stairs. When I reached the control booth, I saw a young man wearing a uniform and a name tag that said Ernesto. He had dark brown hair, a freshly shaven face that didn't seem to need shaving, and innocent brown eyes. He stood up from his stool.

"Can I help you?" he asked in lightly accented English.

"Yes," I said, rubbing my necklace. I was wearing it around my wrist, doubled up like a bracelet. "I work for Justice Alliance. I'm Suzanne Lyon's assistant." I pointed at Suzanne through the glass window. She was standing near the podium talking to a woman in a silk suit. "We gave you an earlier version of our video by mistake. Here's the latest one." I handed him a flash drive. "Pop it in, I'll show you which one."

"You sure? Suzanne herself sent me the video on Vimeo."

"Completely sure. I sent her the wrong one this morning. And if I don't fix it . . ." I made a slicing motion over my neck.

"Ah. Say no more."

He stuck the drive into the computer. "See," I said, pointing to the documents folder. "Just Trade for a Just Economy, Final Version."

"Huh." He downloaded it onto his desktop. We looked at the two versions. *Just Trade for a Just Economy, Final Version*, and *Just Trade for a Just Economy, Final.*

"You guys need a better naming system," he said, more riled up than I would've expected. "You could go by date. Version number. A, B, C. But writing 'final' leaves a big margin for error."

"That's great advice. Thank you."

He erased Suzanne's version, still irritated.

"Do you mind if I sit up here and watch it with you?" I asked.

"There is no problem." He pulled out a second stool for me and gave me a toothy grin, apparently over the file-naming debacle. "Are you avoiding someone?"

"A lot of someones." I sat down and looked out the window. "I find these events very intimidating."

"Me, too," he said. "That's why I'm a tech." He flicked the overhead lights on and off. People started heading to their seats. He pointed to his light board. "This has over ninety different faders and it's still less complicated than people."

Everything was less complicated than people. I pressed my nose to the glass and looked for Matías. I finally saw him in the first row. He was talking to a woman on his right, and there were two empty seats on his left. When Ernesto flashed the lights for the last time, Matías turned around in his seat and scanned the audience. I knew he was looking for me. The lights went off and his face was covered in shadow. A soft light came up on stage, and there Suzanne was, standing behind the podium. Ernesto focused the spotlight on her, bathing her in an orange halo.

"I'd like to say a few words before we start," she said into the microphone, flicking her flame-red hair over her shoulder. "Justice Alliance has been spearheading a campaign in the United States to bring organic, fairly traded coffee to all consumers. We've had a string of successes in progressive cities like San Francisco and Portland. I'm proud to announce that we're about to expand, kicking off a campaign in the Midwest." Polite applause.

"To achieve political success, you must educate the public, and that's why we work so hard on communication. The video you're about to see was produced to promote our newest Truth Trip. These Truth Trips, and the campaigns they finance, wouldn't be possible without the help of many people." She looked toward the front row. "First, I'd like to thank Matías Khalil, our lead organizer. Without your dedication, Justice Alliance would not be the premier nonprofit in the social and environmental justice space." She gave him a warm look. "I'd also like to thank my colleague, Dee, for her tireless work on behalf of the Truth Trips." She smiled insincerely for one second, then looked toward the camera filming her from the back of the room.

"But most of all, I'd like to thank the people who make this all possible in the first place: our partners in the Global South. When these men and women go to work, they're not just producing coffee; they're taking on the global economy. When they offer us their coffee, they're telling us, we *do* have a choice. We can choose fairness. We can choose sustainability. We can choose to build a better world, cup by cup." She found her light and moved into it. "So I want to give my most heartfelt thanks and respect to the pioneering cooperative farmers of Costa Rica. Please help me welcome one of them here today."

Ernesto shone the spotlight on the seat next to Matías—which was now occupied by none other than *Don Manuel*. He stood up and waved at the audience. I had a small heart attack. *Shit shit shit.*

Suzanne waited for the applause to die down. "Thank you, Don Manuel. With no further ado, I am pleased to present *Just Trade for a Just Economy.*" Ernesto dimmed the spotlight and Suzanne sat next to Manuel.

*"We're all aware of the deplorable conditions found in the apparel industry,"* said my voice. *"But are we aware of the equally abominable conditions coffee farmers confront in outdoor sweatshops?"* The screen showed a photo from Café Bavaria of a young boy bent over a coffee bush, his face red and shiny with sweat. Suzanne and Matías looked at each other in surprise; this was not their video.

Another still appeared on-screen: *Doña Belén, looking straight at camera.*

*"When you drink your coffee in the morning, do you taste the suffering in your cup?"* asked my voice.

Suzanne sat upright on the edge of her seat, trying to understand what was happening.

Photos from Café Bavaria flickered across the screen as Doña Belén's voice described the terrible conditions in conventional *cafetales.* Suzanne seemed to be in shock.

*"Fortunately, there is an alternative,"* said the Professor's voice. A still from Las Nubes came on. It was of Clara, Héctor, and Ramón at the mill. *"Cooperative and organic farms like Las Nubes show us that it doesn't have to be this way."*

Don Manuel's face went red at the sight of Clara. He turned to Suzanne and said something, clearly *pissed.* This shook Suzanne out of her stupor. She bolted up and walked toward the back wall, trying to find the entrance to the control booth. She paced back and forth along the wall, looking for a door, until she finally went out the hallway. *She was going to find the door soon.*

Now Clara's voice came over the stills. *"Cooperation is about more than working together. It's about working for each other. It's about the worth and dignity that each person has, and not the worth that each thing has. It's about being fair. And it's about hope."*

More photos faded in and out: Héctor and Ramón raking the beans, kids playing games at the community center, a young couple pointing proudly at their first harvest. I stared in surprise at my own photos; they looked so different. They had just been pictures before. Now they were testimony.

*"But unfortunately,"* said the Professor's voice, *"all is not well in the cooperative kingdom. Some bad actors, like Café Alegre, pose as an ethical, sustainable, organic producer to unfairly profit."* A photo of Don Manuel in Café Alegre's tasting room flashed across the screen.

In the audience, Don Manuel stood, apoplectic. "What the hell is this?!" People turned to look at him. Matías reached for his arm, trying to get him to sit back down. "No, I will not sit!" he shouted. "Stop this video now! This is slander!" Don Manuel ran in front of the screen to try to block people's view. The audience gasped. Professor Ramírez ran toward him. Oh god, I hope he left his machete at home. This was an absolute train wreck. Why, *why* had Suzanne invited Manuel?!

"Sit down!" someone yelled in Spanish from the back of the audience.

"*¡Vete pal carajo!*" said Don Manuel.

Ernesto moved the spotlight to the person who'd spoken in the back. It was Clara! *OH MY GOD.* The Professor must have invited her. "We know you sabotaged our plants, you *hijueputa*!" she said to Manuel. "And you set our warehouse *on fire*!"

The audience gasped in unison. This was by far the best conference any of them had ever attended.

"I will sue the shit out of you!" said Manuel, evading the Professor and running offstage to rush Clara.

Suddenly Héctor and Ramón stepped out of the shadows to block Manuel. Were they going to *fight*?!

I heard a loud thump at the bottom of the stairwell. *Suzanne.* I turned to Ernesto. "Do not let anyone into this room until the video is over. *Please.*"

He nodded.

I ran down the steps and paused at the closed door. I could hear Suzanne arguing with Adrián and Tomás on the other side. "But this is the wrong video!" she was saying. "I need to get in to switch it!"

"I'm afraid it's against company policy to have non-employees in restricted areas," said Adrián's voice, cool as a mud mask from Volcan Arenal. "Why don't we go to my office and discuss this calmly? Then we can get to the bottom of this."

"I'm not going *anywhere* until I put the correct video on."

"Why don't you just give it to me?" Adrián asked. "I'll switch it."

"Because you are totally incompetent! You let this happen in the first place. Tell your employees to get away from that door."

At that moment, Suzanne wasn't just Suzanne, and she wasn't just someone who was insufferably rude and hypocritical. She was everyone who had ever made a decision for me. But I wasn't the same Dee. I opened the door, locked it from the inside, slipped out, and shut it tight behind me. Tomás had been blocking the door and staggered when it opened.

When Suzanne saw me, her face filled with rage. "What kind of stunt is this, Dee?"

"Justice Alliance will contact Ethical Coffee International about decertifying Alegre immediately following this video."

"We'll do no such thing." She tried to push by me to the door.

"I think you'll feel differently once you've seen the whole video." I watched her wrestle with the locked door.

Frustrated, she turned back on Adrián. "Let me in this instant! You see that she was in there."

"This is highly irregular, Miss," said Adrián. "Neither of you is allowed in there. I'm going to have to take both of you back to my office so we can straighten this out." Adrián pulled a walkie-talkie out of his back pocket and took a step into the shadows, pretending to call security.

Suzanne turned back to me. "Just who the hell do you think you are? Let me in that goddamned booth or I'll fire you."

"Go ahead."

Suzanne's body went rigid. "Do you realize what I could do to you? I'll have you blacklisted from every nonprofit in San Francisco, LA, New York, DC. Every city in the whole goddamned country." Fury ran through her body like an electric shock. "And not just the nonprofits. I know people everywhere. You'll be working in a laundromat if you don't let me into that room! You're making an enemy *for life*."

"We're not turning off this video." I could feel my cheeks redden, but I didn't feel scared. I felt *great*. "And when it's over, there will be three hundred witnesses that Justice Alliance has exposed Café Alegre and intends to lobby for their decertification. Plus, who knows how many thousands are watching the livestream. So you'd better start considering your options."

I pushed by her to see what was happening with Manuel and Clara. Suzanne followed me. We both stopped at the edge of the wings, amazed. Héctor, Ramón, and Professor Ramírez were hustling Don Manuel out of the room as he screamed bloody murder.

"Get your paws off me! I wish I'd burned down your whole goddamned farm!" Several attendees were recording his rant with their phones.

Clara looked toward the wings and caught my eye. She smiled: *Got the bastard*. I smiled back. Suzanne grimaced.

I turned my attention to the screen. Photos of Café Alegre flitted by; pictures of kids in the fields, exhausted laborers, the black boxes. The audience gasped at the pesticides.

"Oh my god," said Suzanne, as a photo of Manuel came on the screen, carrying his shotgun.

*"Is Café Alegre really a happy place to work?"* my voice asked. *"When they have conditions equal to that of a conventional farm?"* Photos of tired and sunburned pickers flashed across the screen in quick succession. *"And when a corporate farm like Café Bavaria sells their surplus as fair trade, organic coffee through a backchannel arrangement with Café Alegre, one has to ask, is there any difference at all? Or is Café Alegre merely one more sad face in the deceitful visage of global exploitation?"*

Suzanne closed her eyes in pain, realizing she had been checkmated.

I turned to her. "Go back there and put on a happy face. Accept their congratulations." I smiled, just a bit smugly. "Who knows, maybe this will work out for you. Maybe you'll get more visitors on the Truth Trips. You were so shortsighted about this. Even if all you wanted was power, this was the right move. Taking down Alegre could make you a legend."

"I'm already a legend," she said, all ice. "Something you'll never be."

"The thing is, Suzanne, that was never my goal."

I turned away from her and walked down the steps on the side of the stage, determined to watch the end of the video alone. I looked at the audience and scanned the front row. Matías was sitting with his head in his hands. I wondered briefly if he regretted his decision, but I realized I didn't care. I looked away from him and toward the screen. This moment was too special to waste on him.

The documentary was ending, and I felt like I was tracing a circle that was finally closing. I remembered something my grandfather had said to me the year before he died. He had told my mom he was taking me to the park, but he took me to the Holocaust Museum. When my mom found out, she was furious, because she thought I was too young. But my grandfather said I had the obligation to know. My grandfather didn't treat kids any differently than he treated anyone else. I remember we were looking at a photo of a young girl around my age. She was staring at the camera with big lost eyes. She had a yellow Star of David sewn into her shirt. Behind her the streets were empty except for soldiers. *"Images change people's perceptions of the world,"* he said. *"They start wars. They end them. They can be their own revolution."*

I looked at the screen and thought how true that was. That photo had framed the way I saw everything. I could never look at suffering again and see it as remote, because in some way, that little girl was me. I remembered something else my grandfather had said. He quoted Bertolt Brecht: *"Art is not a mirror held up to reality, but a hammer with which to shape it."*

I looked at the photos. *My hammer.* I was flooded with relief. I finally understood how I could help shape the world I wanted to see. The video finished and the applause was deafening. I scanned the audience. There was the Professor in the back, beaming, with Adrián, Tomás, Mario, Clara, Héctor, and Ramón. My people. To hell with Camus and Sartre; I wasn't alone. When I looked at their faces, I was filled with pride, affection, and a little uncertainty. What would happen next? Would I get a new job here? Would Adrián and I work out long term? I didn't know. But I did know one thing.

I had thought throwing myself over a bridge would make me a new person, but it hadn't. I had thought standing up to guards or stealing documents or facing down the barrel of a gun would make me brave, but they hadn't, either. It was while watching the credits fade from view, and seeing three hundred people with tears in their eyes, sixty of them holding squawking plastic chickens, that I finally understood that I had never needed to be *a different person.* I had just needed to become the person I was always meant to be. I had just needed to be roasted.

# ACKNOWLEDGMENTS

Thank you . . .

Jud Laghi, my smart, insightful agent, who indulges my UFO obsession, and is a great guy, despite being a Mets fan.

The magnificent Blackstone team. Daniel Ehrenhaft, for sharing my vision, making my dreams happen, and always bringing a smile to my face with his unfailing positivity. Christina Boys, for her insight, clever ideas, and great chats. Thank you also to Josie Woodbridge, Lysa Williams, Courtney Vatis, Candice Edwards, Francie Crawford, and Nicole Sklitsis for all their hard work.

Everyone at Echo Lake, especially Amy Schiffman, Zadoc Angell, and Kim Yau for their help and support.

Tod Goldberg, my friend, champion, literary godfather, and person who can make me snort-laugh liquids.

The best writing group in existence, objectively, obviously: Aaron Marshall, Robert Tomoguchi, VJ Boyd.

My readers and cheerleaders: Eleanor Moran, Vanessa Julia Ramírez Inches, Mia Perala, Candice Miller, Sarah Rosenthal, and Amber Klein.

My Spanish-language advisers and *amigos queridos*: Peter A. Padín, Jess Pineda, Jorge Camilo Márquez Solá, and José Corado.

The generous and kind people of Costa Rica who opened their hearts, homes, and farms to me.

And finally, my family. All of my wonderful, crazy family.

Peter McIan, who suggested I write this in the first place.

My dad, who read countless drafts and taught me how to be a writer.

My mother, who taught me magic is everywhere, and who thinks I could fly if I wanted to.

My grandparents, who also thought I could fly.

My aunts, uncles, and cousins, who provide endless encouragement.

My brother, my BFF, the first person I call to understand anything complex, who gave annoyingly good notes.

Braden, for making sure I eat, for believing I could do this, and always picking up the slack so I could do "just a little more writing."

My son, my sunshine, my joy. I love you infinity times infinity. Times infinity. Times infinity.

Everyone fighting to make this world a little more just.

*¡Que vivan los comefuegos!*